MURDER IN THE CROOKED EYE BREWERY

MURDER IN THE CROOKED EYE BREWERY

J.C. EATON

W⊕RLDWIDE

TORONTO • NEW YORK • LONDON
AMSTERDAM • PARIS • SYDNEY • HAMBURG
STOCKHOLM • ATHENS • TOKYO • MILAN
MADRID • WARSAW • BUDAPEST • AUCKLAND

To our relatives, the Lynes and Scher families, who put this
idea in our heads and we couldn't get it out!

W⊛RLDWIDE™

Recycling programs
for this product may
not exist in your area.

ISBN-13: 978-1-335-40548-7

Murder in the Crooked Eye Brewery

First published in 2018 by Camel Press, an imprint of Epicenter
Press Inc. This edition published in 2021 with revised text.

Copyright © 2018 by J.C. Eaton
Copyright © 2021 by J.C. Eaton, revised text edition

This edition published by arrangement with Harlequin Books S.A.

For questions and comments about the quality of this book,
please contact us at CustomerService@Harlequin.com.

Harlequin Enterprises ULC
22 Adelaide St. West, 40th Floor
Toronto, Ontario M5H 4E3, Canada
www.ReaderService.com

Printed in U.S.A.

ACKNOWLEDGMENTS

We are especially grateful to the real Crooked Eye Brewery in Hatboro, PA, for allowing us to use it as a staging ground for murder. Thank you, Paul Mulherin, Jeff Mulherin, Paul Hogan and Jeff Lynes. Readers, if you want to try some amazing flights of beer, the brewery is located at 13 E. Montgomery Avenue, Suite 2, Hatboro, PA 19040. Find them at crookedeyebrewery.com and watch out for any Wild Turkey Bourbon Beer!

ONE

Office of Blake Investigations, New Ulm, Minnesota

"THERE'S A CALL for you on line one, Marcie." Angie's voice rang out as I started to check my emails.

"We only have one line, Angie," I yelled back, catching a glimpse of her as she walked toward the coffeemaker. Short frosted hair, silver studded earrings and a sharp pants suit.

"I know, I know, but I think it gives our company more prestige. You know. Having lots of phone lines. Anyway, the call is from an Iris Krum. Is that one of our clients? The name's not familiar. I'm still just getting used to working here."

Oh, that name will be familiar, soon enough.

Iris Krum. The two words I didn't want to hear so early in the morning. Iris-I-won't-give-up-until-I-nag-you-to-death-Krum. I should have warned Angie about her. Then again, she might have quit her job as receptionist/secretary for our small private investigation business. My boss, Max Blake, was a retired police officer from New Ulm, Minnesota, and I was his investigative assistant until I got my official license.

I took a leave of absence from my former position in the Office of Public Safety at St. Paul Community College following "The Failed Marriage." It failed because my ex-husband cheated on me with more coeds than I cared to imagine and, believe me, I have quite an imagination. I also had a pistol permit and good aim. I took that leave because I didn't want to tempt myself. And as far as the marriage went, all I took was my ex's last name—Rayner. I liked the sound of it better than my maiden name. Marcie Krum sounded like some stuffy schoolgirl with clunky shoes and I was anything but that. Marcie Rayner, however, was sharp and bold. It seemed to fit my tall, svelte frame and my attitude.

Max was my father's best friend, the best man at his wedding, and one of his pallbearers. He convinced me to take a leave from the community college in order to work with him in his investigative firm. As he put it, "You have a degree in criminal justice, but you're not using it sitting behind that desk running crime statistics."

"I don't just run them," I said. "I analyze them and make predictions that impact the way in which the college campus provides security for its students."

His response took me totally off guard. "You've been at that job for over four years. Do you really want to spend the next four doing the same thing? You've got all the makings for one hell of an investigator. Plus, with all that field work, you wouldn't need to take those Zumba classes of yours, the running around constitutes as a fitness program."

Who could argue with that? Now, seven months into the job, I had less than three to let Max and the community college know if I planned to return. Not to mention the Bayberry Apartments. I had less than two months to let them know if I planned on renewing my lease.

Byron, my six-year-old tuxedo cat, who had been with me from before and after the marriage, liked the Bayberry Apartments. My place overlooked the courtyard where all the action took place. And by action, I meant loose dogs, screaming kids, late-night teenage make-out sessions and the occasional police search for one thing or another. Yep, if nothing else, the place I was now beginning to call home in New Ulm was the entertainment source for my cat.

Clearing my throat, I yelled back to Angie. "No, thank God. She's not one of our clients. It's my mother. Do you mind shutting the door as long as you're up?"

"No problem."

I lifted the receiver, certain the first words out of my mother's mouth would be "So, have you made up your mind yet about the job?"

Biting my lower lip, I forced myself to speak. "Hi, Mom. I've told you before, I haven't made up my mind about the job yet."

"That's not why I'm calling. I'm calling because I need you to solve a murder. And, before you say a word, you need to listen."

I couldn't force a single syllable out, let alone a full word.

"It's a real honest-to-goodness murder, Marcie. One in Minnesota. Just an hour or so from New Ulm, so you won't have to drive too far. It was horrible. Simply horrible. Took place at the Crooked Eye Brewery in Biscay. Maybe it was on the news. Anyway, it was one of my neighbor's former students from when she taught elementary school. Such a nice boy, according to Alice Davenport. That's my neighbor. I don't think you met her. She was visiting her niece the last time you were here in Delray Beach. Which reminds me, it's not such a long flight from Minnesota to Florida. Well, anyway, Alice is beside herself and those bumbling sheriff deputies in Biscay haven't been able to solve a darned thing. That's when I told Alice you were a private investigator."

"Whoa. Slow down. And to begin with, I'm not a private investigator. I'm Max's investigative assistant. There's a difference."

"I'm not about to argue semantics with you. I need you to get on this case. I promised Alice."

"Look, in order for us to investigate, someone has to hire us. Contract and all."

"Oh, for heaven's sake, Marcie. I thought I was clear. Alice Davenport will be hiring you. She'll be calling you in a few minutes. As soon as I get off the phone."

"Don't tell me she's right there with you!"

"Of course not. She's at home waiting for my call. So…are you going to take this case or what?"

"I can't make any promises. First, let me get the information from Alice and speak to Max, okay?"

"It'll have to be okay. I'll call you tonight. And don't let it go to voice mail. I hate when that happens."

I was about to tell my mother I couldn't guarantee I'd be able to pick up her call at the exact moment, but I didn't feel like arguing. Instead, I asked her for the one pertinent piece of information she had neglected to give me. "Before you hang up, what was the name of the guy who was murdered?"

"Billy Hazlitt. Forty-five years old. Divorced. Twice. No children. Retired from the service. He was one of the co-owners of the brewery."

"And how exactly do you know he was murdered?"

"Because the cleaning crew found him face down in the walk-in refrigerator. Shot in the back. Or maybe it was the neck. Anyway, if that doesn't constitute murder, then I don't know what does."

I could tell my mother was getting exasperated. "Guess that about sums it up. All right then, I'll talk to you later. Have a good day, Mom."

Knowing my mother, I had less than five minutes before the phone would ring again. This time with Alice Davenport on the other end. I charged over to the coffeemaker for reinforcements just as Max came through the front door. For a man approaching sixty, he had the build and energy of most forty-year-olds. I attributed that to his wife, Doris, who kept a tight grip on his diet.

"Hey, Marcie. I got the strangest email from your mother. All it said was 'I'm giving you a murder.'"

"What she's giving you, or I should say us, is a headache so you'd better pull up a chair and listen quickly. We don't have much time. Someone is about to hire us."

Max chuckled as he followed me into my office. It was a space I really liked with a window facing the street and a view of small gift shops and a bakery. The office was once the temporary digs for a tax preparation company, but they moved into the Walmart just outside of town. Max was more than thrilled to be able to rent this space for his business a few years ago.

Angie was new, too, having moved to New Ulm from a suburb of Minneapolis when her husband passed away. She wanted to be closer to her grandkids but not become their babysitter. Her secretarial skills were top-notch, and Max hired her on the spot. So far it seemed to be working out.

"Angie," I said. "When the phone rings in the next five minutes, it will be an Alice Davenport. Tell her I'll be right with her."

"Okay, Marcie. And good morning, Mr. Blake."

I turned to Max and whispered, "How come you get the Mr. Blake treatment and I'm on a first name basis with Angie?"

"I think it's because I'm the one who writes her paycheck. Besides, she's at least thirty years older than you. Anyway, what's going on with this message from your mother? It has 'caution' written all over it."

"Grab some coffee. You'll need it."

I then proceeded to tell him about my mother's phone call and the unfortunate demise of one Billy Hazlitt.

Max ran a hand through his thinning brownish-gray hair and listened. "Hmm, I remember hearing about that. It wasn't too long ago. A month or so, maybe? They never figured out who killed the poor guy. Of course, communication in Biscay is the virtual dead zone."

"Huh? Are you being funny?"

"No, I'm serious. They call it the 'Biscay Triangle.' People can't seem to get cell phone service so they rely on CB radios and AM/FM for communication. Not only that but, for some reason, plants don't seem to grow in the soil at a normal rate and funnel clouds change direction when they approach that area. Not that the plants or funnel clouds have anything to do with this, but not having cell phone service probably disrupted the investigation in more ways than we can imagine."

"You're making it sound like *The Twilight Zone*. I've lived here all my life but I've never been up that way. How come you're so familiar with it?"

"I had an aunt who lived in Hutchinson. We had to drive through Biscay to get there. And yeah, if you blinked, you missed it."

"Seems the murderer didn't miss it. That's for sure. So, should we take this case, Max?"

Judging from the expression on his face, it was like watching a salivating dog. "It's a no-brainer. I don't know about you, but I'd rather deal with Biscay's antiquated communication than the never-ending communication from your mother if we don't take the case. Let's face it, Iris can be quite formidable."

Formidable. I could think of a dozen adjectives to describe my mother, but I suppose "formidable" wasn't too far off. "She'll be pestering us every day to see how it's going. Are you sure you're up for that?"

"We'll manage. This year we've dealt with fraud, theft, cheating spouses and extortion. All good, well-paying jobs. But solving a murder? That's what I was trained to do. And you're a quick study, Marcie. So, yeah, give your mother's friend the green light when she calls, okay?"

Just then, the phone rang, followed by Angie's familiar response. "There's a call for you on line one, Marcie."

Max snickered as he stepped out of the room.

Before I could finish my usual greeting of "Hello, this is Marcie Rayner of Blake Private Investigations," Alice Davenport cut in like a meat slicer with a chunk of salami on its blade.

"Marcie. Your mother said you're expecting my call. Thank you for taking this case. Write down my fax number immediately and send me the contract. I can't afford to waste time and neither can you."

My fingers fumbled as I wrote the number, and I repeated it once to be sure I had written it down correctly.

"Yes, yes. That's the number. Your mother told me

you had a great deal of experience with this sort of thing and honestly, that's a relief. I don't know if it's incompetence, laziness or a lack of resources, but all that sheriff's department in Biscay could figure out was Billy Hazlitt had been murdered. A fourth grader with a magnifying glass and a notebook could have figured out as much!"

I was still trying to process her comment about my having experience with murder investigations. Thank you, Mother, for managing to exaggerate to the point of no return.

"So which one will it be?"

"Um, er, a…what?" I had obviously missed the first part of her question.

"The reports. The reports you're going to provide me with. Will they be daily or weekly?"

I took a quick breath, relieved she wasn't asking for an hourly report. Heck, we hadn't even begun the investigation and I had no idea what we'd uncover or when.

"Our office will keep you updated weekly, unless something comes up." *Yikes. I can't believe that came out of my mouth. It was like saying "Things will remain the same unless they change."*

"Good. Good. Now, let me tell you about Billy Hazlitt."

For the next twenty-five minutes, Alice Davenport expounded on all sorts of details regarding Billy Hazlitt. Unfortunately, none of them were pertinent and none of them were current. He was in the fifth grade the last time she'd seen him. I made a mental note that he disliked creamy peanut butter, could whip a spitball across the room in record speed and was liked by absolutely everyone in his class. My eyes had started to

glaze over when she began to tell me about his penman-
ship, so I cleared my throat and broke in.

"How exactly did *you* find out he was murdered?
Are the local Minnesota papers mailed to you in Delray Beach?"

"Papers? Mailed? Listen here. I may be old but I'm
not a relic. I go online to check the obits columns from
time to time so I can see who I've outlived. But I never
expected it to be one of my former students. And such
a good boy, too. That's why whoever killed him needs
to be apprehended."

"I understand."

"Aren't you going to ask if he had any enemies?
That's usually how these investigations are started."

I didn't want to rile her by asking how on earth she
knew the way in which investigations were conducted.
Plus, I doubted she'd be much help regarding any enemies the guy might have had thirty-five years after
he completed the fifth grade. However, I played along.

"Yes. Yes. Naturally. Do you know of any enemies?"

"None whatsoever. As I mentioned earlier, Billy Hazlitt was liked by everyone."

It was hard to tell what was going to be more
challenging—conducting the investigation or dealing
with Alice Davenport.

I pulled my shoulders back, trying to release the ten-
sion in my body as I focused on ending the call. "Well,
thank you, Miss…er…Ms. Davenport. You have my
word we'll begin immediately."

"Of course you will. And it's Miss. I can mail your
company a check with the contract or I can send the
money immediately with PayPal."

"A check and the signed contract will be fine. I'll be in touch. Have a nice day."

I think she said, "you as well" before hanging up but I wasn't too sure. Frankly, she scared me. My hand was still on the phone when Max stuck his head back in the doorway.

"Two words I like to hear, especially in the same sentence—check and contract. So, it's a go, huh?"

"Looks that way. Oh my gosh. I'd better have Angie fax that contract immediately. I have a feeling Alice Davenport is standing over her machine. Give me two seconds and then I'll fill you in on this case."

By mid-morning, Max had already contacted the sheriff's department in Biscay and informed them we were hired to investigate Billy Hazlitt's death. He got the verbal rundown on the case and they agreed to provide us with copies of their written findings.

So, Max set up a time to meet with one of them in the afternoon. "It's only about an hour and a half from here. Good thing it's June or that hour and a half would've turned into two or three with those winter storms."

"Please tell me we'll have the case wrapped up by then."

"I'll do one better. I'm aiming for the fourth of July. Got the usual family picnic at my brother-in-law's place and, for once in my life, I'd like to sit back with a hot dog and beer. Last year Doris pitched a fit when I had to leave early for a stakeout. You'd think she would've been used to it after twenty-seven years of marriage. Come on, grab your things. We'll get a bite to eat in Biscay. If my memory serves me well, there's an old diner on the main street that's been around since the Depression."

"Okay, coach." I grabbed my purse. "Anything to get out of the office in case Alice Davenport calls again."

TWO

MAX WAS RIGHT. Biscay was a tiny little dot on the map and without a good magnifying glass, easy to miss. It was north of New Ulm and equidistant from Glencoe and Hutchinson. If we were starting out in Minneapolis we'd have a straight shot heading west, but New Ulm was southwest of Minneapolis and in order to reach Biscay, we'd have to drive to Glencoe and take Route 22 to Biscay. At least my boss would be in familiar territory.

By the time we left New Ulm and got onto the highway, Max and I had already shared all the information we had gleaned. It was pretty much the same stuff my mother had told me and that came from her conversation with Alice Davenport. What Alice didn't know was that Billy Hazlitt was shot in the temple with a .357 Magnum, his body lying all twisted up in front of one of the brite tanks used to chill and carbonate beer after fermentation. The sheriff said it looked as if someone tried to slide the body behind the tank but gave up.

The whole thing made no sense because it wasn't as if the tank could conceal the body from view. According to Max, those tanks were tall and cylindrical. No way to hide a body. Apparently the sheriff's department was baffled, too.

"I can't add much more to that." I adjusted the seatbelt so it wouldn't burn my neck. "Unless Billy's ability to hurl a spitball somehow plays into all of this. Other than reiterating milestones in his life over the years, Alice Davenport wasn't much help. She knew he had gone into the service as soon as he got out of high school and that he was married twice with no children. You don't think it was a jealous ex-wife, do you?"

"Right now the field is wide open for speculation. It could've been anything from a robbery gone bad to an unbalanced girlfriend. Or, as you said, 'a jealous former spouse.' Not that it's any of my business, but you're over your ex, aren't you?"

"Over and out. I can't believe I was so naïve not to pick up on the clues sooner. He cheated right under my nose but I didn't want to admit I saw the signs. Not a great reference for a neophyte investigator, huh?"

"It's always tougher when it's firsthand. Our minds are wired to ignore the evidence. Self-preservation and all that crapola. I'm sure there's a fancy psychology term for it but I'll be darned if it comes to mind."

"Denial. I think the word is denial."

"Well, nothing to deny as far as Billy Hazlitt's death goes. We don't have any personal ties that would cloud our thinking. And we've got a big advantage as far as sleuthing is concerned. Biscay is a really small town. A hundred people or so and, from what I know about small towns, someone is bound to talk."

We spent the next half hour gabbing about jealous exes and the bizarre stories we'd heard before we finally got back on track discussing the investigation. Since Max was a retired police officer and had already spoken with the McLeod County Sheriff's Department, it made more sense for him to drive to their station and get copies of the reports while I introduced myself at the brewery and tried to get some initial information from one of the other owners.

"You've got a good knack of speaking to people, Marcie, without putting them off. See if you can unofficially interview whoever happens to be working and set up a time this week to return."

I wasn't so sure anyone was going to open up and tell me about the murder. "What if they refuse to say anything?"

"They'll talk. Don't worry. From what the sheriff's deputy said, the other two owners were pretty shaken up as well as the part-time employee who works there. They'll want to know who did it."

Max pointed to a small cluster of clapboard houses on the right and announced that we had arrived.

"Oh my gosh," I blurted out. "You were right. There's nothing here."

"I wouldn't say nothing. There's the Triangle Diner, as well as the Crooked Eye Brewery. That little diner gets all the traffic between Glencoe and Hutchinson. And I imagine all the gossip, too. Come on, I'm starving."

As Max pulled off the road and onto Front Street, the Crooked Eye Brewery literally jumped out at us. It was the giant sign of a red and yellow eyeball high above the entrance to the flat-roofed building that got my attention, followed by the words, "Ale Away at the Crooked Eye."

There were a few cars parked out in front of the building, a bright yellow structure that looked as if it might have been a garage at one time. Someone went to an awful lot of trouble to restore and refurbish the place.

Two small pine trees framed the entrance with smaller potted plants decorating an outdoor patio.

"Eye catching, huh?" Max asked.

"Very funny."

"The diner's right across the street. I'm dying for a juicy burger and maybe a clue or two to wash it down with."

Compared to the brewery, the Triangle Diner was pretty nondescript. It had a green and blue sign in the shape of a triangle strategically placed over a large picture window in the front. The place looked as if it had always been a diner. Max pulled up to their small parking lot and turned off the ignition. It seemed as if most of their customers parked on the street in front of the diner.

"Okay, Marcie. We're on. We're not just eating, we're on duty. Listen to everything you hear from everyone."

"Roger that, boss." I approached the steps to the diner.

As Max swung the door open, it was like walking back in time. Only I wasn't sure what time—the thirties? Forties? Everything looked old and brown from the seats at the counter to the booths along the edge. But the place was spotless. Gingham valances framed the windows and cutesy cow and pig salt and pepper shakers dotted each of the tables. There were at least eight or nine people eating when we stepped inside to find a booth.

No one noticed us. The customers were too fixated on the conversation between the owner and his two waitresses. The three of them were standing off to the side of the counter near a door that I presumed led to the kitchen.

The owner's voice could drown out an F-16. "Cut it out, you two. It's freaking daylight with a diner full of customers. No one is going to gun you down in the walk-in. You can't keep asking me or Frankie to stop cooking and get you something. I've got a business to run and this is getting ridiculous."

The skinny waitress, who couldn't've been older than eighteen, let out a small huff and replied as the other one, noticeably better developed, took a step closer to the counter. "I can't help it if Trudy and I get the feeling someone has a gun to the back of our heads every time we go in there. Until they catch whoever killed Billy, I'm not about to set foot in the walk-in refrigerator. And neither is she."

"Trisha's right," the other waitress said, turning her head to survey the diner. "For all I know, a psychotic murderer could be in here right now."

The owner's face had started to turn crimson. "Give me a break! Even if someone was in there brandishing a weapon, they wouldn't be stupid enough to gun down either of you unless, of course, the service gets worse, so come on, get going. Two new customers just walked in."

The waitresses looked as if they'd been caught smoking in the girls' room. The skinny one, Trisha, approached our booth as the other one leaned over the counter to refill a customer's coffee.

Trisha spoke softly and looked as if she was about to cry. "Sorry you folks had to overhear that. You must be passing through or you'd know that one of the brewery owners from across the street was murdered in their walk-in refrigerator. Shot in the head. Less than a month ago. And the killer is still loose. I don't care what our boss thinks. It's like it happened yesterday. Anyway, can I get you some coffees or something to start with?"

"I'm about coffee'd out," I said, "but I'll take a Coke."

Max nodded. "Same here."

Trisha handed us two menus and started to walk toward the kitchen when Max spoke.

"About that murder, are there any suspects? Any leads?"

The waitress shook her head. "No. Nothing. Or nothing the sheriff's department is willing to share. They're so pokey and slow. I don't think they'll ever catch who did it."

"That's too bad," Max said. "Did you know the victim?"

"In case you haven't noticed, Biscay is a really small town. Everyone knew him. Billy. Billy Hazlitt. One of the nicest guys you'd ever meet. And a good tipper, too. Who would want to kill him is beyond me."

A voice screamed across the diner just as I was about to say something. "Hey, Trisha! Order up!"

"I'll be right back with your drinks. Meantime, check out the menu. And again, sorry about what you overheard when you came in."

"Should we tell her we're investigating this case?" I asked Max as I scanned the menu.

"Not right away. Sometimes when people hear the words 'private investigator,' they get all spooked. Let's see if she can give us any more info when she takes our order."

Seconds later Trisha reappeared with our drinks. "So, what are you having?"

Max ordered a cheeseburger with fries and I had what I liked to refer to as "my safety sandwich"—a

BLT. It would be difficult to ruin bacon, lettuce and tomato.

As the waitress turned toward the kitchen, Max tapped her on the elbow. "I can only imagine how unsettling it is to have someone murdered in such close proximity to your workplace. Do you remember exactly when his body was found?"

Trisha bit her lip and took a deep breath. "I remember all right. I wish I didn't. It was real early in the morning. Around five thirty. We have to report at five thirty and start prepping. You know, get the coffee going and all that stuff. That's 'cause we open at six. Anyway, there's a cleaning crew out of Hutchinson that goes into the brewery every morning about the same time as when I get here. They usually finish up around seven, stop in for coffee and then head to their next job. Only that day, they never came in. Instead, they stood outside the brewery and Trudy and I wondered what was going on. Then the sheriff pulled up. And a few minutes later, another sheriff. And I knew something really bad had happened. 'Cause if it was a theft, they would have only sent one car."

Trisha looked around, making sure she wasn't needed at another table. "The next car that pulled up wasn't a car. It was the county coroner's van. And I knew. I knew right then someone was dead. But I didn't know who. I mean, there's Billy. Um…*was* Billy. And his older brother, Tom, and Hogan Austin, a friend of theirs, who was the third owner. It had to be one of them the coroner came to get and not the part-time kid."

"What made you think that?" Max took a sip of his Coke.

"Because it was Monday morning. The kid they

hired doesn't usually work on Sundays. I knew whoever was dead had to be Billy, Tom or Hogan. And I figured maybe Tom had a heart attack, being so overweight and all. But Billy? And then to find out he was murdered? And my boss doesn't understand why I'm afraid to go into the walk-in refrigerator?"

Trisha was on the verge of a breakdown, tears and all. I had to do something. Say something. So I blurted out the first words that came to mind. "Onion rings! Do you have onion rings? I'd really like to add them to my order."

It was enough to jolt Trisha back into action. "Sure, sure. I'll get that going right away."

She marched toward the kitchen.

"Sorry, Max, if I ruined the flow, but I thought she was about to lose it right in front of us."

"No, you did the right thing. Last thing we need is to create a scene. After we're done eating, I'll have a word with the owner and ask if we can speak to his staff one afternoon this week when they get out of work."

"I don't blame the waitresses, though. I wouldn't want to walk into one of those refrigerators either. Murderer on the loose or not."

THREE

GEORGE BOWMAN, the owner of the diner, was more than relieved to talk with us about the investigation. According to Max, who spoke with him while I stepped into the ladies' room, the guy just wanted to get things back to normal around the diner because "everyone was as jumpy as a kid in a Halloween spook house," himself included, although he didn't want to admit it to his employees. Judging from his appearance, it looked as if very little would rattle him. He was a large man with a round face, a receding hairline and a protruding stomach. I imagined he didn't miss too many meals. The guy said he would ask the waitresses and his cook to give us as much information as possible when we came by later in the week. He also told my boss Thursdays were best since the waitresses didn't have to rush off to classes at the community college and the part-time waitress would be available as well.

"So, we're sticking with the same plan, right?" I asked Max as he picked up the check and walked it over to the counter.

"Yep. I'm going to head over to the sheriff's station near Hutchinson while you find out as much as you can at the brewery. Might as well be upfront with them since the murder took place in their establishment. I should be back in an hour or so. If it gets to be much longer, grab yourself a coffee or something in the diner. Won't be able to call you since they don't get cell phone service. I'll look for you in the brewery or the diner."

"Sounds good. I might as well walk over there. Thanks for the lunch."

"Hey, it's a business expense, but don't get too used to it until we make our first million."

I was still thinking about Max's remark when I reached the parking lot in front of the brewery. His business had to be doing all right considering he added me to the payroll. And who knew? Solving a high profile murder case could certainly be a boon.

For me, Damocles' sword hung like a halo on top of my ultra-fine hair. Or wispy blond, according to my mother. At least she'd have to admit the layered bob looked pretty cool. Anyway, I had to decide if I wanted to remain working for Max and learn how to become an investigator for real or go back to campus security and take my chances that I might run into my philandering ex-husband who still worked at the college. No rush. There was plenty of time. Thankfully, my mother stopped referring to me as a "ruined woman." At least to my face.

My thoughts were interrupted when a girl with long brown hair came storming out of the brewery. Faint purple highlights on the tips of her curls gleamed in the sunlight. Her denim jacket covered a low-cut tank top and was as faded as the jeans she wore. She swung open the door to her pickup and started to get inside. At her heels was a guy who didn't look old enough to buy beer legally.

The girl turned and lashed out at him. "Don't expect me to cry at your funeral, Tyler, because I won't!"

"For cryin' out loud, Kimmie. I'm not going to get

shot up. I told you before, it wasn't a robbery or any-thing. No one's after me."

"And how do you know that?"

The girl was almost as hysterical as Trisha from the Triangle Diner. I stood off to the side, hoping to remain inconspicuous while the two of them hurled comments back and forth. By now, Tyler had placed his hand over the frame of the door, preventing the girl from going anywhere unless she planned on pulling out with him only inches away.

"Look," he said, "I need this job. Don't you get it? It's not like there are a zillion jobs around here. This is the business I eventually want to get into."

"Don't come crying to me when you're face down in front of a big old beer tank!"

"Yeah, I'll remember that, Kimmie!"

The next sound was the squeal of truck tires on the pavement as Kimmie took off, driver's side door wide open and Tyler staggering back, catching himself be-fore falling to the ground.

We were a few feet away from each other in the park-ing lot and from the look on Tyler's face, he hadn't re-alized I was there. "Whoa. Girls, huh?"

Talk about bravado. Do these guys learn it at an early age or does it come naturally to them? I rushed over and asked if he was okay. "I sort of heard everything," I said. "Was that your girlfriend?"

"Yeah, that's my girlfriend. Or maybe *was*. She'll get over it. I didn't hear anyone pull up in a car or I wouldn't't've gotten into it with her in front of custom-ers."

"Um, that's because I walked over from the diner. I didn't drive in."

Tyler glanced at the diner. There were a few cars in front, so he must have figured one of them belonged to me.

"So, I guess you're coming in to taste some beer. I'd better get back to the counter. Good thing there weren't any other customers inside to watch Kimmie's meltdown of the week."

"It sounded like she was really worried about you."

"Yeah, well…ever since one of our owners was murdered, Kimmie comes in here trying to talk me into quitting my job. You don't look too surprised to hear someone was murdered. If you're coming from the diner, I suppose Trudy and Trisha gave you all the details. Those two can't help running their mouths."

"The only thing I know is that one of the owners, Billy, was found shot in your walk-in refrigerator a few weeks ago. A gunshot wound to the head, I believe."

Tyler let out a long sigh, rubbing his hands against his jeans. "Well, lady, you know as much as I do. As much as anyone, I suppose. At least it was a clean shot or I'd be kind of freaked to go back and forth to the tanks in there."

"What does a clean shot have to do with not being freaked out?"

Tyler answered as if he was explaining something to a five-year-old. Under ordinary circumstances, I would have been annoyed but, number one, I needed to learn as much information as possible and, number two, the kid had to redeem his bravado. I wanted him to talk and he did.

"A clean shot means instantly dead. Like snipers or hired killers. Or at least someone who was real, real good at it. Even if it was close range. This wasn't just any old guy shooting to kill. This was someone who knew his business. Someone who'd had practice. Someone who knew how to get a bullet straight to the head. One shot. They had to know their target. That's why I keep telling Kimmie I'm not worried. No one is after me."

"What makes you say that?"

Tyler let off a huff of air. "Because I only work here. I don't own the place. And besides, I haven't done anything to piss anyone off. Except maybe Kimmie."

"Do you think someone was after Billy? Could he have done something?"

By now we were inside the brewery and Tyler had moved behind the counter.

"I think someone left him a calling card to the right temple. That's what I think. As for who, it's anyone's guess. As far as I know, Billy didn't have any enemies. At least none that any of us in the brewery knew about. Anyway, I'm sure you didn't come here to talk about my boss getting shot. So, what would you like to taste? We've got incredible beers on tap—pale ale, chocolate stout, Scotch ale, India pale ale and our newest addition—Wild Turkey Bourbon Beer. It's a brown ale aged in a Bourbon barrel."

"Actually—" I reached into my bag for my business card "—I *am* here to investigate Billy Hazlitt's murder. I'm with Blake Investigations in New Ulm and we've been hired to look into this case. My boss is meeting with the sheriff's department right now. Is there anything else you can tell me? Anything at all?"

Tyler shook his head and swallowed. He didn't appear to be too surprised at my revelation. "Nope. That about sums it up. But Hogan Austin's in the back, cookin' up some grains in the mash tun. If you guys aren't familiar with brewing, it's a fancy name for a big pot. Anyway, Hogan's one of my bosses. Billy's brother Tom is the other one, but he won't be in till later on. Hold on. I'll go get Hogan for you. Sure you don't want to try something?"

"Maybe another day. They do sound delicious. Do you sell them by the bottle?"

"No, we're too small a business for bottling. We produce kegs and sell them to local bars and restaurants. Oh, yeah, and to the German Club over in Willmar. But we're licensed to serve pints and flights in here as well as growlers."

"Flights of beer" were small samples going from light to dark, sort of like wine tasting, but I'd never heard of growlers. "Growlers?"

"Yeah. Those are thirty-two and sixty-four ounce refillable bottles. Wait a sec. I'll get Hogan for you."

Tyler opened a large wooden door behind the counter and disappeared just as three customers walked in— all men in their late fifties or early sixties. I nodded to them and said someone would be right back.

Before anyone could say anything, a tall sandy-haired man, who looked to be in his thirties, approached me and held out his hand. Broad shoulders, narrow waist and toned arms. He had the same Scandinavian features I did including the high cheekbones, only his eyes were definitely darker than my arctic blue ones.

"I'm Hogan Austin and I understand you want to speak with me."

I looked straight at him and gave him a slight smile. "Yes, I'm Marcie Rayner from Blake Investigations in New Ulm."

"Nice to meet you, Miss Rayner."

"Call me Marcie. Everyone else does. I'm here with my partner, well, actually he's with the sheriff, but we're both here looking into Billy Hazlitt's death."

"You can say it. You can say *murder*. It's not a secret. Come on. Let's talk where it's more private."

As long as it's not the walk-in refrigerator.

I stood frozen on the spot with only my eyes darting back and forth to the walk-in where Billy was killed. I wasn't about to follow anyone into a place where someone had been shot to death. Not alone, anyway. Hogan must have noticed my apprehension because he took a step forward, motioned for the front door and touched my elbow. "No one's on the patio. Let's grab a seat and you can ask me anything you'd like."

There was something comfortable about the guy and the easy way he seemed to be around people. Even those who were poised to question him about his partner's murder. I figured this could work to my advantage.

FOUR

"So," Hogan said, holding out the chair for me, "I suppose Tyler gave you the rundown already about Billy's murder. Hey, before I sit down, did you want anything to drink? I can get you bottled water if you don't feel like tasting one of our beers."

"Um…thanks. I'm fine. I had more than enough Coke at the diner."

I clasped my hands together and leaned forward. Max told me to be diplomatic when questioning potential witnesses, victims or killers, and if that didn't yield results, then go for the jugular. Hogan gave me a nod and I continued to speak.

"Yes," I said. "Tyler told me that one of your partners was found shot to death in the walk-in refrigerator. The same information my partner and I had gotten from the waitresses across the street and the sheriff's office. It seems as if Tyler knew that your partner, Billy Hazlitt, was shot in the right temple. Was that common knowledge?"

"Everything about the murder is common knowledge around here, including the fact the sheriff's office ruled out robbery. That was a no-brainer. Nothing was stolen. Yeah, everyone knows everyone's business. Biscay has a population of a hundred or so and the town's most well-known export is gossip. If you haven't had an earful yet from Trisha and Trudy across the street, you will. But they're amateurs compared to Kaye."

"Kaye?"

"George Bowman's sister. You'll meet her soon enough, I'm sure. Looks like her brother, too, only with a skirt and more facial hair."

I tried to not to laugh but it wasn't easy. Hogan gave me a faint smile and continued. "She worked at this diner when it used to belong to the first owner. Eons ago. Before George bought it. Now she works part time for her brother, waiting tables. Gives her something to do, I suppose. But I'm warning you, don't let her take you down memory lane unless you've got an hour to spare."

"Thanks for the heads up," I said, opening my bag and taking out a pad and pen. "Do you mind if I write down the information you're giving me? I want to be sure I get everything right."

"No problem. Funny, but I figured you'd be taking out one of those recording devices."

"Nah, I'm not that high tech. I'd probably screw it up and wind up erasing everything."

"You wouldn't be the first person. Half the time I wind up deleting phone messages from my answering machine at home."

I smiled. "So, um…getting back to the murder… Tyler mentioned that the shot was clean. Possibly close range. What do you know about that?"

"The sheriff's office should have all the forensics for you, but yeah, I'm guessing six feet or so. Whoever took that shot had to be standing in the walk-in. It was deliberate. Look, I hope this doesn't upset you but… the blood from the bullet wound was in a pool by the brite tank. Someone had to have followed Billy into that refrigerator and pulled the gun. Our walk-in isn't very large so whoever fired the gun did it up close and personal."

I watched for any sign of emotion on Hogan's face but I didn't see anything, almost as if he was detached from the entire situation. He gave me the same time-line that Tyler did, adding one piece of pertinent information.

"Billy Hazlitt was the last one in the brewery that Sunday. We close at five. Tom was off that day and I left a few minutes after we locked the front door and put up the 'closed' sign. The back door was open and unlocked when I left so whoever killed Billy must have known our routine. The last guy in the brewery makes sure all the equipment is running okay and cashes out."

"Did anyone know Billy would be the one staying late?"

"Not really. It's not as if we have a fixed schedule. But I had tickets to the Willmar Stingers game that night so Billy was the one who locked up."

"The Willmar Stingers?"

"Uh-huh. They're a baseball team. Part of the North-woods League. And the only reason I had tickets was that my nephew was in the line-up. The teams don't usually play on Sunday nights but there was a huge fire in Willmar on Saturday so they had to move the game to Sunday. Anyway, to get back to your question, it wasn't as if our work schedule was posted anywhere. You sure you don't want something to drink?"

"No, I'm fine. Really."

I was writing as fast as I could, all the while trying to figure out what to ask him next. Not being the seasoned detective Max was, I resorted to the cliché that every detective in every book, TV show or movie ever asked. Alice Davenport would have given me a plus.

"Do you know if Billy Hazlitt had any enemies? Anyone who would want to harm him?"

Hogan crossed his arms and rubbed the muscles above his elbows. "Off hand, no. But Billy kept a lot of things to himself. Never let on if he was having a bad day or anything."

"I know he was married twice," I said. I also couldn't help but notice Hogan wasn't wearing a wedding ring. "Maybe one of the exes wasn't too happy."

He stopped rubbing his arms and instead, folded his hands and stretched them out in front. "I think you can scratch them off your list."

"What do you mean?"

"He married his first wife, Jennifer Midland, when he got out of basic training. If you ask me, they were too young and too stupid. From what I heard, Billy's older brother Tom tried to talk him out of it but Billy wouldn't listen. I was in high school when they tied the knot. We all grew up here, you know. And it's a really small town so everyone knew each other's business. Anyway, about that marriage…well, you can imagine how the story went."

Believe me, I can imagine just about anything when it comes to marriages.

I nodded and pretended to write something while Hogan continued talking.

"After basic training, Billy got stationed in Lubbock, Texas, then somewhere in Virginia. By that time, Jennifer was tired of moving around and being an army wife. She wanted to live in a big city with all the fancy trappings and that wasn't going to happen if she stayed married to Billy. So, two years later they divorced. That was over a decade ago. Jennifer re-married some wealthy investment banker and moved to Seattle. I doubt she had any reason to kill her first husband."

Just then, two cars pulled up and five people headed into the brewery. Two women and three men. Hogan and I stopped talking and nodded to them as they walked past us. Once the front door closed, I leaned in and whispered.

"What about the second wife?"

"You don't have to whisper. They can't hear us. Listen, I don't think some people are meant to get married. Billy's second wife is a school teacher in Minneapolis. Their marriage lasted about two years. Then, they split up. No blow-up. No cheating. No nothing. It just fell apart, that's all."

Two years. That must be the track record for marriages on the rocks.

Hogan's comment of "I don't think some people are meant to be married" explained the lack of a wedding ring. I wondered for a moment if he was talking about himself and realized I might care what the answer would be.

"Um…yeah…well, I suppose."

"Is there anything else you wanted to ask? And are you sure I can't offer you anything to drink?"

If nothing else, Hogan Austin was certainly accommodating. "I'm fine. Really."

He was looking right at me and I had the oddest feeling he wasn't thinking about the murder investigation. Then again, it was probably my imagination. I brushed the hair from my face and paused for a second. "You mentioned nothing was stolen. What about data from your computer?"

Hogan let out a quick laugh. "Computer? We don't have a computer here. We use our smartphones at work and I track the data on my iPad at home. We go through a credit card processing company that handles our inventory and sales, whether people charge or pay cash. We all take our own devices home. It's a lot easier that way."

"What about Billy? What did he use?"

"A smartphone. Password protected. They found it in his pocket. It's hardly evidence but the sheriff's department has it."

My brain kicked back into gear and I remembered to ask him who was the first person at the brewery after the cleaning crew had gotten there. Hogan explained it was Billy's brother Tom who had to identify the body and that Tom was having the worst time possible dealing with the murder. Judging from Hogan's demeanor, I knew he wasn't having an easy time either.

"It's like Tom's on automatic pilot if you know what I mean. He comes in, usually later in the day, does the routine stuff, even talks to the customers, but it's as if he's lost every bit of his personality. I'm trying to pick up the slack but I don't know how much longer I can take it. So you see, it's really important to find out who killed my partner and my friend."

Normally, I keep my hands, feet and objects to myself, but something made me want to reach across the table and give Hogan's hand a squeeze. Not a romantic *I want you to take down my phone number and give me a call* squeeze, but a compassionate *I'm really, really sorry for your loss* squeeze.

Another vehicle rolled into the parking lot. This time a van. I heard the crunch of gravel before I noticed the vehicle. Hogan stood up and sighed. "I've got to get back inside and give Tyler a hand. Hey, I don't know how helpful I was but you know where to reach me if you have more questions. Or if you just want to run something by me."

"Hogan," I said as he started toward the door, "Do you think Tom Hazlitt would be in any shape to speak with me or my partner? We're planning to stop back on Thursday."

He shrugged and shook his head. "Hard to say, but you can try. I know the sheriff questioned him right after the incident but when Tom and I spoke later, he told me that he didn't remember anything he had said."

"I see. I mean… I understand. Well, thanks for everything. I appreciate it."

"You're welcome," he said. "To be honest, I wasn't all that thrilled having to answer the same questions I did with the sheriff's deputies but talking with you was… well, not as bad as I expected."

Not as bad as he expected. Wow. That's quite a reference for me. *Maybe I could put that on my résumé. "Talking with Marcie Rayner is not as bad as you think."*

I tried to smile but I think I might have grimaced. "Well, um, thanks again."

Hogan nodded and stepped back into the brewery. The sound of another car pulling into the parking lot grabbed my attention. It was Max. Either I had spent a longer time at the brewery than anticipated or his visit at the sheriff's office was really brief. I walked across the lot and opened the passenger door.

"Everything go okay, Max?"

"Sure enough. What about you?"

"I'd say it was productive."

How productive? I wasn't sure. I had managed to pick up a few more tidbits about Billy Hazlitt and some keen observations about his partner. My gut told me Hogan was on the up and up and his grief was genuine. Then again, my background was in crime stats and not crime psychology. However, I didn't need a degree to read body language. Hogan Austin was either one heck of an actor or still reeling from the shock of losing his partner.

FIVE

THE RIDE BACK to our office in New Ulm was uneventful. Max and I tossed around the few crumbs of information we were able to get and re-hashed them over and over again before he changed the subject.

"I've got to drive over to Minneapolis tomorrow and testify in the Klemmer fraud case. God knows how long that will take. I figured with my luck I'd be stuck in the courtroom most of the day waiting for them to call me to the witness stand."

The Klemmer fraud case was one of our first assignments. Lester Klemmer and his wife had perpetuated a phony lender scheme and finally got caught. It was one of those cases where a background in accounts receivable would have really come in handy. Nevertheless, Max and I knew enough math between the two of us to recognize doctored account keeping.

"Sounds like you'll be back really late."

"Actually, I'm going to get a hotel room and spend the night. Don't feel like driving back in rush-hour traffic. Meanwhile you can review the sheriff's notes and the coroner's report. That way you can get the timeline charted out and see who else we need to contact. George Bowman is expecting us on Thursday so we only have a day in between."

"No problem."

Angie was closing things up at the office when we

walked in. She acknowledged Max immediately and smiled at me.

"Hi, Mr. Blake. It was pretty quiet in here this afternoon but you got four calls. I left the information on your desk. And Marcie, you got one phone message. It was Alice Davenport and she insisted I write it down verbatim."

My stomach began to churn. We had barely started on the investigation and Alice Davenport was going to give me the kind of indigestion that no Tums could handle. I swore I saw Max smirking as he strolled into his office.

"What was the message, Angie?" I asked.

The secretary let out a long, painful sigh and walked over to her desk. She read the note without stopping to let in any air.

"Regarding my weekly reports. I've decided they do *not* have to be chronological according to your investigation, unless of course you deem that to be the most effective means of communicating your progress. The reports may be written thematically, in which case some chronological order may be necessary, or they may be written according to high and low importance as quantified by your judgment."

My jaw dropped to the ground while Angie added, "I left you a copy next to your computer. Don't look so stunned, Marcie. At least she didn't specify the font."

"That's probably because she's expecting it in cursive."

Angie laughed. "So, do you or Mr. Blake need me to stay any longer? It's already past five."

"Um, no. We'll be fine. That is, Max will probably be fine. I'll be in my office trying desperately to restrain myself from pulling the hairs out of my head. Anyway, thanks. See you in the morning."

My God! Alice Davenport's demand was worse than any assignment I had in senior English. Chronological order? Thematically? Quantified by my judgment? I wasn't even sure what that meant. All I planned on doing was keeping her informed with little "bullets" of information. Apparently that wasn't her idea of communication but who the heck had time for a dissertation each week? I grumbled and muttered to myself as I read her note again before checking my computer for emails.

Nothing on the screen that couldn't wait for the next day. I walked into the small workroom that doubled as a storage area and pulled out a few dry erase pens from a cabinet. It was serendipitous that the tax preparation company had left their large white dry erase board on the wall in that same workroom. Shoving a few boxes out of the way, I walked to the board and wrote three words across the top—Billy Hazlitt Murder. Then, I drew a long horizontal line across the board before turning out the lights and heading home. I expected to have that timeline completed the next day. I figured it couldn't possibly take me that long.

If Alice Davenport's phone message wasn't enough to annoy me, Iris Krum's was. I could see the little red dot flashing on my landline when I got home and walked into the kitchen. Byron rubbed his head against my calf and meowed, forcing me to open a can of mackerel morsels before I could get to the message. I knew immediately the call was from my mother. Rather than have her call back, an absolute "given," and disrupt any hopes I had of eating in peace, I returned the call as soon as I took my shoes off and threw on a pair of jeans.

"Well, have you made any progress on the case yet?"

"It's only been a few hours, Mom."

"I don't know about you, Marcie, but I've been giving it some thought. Do you want to know what I think?"

"Like I have a choice."

"Don't be snippy. I'm trying to help. This is what I think. It had to be a sniper. A trained mercenary sniper. Alice Davenport told me her student was shot in the head and that he was in the service. Who else can shoot you in the head like that? If I were you, I'd be contacting Homeland Security."

And there it was. The immediate leap into the absurd.

And here I thought chronological order was going to be a pain in the neck. I took a slow deep breath and reminded myself that my mother was hours away. In Florida. Hours away. It wasn't as if she could walk through the door.

"First of all, Mom, Billy Hazlitt retired from the service years ago and worked for a brewery in Minneapolis before starting his own microbrewery in Biscay so I seriously doubt it was any sniper from some unknown government."

"You don't know that. You don't know what any of these people are into. Sleeper cells. Stashes of weapons. Secret government workers…"

"I'll keep all of that in mind, Mom."

"Good. And call me with an update. I've got to go. I've got a Mah Jong game in a half hour. Oh, and before I forget, I mailed you something. It should arrive any day now."

"What? What did you mail me?"

"One of those laser pointers on a key chain. You know, in case you have to give a presentation. I saw it in a catalogue and immediately thought of you. Put your keys on it and that way you'll have it when the time comes. You'll be prepared, unlike the last time."

The "last time" was in King's Point Retirement Community in Delray Beach when I got roped into doing a presentation on personal safety for my mother's Mah Jong club. Not my ideal way to spend a vacation. I still shudder when I remember getting kicked in the foot by my mother's friend, Mabelle Hoffmeyer, who told me, "Kick'em in the ankle first and work your way up."

"Um…well, thanks, Mom, but I doubt I'll be giving any presentations."

"Then you can use it to play with that cat of yours. I saw the cutest little YouTube video of a man playing laser tag chase with his cat. Put it on your key chain. These things come in handy."

"Okay. Okay."

"And about my theory…none of us can be sure of what certain people are up to, so be careful."

"I will. Thanks again. Love you."

In spite of her "go to the extreme and work backwards from there" philosophy, my mother was right about one thing. We really didn't know what Billy Hazlitt might have been into and if that's what caused his death. I thought about it most of the evening until I turned down the covers and crept into bed, shoving Byron off to the side. That's when the phone rang again and this time it wasn't my mother.

"Miss Rayner? Is this Miss Rayner from Blake Investigations?"

It was a woman's voice. Kind of young and almost panicky. I thought I recognized it.

"Yes, I'm Marcie Rayner."

"This is Trisha from the Triangle Diner. I'm the one with the ponytail. My boss said you were going to speak with me and Trudy on Thursday but it can't wait."

I was momentarily stunned. "How did you get my number? The card only had the office."

"From the internet. The white pages in New Ulm. There aren't many Marcie Rayners and I only woke up one other lady."

The internet. My landline. I made a mental note to relist my name as M Rayner and leave off my address.

"What's so important, Trisha, that it can't wait?"

"I think I know who killed Billy Hazlitt."

I threw back the covers, turned on the lamp next to my bed and started to reach into my nightstand for a pencil and paper. I wanted to be sure I got everything right.

"Who do you think it was, Trisha? And more importantly, how do you know?"

Her voice got softer and I thought I could hear someone in the background. "It's complicated. I can't talk here. Can you meet me tomorrow morning at the Hennepin Coffee Shop in Glencoe? It's just off of the 212. I can be there when it opens at six. Trudy will cover for me at the diner."

"Six? AM?"

That meant I would have to get up by four in order to shower, get dressed and make the drive. I didn't want to sound disinterested, especially when someone may have dropped the murderer right into my lap. Geez… I'd be a walking zombie at that hour.

"Trisha, is there any chance we could meet a bit later?"

"Okay, fine. Six thirty. I can't make Trudy cover for

me much longer or I'll really owe her and believe me, she cashes in on favors."

Out of nowhere, the voice in the background got louder and I could hear every word.

"Who's on the phone? It that you, Trisha? Who are you talking to this late at night? I didn't hear the phone ring."

"It's someone from school. They needed an assignment."

"At this hour?"

Then the voice in the background faded and the only words I heard were Trisha's before the line went dead.

"Hennepin Coffee Shop. Six thirty."

SIX

THE NEXT MORNING I left Angie a message telling her I would be in late. It was one of the few coherent things I did along with brushing my teeth, feeding the cat and getting washed. Not necessarily in that order. Then I got into my car and drove to Glencoe, pausing from time to time to make sure I was actually dressed.

It was such an obscene hour of the day that there wasn't too much traffic on the highway. I arrived at the coffee shop a few minutes before six thirty to find Trisha sitting at a corner table. She waved me over and then stood up.

"If you don't mind, I'm going to sit down and face the wall. I'd rather not have anyone see me talking. I got you a cup of coffee but didn't know if you wanted any donuts. They're wonderful—homemade and huge."

If you could deliver the coffee to me intravenously, it would be ideal.

"That's fine, Trisha. I'll get us some donuts and then you can tell me what you know."

The coffee shop was filling up quickly. Apparently this was *the* place to be at the crack of dawn in Glencoe. As I lifted my coffee cup to my lips, Trisha leaned into the table and said two words, then looked at me as if the words were supposed to mean something.

"Skip Gunderson."

"I don't understand. Who's Skip Gunderson? Is that who you think murdered Billy Hazlitt?"

"Shh." Trisha fidgeted with her spoon and motioned for me to lean closer into the table. I was afraid we were going to bump heads.

"I don't think anyone can hear us," I said before taking a bite out of my donut. "Who's Skip Gunderson?"

"Skip Gunderson owns the feed and grain store in Hutchinson. He loaned Billy the money for a new truck when Billy's old one died. I overheard them three months ago when they made the deal. I was changing the filter in the coffeemaker. Even though your back is turned to someone, it doesn't mean you can't hear them."

Then, as if to prove a point, Trisha turned around, taking in the entire coffee shop.

"What makes you think he's the killer?" I asked.

"Because of what Skip said."

"So what did he say?"

"He *said* that if Billy didn't make the payments on time, Skip would see to it Billy would be meeting Saint Peter at the Pearly Gates."

"I think that's just a figure of speech, something to reiterate that the guy wanted to be paid on time."

Trisha shook her head. "Not if you know Skip Gunderson. It had to be a last ditch effort on Billy's part to borrow money from that guy in the first place. Billy must have been really wiped out from his last divorce and the bank loans for the brewery. People in this town don't go asking Skip Gunderson to loan them money unless they're desperate."

I took another swallow of coffee and continued. "Has Skip ever done anything to hurt anyone?"

Trisha tore off the edge of her napkin and rolled it between her thumb and index finger. "He's beaten up a few guys over the years although people say he's mellowed. Whatever the heck that means. I wouldn't so much as borrow a dime from him."

"I know you believe he may be responsible, but it's a longshot. And no evidence."

"There's evidence all right. I saw his truck parked outside of the brewery the Sunday night before they found Billy's body. I was on my way over to my boyfriend's on Grant Street. We had a big fight so I turned around and left. When I passed the brewery again, the truck was gone."

I all but choked on my doughnut. "Why didn't you tell any of this to the sheriff?"

"Are you crazy? Don't you know who Skip Gunderson *is*? He's my boss's brother-in-law! I don't feel like losing my job. I figured you'd kind of investigate and find out for yourself. Look, I can't stay. I'm already way late for work. Trudy's probably pitching a fit. Do me a favor and wait until I'm gone for a few minutes before you leave. Okay? I don't want to take any chances."

The verdict was still out as to whether or not Trisha was a bona fide drama queen or if she was really scared. I did as she said. I waited it out and wound up eating two of Hennepin's enormous donuts before deciding to take a little drive into Hutchinson to check out the feed and grain store. If Trisha's accusation was on the money, I had to act fast.

Passing by the local gas station a few yards from the donut shop, I was glad I had checked my tires and filled up in New Ulm the day before. Prices were at least five cents more a gallon in these small towns. I got back on the highway and tried to figure out how to approach Skip Gunderson. I pictured a cross between a medieval henchman and a prize fighter. I was right on both counts.

Skip Gunderson stood at least six feet tall and looked as if he had been benching weights as soon as he had been weaned. He was tossing around forty pound bags of grain as if they were beach balls. I knew it was him even before I asked at the counter.

"Yeah," a twenty-something guy said as I walked into the store, "Skip's loading up a truck. He'll be done any second."

If I'm not professional and direct he'll be tossing me into one of those grain delivery trucks. It doesn't look as if this guy takes any prisoners.

I used the same tactic on Skip I did in second grade when a growling dog came at me. I refused to show him I was afraid.

"Excuse me," I said as I walked across the gravel lot. "Are you Skip Gunderson?"

His eyes caught mine and for an instant I thought I could discern some softness. In spite of the small wrinkles around his narrow face, he didn't have any glaring frown lines or deep set furrows. Only a day's overgrowth. Ruddy red stubble. I hoped Trisha was wrong about him.

"That's me. How can I help you?"

"I'm Marcie Rayner," I replied, "from Blake Investigations in New Ulm. We're looking into Billy Hazlitt's death." I didn't use the word *murder*. Death sounded more businesslike. More textbook. *Murder* on the other hand, could be taken as accusatory. It didn't matter. Skip wasn't about to be fooled.

"I don't know why you'd be asking me about that. I don't know anything. I don't have any business with the brewery."

"Not the brewery, exactly. But with Billy."

"What are you talking about?"

I took a deep breath and tried to remain as composed as possible. "My understanding is you loaned Billy Hazlitt money in order to buy a replacement truck when his died."

Skip Gunderson's face turned waxen and took on a hardened look. Cold and steely. I was beginning to have second thoughts about him.

"Damn it. Never tell your wife a stinkin' thing. Is that where you heard it? From Corrine? Oh what the hell. She probably blabbed it to one of her friends and no one can keep their yaps shut around here. Yeah, I loaned him some money but if you're thinkin' I killed him because he didn't pay up, you're wrong. What good is it to kill someone who owes you money? You'll never get the money back."

Skip Gunderson had a point but it still didn't explain why he was at the brewery during the alleged time of death. I tried to figure out how I could weasel that information from him, keep Trisha out of it and manage to leave with no broken bones.

"I don't know quite how to say this, Mr. Gunderson, so I'll be frank. Someone left a message with our agency indicating they had seen your truck in front of the brewery on the night of the murder. Can you explain that?"

"Bunch of old hens flapping their mouths! GEEZ! You can't take a fart around this place without it making national news. Yeah, I can explain it. It was Sunday night all right. I was driving back from a poker game with some buddies in Glencoe and had to take a whiz. Did you know you could get arrested for doing that in public? So I pulled into the brewery, went around back and drained the monster in some bushes. I never set foot inside. If you want to verify my story with my poker buddies I'll be happy to give you their names."

"Um, no. That won't be necessary. When you left the brewery parking lot, did you see anything at all? Anyone walking? Any cars?"

"Nope. Nothing. It was real quiet. Like I said, I did my business and drove straight home."

"Thanks Mr. Gunderson. Sorry to have taken up your time. Here's my card. If you can think of anything, please give me a call."

He muttered something, shook his head and headed back into the store. So much for Trisha's revelation. Yet, he could have been lying. After all, Trisha's car drove by. Wouldn't he have noticed that? Unless she was the one spinning tales. But why? Given the choice between her version of that night and Skip's, I was placing my bets on Trisha.

SEVEN

I GOT BACK in my car and headed to the highway, making a mental note that Skip Gunderson could be *a person of interest*. It was easy to see why Trisha would suspect him. I couldn't find anything likeable about him. In fact, his entire mannerisms screamed out "rough around the edges." Still, adolescent crudeness didn't make him a murderer or the police would be targeting every college frat house. Images of weapon-wielding frat boys crossed my mind as I drove back to New Ulm.

Up ahead was the exit for Biscay. I knew Max and I would be there the next day to talk with the rest of the diner employees. At least I'd have the better part of the morning to review the sheriff's notes and establish a solid timeline. Then, out of the blue, another image crossed my mind and I started to laugh. I pictured the scene from *The Music Man* with all of those gossipy women singing "Pick-A-Little-Talk-A-Little." It was something Skip Gunderson said—"Bunch of old hens flapping their mouths." What old hens? He wasn't referring to his wife's friends. Did Skip believe someone near the brewery saw him pull off and head for the bushes? If so, who were they and what else did they see?

Jumping on my brakes, I slowed the car down in time to pull off of the highway without causing a major accident. I had to take a better look at the street where the brewery and diner were located. Maybe someone in one of the neighboring houses saw something or heard something that night.

Judging from the parked cars along the street, the diner was pretty packed. After all, it was fairly early in the morning. The breakfast crowd was still there. Across the street, only one truck was parked in the brewery lot. I assumed it was Hogan's or Tyler's. Or maybe Tom had decided to come in to work. No matter, I wasn't going in there. Not today. I looked like I belonged with the zombie apocalypse with my fair skin and only lip gloss and sunscreen tint on my face. Phooey. I should've kept Trisha waiting and put on some eyeliner and blush.

What the heck was I thinking when I raced out of my apartment? Thankfully my hair, with a new layered chin length cut, always seemed to work and my clothes were stylish for summer wear—khaki twill pants and a gorgeous green Lafayette Zoey topstitch blouse from Neiman Marcus that I snagged on sale last month. A lucky find for someone who's tall and on the thin side like the rest of the relatives in my family. Unless, of course, I count my two heavyset maternal aunts, who, according to my mother, "have never shied away from the dessert table."

Driving a few yards past the diner and brewery, I pulled over to see if any houses were in the sightline of the brewery. There was a vacant lot to the left of the brewery and a row of large junipers that separated the building from the small clapboard house on the right. A house with a For Sale sign in front. From the look of things, its last occupant probably left the place when Jimmy Carter was still president. The house was literally falling apart with a roof that was leaning to one side and a side porch that looked as if it had been invaded by termites. The dead giveaway was the sea of weeds that led to the front door. Nothing but woods behind the brewery.

Across the street was a different story. The diner was flanked by two houses, both of them with neat little flower gardens and carefully manicured lawns. Both had large front windows with bird's eye views into the brewery. I pulled farther down the street, turned off the engine and reached into my bag for my phone. Taking a chance that the sporadic cell phone service might work, I sent Angie a text explaining I wouldn't get to the office until much later in the morning. Later than I had expected.

Making sure my business cards were within easy reach in my bag, I walked up to the first house and rang the bell. Standing on their porch, I could see the house belonged to a family with kids. Plastic toys, a soccer ball and one shoe were crammed into the corner along with a pile of wadded up clothes. I waited patiently hoping someone was home and that they would answer the door.

Seconds later, a twenty-something woman holding a baby opened the door. It looked as if she had just washed her curly brown hair but didn't have time to comb it. The infant was sucking frantically on a pacifier as the woman looked at me.

"Yes?"

I explained who I was and that my partner and I were looking into the death of Billy Hazlitt from the brewery. She took my card, read it and looked directly at me. "Nice top. I forget what clothing looks like without stains. You'll have to pardon me," she said. "I have three kids. Nothing I wear looks clean or decent any-more. They don't tell you this about having kids but you'll never be able to have a moment to yourself. Not in the shower or on the toilet for that matter. So, want to come inside?"

It turned out the woman's name was Marisa and she and her husband had moved into the place weeks after Billy Hazlitt's murder. The house had been on the mar-ket for months and no one was living there when they purchased it. She shuffled the baby from one arm to the other and adjusted his pacifier.

"Maybe the two sisters who live next to the diner can help you out," she said, pausing once to yell at two older children who were inches away from me, about to crayon the wall.

"Two sisters?"

"Yeah, they're both really sweet—Rose and Lila Bar-ton. They must be in their seventies or eighties. They brought us a casserole when we moved in and some wonderful cookies. You might try talking to them."

"Thanks," I said. "I will."

Marisa held the door open for me and I thanked her again before heading past the diner to Rose and Lila's place. I made it a point to shield my face from the brew-ery just in case Hogan Austin stepped outside and no-ticed me.

If Rose and Lila were the "old hens" that Skip was referring to, I could see his point. If ever there was a stereotypical description of little old ladies, those two matched the bill. Short. Stout. Perfectly combed gray-ish white hair. Floral dusters. Marisa was being diplo-matic. They had to be pushing ninety.

The sisters didn't stop babbling from the moment

they invited me inside their house to the minute I left. I was certain I was developing tinnitus in both of my ears as a result of their non-stop talking. I literally had to force myself to pay attention because neither of them could answer any of my questions without going off on unrelated tangents, including how they learned to crochet doilies, their grandfather's penchant for hunting, and who won the spelling bee when they were in grade school. They never let up. I did, however, get to enjoy some of the amazing chocolate chip cookies they baked. Marisa was right about that part but I wished she had warned me about the ladies' endless jabber.

Finally, I caught a break. Or at least a short interlude and I asked them if they had noticed anything unusual the night of Billy's murder or if they had heard anything.

"The only thing I heard was the infernal sound of the muffler on that waitress' car," Lila said as she motioned toward the diner. "I've told her over and over again she needs to get it fixed but you know what she told me? I'll tell you what came out of her mouth. She said, 'Until I get pulled over and ticketed, I've got better things to spend my money on.' And I told her it was a matter of time before she got arrested for disturbing the peace and *she* had the audacity to tell me that as long as her radio could drown out the noise, she wasn't about to spend money fixing a muffler."

Then Rose added, "She should be spending her money on food. That girl is as thin as a toothpick."

They had to be referring to Trisha but I needed to be sure. "Um…how do you know that the car belonged to the waitress?"

Rose was adamant. "She drives a blue beat-up Ford Taurus with some ridiculous pink slogan on the back window. Who puts things like that on a car window? Anyway, as soon as we heard the noise, Lila and I pulled back the curtains and looked outside. Sure enough, we saw that blue car go by—silly slogan and all."

Please tell me you ladies kept track of the time.

"About what time was this?"

"The *first* time was a little after eight. *Masterpiece Theatre* had just started. And the *second* time was about a half hour later."

Trisha's story was holding up. It was summer. With daylight savings time, her car was clearly visible and for that matter, audible. She had driven to the boyfriend's house, got into a fight with him, and drove back. The Barton sisters heard that muffler even with the television on. Then why didn't Skip Gunderson? It was becoming pretty obvious to me. Even though the sisters hadn't seen Skip Gunderson's truck, Trisha did. That had to count for something.

I thanked Rose and Lila profusely, told them that if they remembered anything else to please call me. I gave them my card. Then I hustled back to my car, once again turning my head away from the brewery. Unfortunately, I didn't turn it fast enough.

EIGHT

"MARCIE! MARCIE!" A voice rang out from across the street and I recognized it immediately. I was stuck. Hogan was running toward me from the brewery's parking lot. Marisa might've thought I looked fine, but I really wished I had taken the time to put on eyeliner and blush.

"I thought that was you a while back heading over to the Barton sisters but I wasn't too sure. I had to unload some things from my truck and your head was turned the other way. So, did you find out anything earth-shattering from Rose or Lila?"

He had a broad smile on his face as he waited for my response.

"Um, er…just the same information we already had but my partner and I like to be thorough. I don't suppose Tom is working this morning, is he?"

"No, if he decides to come in, it'll be in the afternoon. If I had known you were going to be here I would have tried to convince him to stop in. I don't recommend you pay him a visit at his house. He's probably sleeping and if he isn't, I doubt he'll open the door. I thought you said you were coming back to Biscay tomorrow. Thursday."

"We were. I mean, we are. But I wanted to speak with the neighbors and I thought I'd save some time by getting an early start today."

Hogan studied my face for a minute and then glanced at my outfit. "Cool top. Biscay isn't exactly the fashion capital as you've probably surmised."

"Um, thanks. A lucky find."

"Listen, if you're not in a hurry, the brewery is officially opened for business since it's after ten. Why don't you stop in and try a flight of our beers?"

"Beer? Right now? I can't. All I've had to eat today were a few of the Barton sisters' cookies." I neglected to mention the donuts in Glencoe or my reason for being there in the first place. I wanted to get back to the office and salvage at least part of the day. Then, my stomach began to rumble and there was no way I could cover it up. City street excavations were quieter.

Thankfully, Hogan didn't hear it or he pretended not to notice. "Trust me. There's not enough alcohol in a flight of beers to render you unconscious or evenly mildly buzzed. But I understand. Tell you what. Come inside, I'll make you a ham and cheese sandwich and then you can wash it down with our beer. If that doesn't soak up the alcohol for you, you can stuff yourself with pretzels. We've got bowls of them."

"Do you always offer your customers sandwiches?"

"Only the big spenders. Seriously, we keep ham, cheese, bread as well as peanut butter and jelly in our back fridge in case we get hungry and don't feel like waiting at the diner. Crunchy peanut butter because Billy couldn't stand the creamy kind."

He paused for a second. "I suppose that doesn't matter anymore but I couldn't bring myself to buy the creamy kind. Geez, I can't believe I'm going on about peanut butter. Anyway, what do you say?"

I'd say Alice Davenport has a good memory.

I watched as he took a step back and waited for my response.

"How can I possibly turn down a culinary delight like ham and cheese? Okay, I'll try a sampling of whatever the Crooked Eye Brewery is serving. I'll be over in a minute. I need to call my office and let them know I'm running late."

"Great. I'll get the beers lined up and get started on the sandwiches. You may want to place that call after you leave Biscay. You do know about our infamous cell phone service, don't you? Or, just use our landline and make a real call."

"I'll give it a try and if it doesn't work, I'll take you up on your offer."

Watching Hogan cross the street I reminded myself not to get involved. After all, he was a suspect along with everyone else who might have known Billy Hazlitt; and until Max and I could figure out who put the bullet in Billy's head, no one was in the clear. Nonetheless, there was a certain charm to Hogan and I had to be careful not to lose focus about the investigation.

I took out my phone and sent another text to Angie. This one indicating it would be early afternoon when I'd be back in the office. The text seemed to have gone through.

Hogan had already set out the small glasses for the beer tasting flight and I could hear him in the kitchen area preparing my lunch.

"Eat a few pretzels in the meantime," he called out. "I'll be right there."

A few minutes later, Hogan appeared with two plates and two generous sandwiches. He must have seen me glancing at the door. "Don't worry. We usually don't start to see customers much before noon on weekdays. That gives us time to check on the machinery and the brewing. Tyler won't be in till the afternoon either."

I reached for a ham and Swiss. "Is it an awful lot of work for one person? Without Tom here to help...and of course, Billy..."

"Only when we're pouring grains into the mash tun or using the sparge tank."

"I'm totally lost," I said, biting into my sandwich.

"It's the machinery used for brewing. Anyway, I'm sure you don't want to hear about the chemical process for making beer when you could be tasting the results. So, here goes!"

I watched as Hogan filled each of the small glasses with a different beer. There were four in all, going from a pale wheat color to a dark amber tint.

"Go ahead, Marcie. They won't bite. Honest."

I picked up the first glass and put it to my lips. "I'm really not a beer connoisseur. I mean, I'll have an occasional Coors or something with pizza but that's about it."

"Well, maybe this will change your mind."

The first beer was malty and biscuity, if there even was such a word. It was light and pleasant with no heavy aftertaste.

"Not bad," I said. "I expected something heavier."

"That's our pale ale. Keep going."

The next sip was different—rich with chocolate overtones. I took another sip.

"Looks like that one agrees with you."

"Anything with chocolate agrees with me."

"Good. It's our chocolate stout."

The third taste was equally good, a combination of

coffee and caramel. I had no idea that beers could be so complex. Finally, I reached for the darkest beer and tentatively put it to my lips. A pungent flavor hit my palate like molasses and smoke. I wasn't sure if I liked it or not.

"That's our Scotch ale. It's an acquired taste."

"I'm impressed, Hogan. I mean it. You could have just served me the first beer and I would have signed up on your customer list."

"Then you're in for a surprise. I've got one more beer for you to sample."

I finished off my sandwich in two bites and waited while he took a small cylinder and poured out a dark, reddish liquid. The aroma of clove and cinnamon filled my nostrils before the first bit of liquid reached my mouth. It was heavenly—spicy and savory with a peppery black chocolate finish that seemed to tease my senses.

"Holy cow! What *is* this?"

"This is our Wild Turkey Bourbon Beer. Not bad for an aged brown ale, huh? It's a formula Billy developed."

I took another sip. "Formula?"

"No pun intended, but it all boils down to math and formulas. The ratio of liquid malt to dry malt, the ratio of grain to liquid extract… Anyway, Billy developed his own formula for this one and there's nothing like it."

"Is this fairly new or have people been tasting this?" I asked.

"We introduced it a few months ago. Why?"

"Nothing. I was wondering, that's all. It's an amazing flavor."

I didn't say it out loud but I certainly thought it. *Could someone have murdered Billy Hazlitt for his for-*

mula? I took another sip but this time I let the liquid roll around in my mouth. "Tell me," I said, "Are the formulas common knowledge?"

Hogan shook his head. "No. Well, not exactly. The big name brand breweries have standard formulas that they've been using and tweaking for decades. But microbreweries like ours develop their own formulas and keep revising them. In fact, Billy's formula is hanging from a small hook on the wall near the brite tank."

"Bright tank?"

"Not bright like in a color but b-r-i-t-e. It's a large stainless steel tank that's used to condition and store beer until it's mature."

Then, as if to verify what he said, Hogan pointed to the walk-in refrigerator, got up, and opened the door. "See? The large stainless tank? Look at the wall next to it. You can't miss Billy's notebook. It's the frayed one with all of our formulas."

I saw the notebook hanging from the hook but it was the red stain on the concrete floor that caught my eye. It had been bleached to a lighter hue but no amount of Clorox was going to erase Billy's blood from the concrete.

Just then, three customers came through the front door and headed for the counter.

"I'll be right with you," Hogan said.

It was my cue to get going. I tapped Hogan on the arm, turning my face away from the customers. "I've really got to be on my way. Thanks for the sandwich and the beer flight. I'll talk to you later. And thanks for not pointing out my grumbling stomach was louder than a 747 on takeoff."

"I hardly noticed," he said, closing the walk-in door behind him. "I was too busy staring at the crumbs of cookies on your mouth. Chocolate chip? Those Barton sisters sure know how to bake." Then he gave me a wink before turning his attention to the customers. Yep. Had to admit, he was a charmer.

NINE

A PLEASANT AFTERTASTE from those beer samples lingered in my mouth even though Hogan's ham and Swiss sandwich absorbed most of the alcohol. This was a first. Drinking on the job. Actually, it *was* the job. Not the beer tasting but certainly the sleuthing. I reached into the catch-all between the driver's seat and the passenger's to grab a peppermint. There were at least a dozen of them, the small tokens that came with the check following last month's restaurant meals. I popped one in my mouth and spit the plastic into my hand. Very lady-like. At least Hogan wasn't here to witness that. Or my mother, for that matter.

The traffic, although fairly light, had certainly increased since this morning's pre-dawn ride. I was back in the office by early afternoon and announced myself as I came through the door.

"Hey Angie! How's it going? You got my message, right? I was in Biscay on that murder case. Oh, and in case you're wondering, I already had lunch."

"Okay, but if you get hungry, let me know. I'll be heading to the deli in a little while. The office has been pretty quiet but you've got a message. I left it on your desk."

"Alice Davenport?"

"The very harpy herself. Look, I don't want to tell you how to run your business, but if I were you, I'd call her back right away. Before she decides to storm in here or something. She frightens me."

"Yeah, me, too." *And she wouldn't have to storm in here, just fly on a broomstick.* "Don't worry. She's miles away in Southern Florida. But I'll get right on it. Why take a chance? Anything else going on I should know about?"

"We've had a few queries about our business but nothing definitive."

"Thanks."

I flung my bag over one of the chairs in my office, booted up my computer and dialed Alice Davenport's number hoping she wasn't about to demand daily chronological reports. She answered on the first ring.

"Miss Rayner. Thank you for getting back to me. I've been waiting for your call."

Probably sitting inches from the phone.

"How did you know—"

"I have caller ID. Those telemarketers aren't going to fool me. Anyway, I called you because I had forgotten to mention something. Something important."

My hand reached for a pen as she continued.

"I know I told you Billy Hazlitt was liked by everyone but I forgot all about Lucas Rackner."

"Who?"

"Lucas Rackner. He was in the same class as Billy and they never got along. Once, during lunch, they got into a fight and the principal had to break it up. Both boys stayed after school for two weeks as punishment. Track down Lucas Rackner and send me a report."

"That was decades ago. I hardly think that some schoolyard brawl would result in murder."

"That's what you need to find out. For all I know,

Lucas Rackner could have been carrying a grudge all those years. Festering. Boiling. Stewing. And then…"

What? No cooking, baking or braising?

I didn't want to hear anymore. "Okay. Okay. I'll put him on my list. Do you have any idea if he's still in Minnesota?"

"Of course not. You're the investigator. Remember, send me a report at the end of the week."

Before I could utter a single syllable, she had ended the call. Unbelievable. A left over grudge from the fifth grade? It was preposterous. A complete waste of my time. Nevertheless, Alice Davenport was paying for our services so I stood up, walked into our outer office and did the only thing a reasonable person would do. I asked Angie to contact Billy and Lucas' former school district to find out when Lucas Rackner graduated and where he wound up. A decent internet search could take it from there.

I returned to my desk but kept mulling over her call. Finally, I got up again, this time planting myself in front of Angie's computer monitor. "Say, Angie, you've got grandkids in elementary school, don't you?"

She gave me a funny look. "Yeah. Two boys. One in first grade. One in third. Why?"

"Do you think they would hold a grudge for years and years if they had a fight with one of their classmates?"

"Heck no! Wait till you have kids. One minute they're duking it out, the next they're raiding someone's refrigerator. Of course, that's boys. I have no idea about girls that age but I doubt it. Why?"

"Ah, something Alice Davenport thought up."

"Oh. I see."

As Angie started to look up the phone number, I went into the workroom to begin the project I should have started in the morning—completing the timeline. No sooner did I draw a long horizontal line across the whiteboard when Angie knocked on my doorframe.

"Hey, I know this is none of my business so feel free to stop me at any time. I just wanted to put in my two cents for the record."

I stopped writing. "What do you mean?"

"I wanted to tell you that I think you're doing a hands-down job with this investigation and I'm not saying that to waste my breath or make you feel better. I watch how you work, Marcie, and you've got a talent for getting right to the crux of things. Plus, I've seen you with clients and you've got a way about you that puts people at ease. That matters in a job like yours. Look, I'll get right to the point—I'd hate to see you return to your other job."

"Wow. Sure you're not saying that because you're afraid Max will hire some stuck-up namby-pamby or worse yet, a really high maintenance investigator?"

Angie laughed. "Give me some credit. Max would never do that. Besides, how am I going to keep up with the latest fashion footwear if you leave?"

"Ah-hah! The real reason comes to light. I think you'll be seeing lots more of my shoes before this murder gets solved."

"Good to know."

"Seriously, thanks Angie. It was a nice thing to say."

She gave a nod and walked to her desk. I turned to the whiteboard and entered the events from Sunday afternoon to that Monday morning at dawn, the week before Memorial Day.

Billy Hazlitt was last seen alive when the brewery closed. Sometime before dusk Trisha drove to her boyfriend's, got into a fight and drove back. Her drive was substantiated by the Barton sisters who were aggravated by the noise from Trisha's muffler. Then there was Skip Gunderson who went behind the brewery to relieve himself following a poker game in Glencoe. Trisha had seen his truck in front of the brewery on her way over to the boyfriend's.

The coroner had placed the time of death somewhere between eight at night and two in the morning. It was a broad "window" and even though Skip Gunderson was there during that time span, it didn't mean he was the killer. I believed him when he said there was no motive to kill someone who owed you money.

Then who? Not that Skip was totally off the hook as far as I was concerned, but there had to be something else. I started to review the notes again when Angie called out to me.

"I located Lucas Rackner for you, Marcie."

"What? That fast?"

"It was easy. Fell right into my lap, so to speak. Lucas graduated from high school in the same class as Billy. Went to state college for physical education. Owns a fitness business in Willmar. You know, personal trainers, weight loss, the whole works."

"How on earth did you find all of this out so fast?"

"Turns out the secretary at the high school used to work in Willmar and took exercise classes there during her lunch hour."

"Amazing. That's amazing."

"Not really. Glencoe, Biscay, Hutchinson…they're

all such small towns that everyone knows everyone
else's business."

Yeah, I thought. *Then how come they don't know who
murdered Billy Hazlitt?*

At least Willmar was in driving range of New Ulm
and not in South Dakota or Iowa. Lucas Rackner never
left the state. I figured I'd give him a call and see if he
had had any contact with Billy over the years. I was sure
he'd say no and spare me the road trip. I was wrong.

TEN

THE REST OF my afternoon was spent mulling over the notes, adding tidbits to the timeline and trying to figure out if Hogan Austin was really as nice as he seemed or if it was a ruse to shift the attention away from him as a possible suspect. I certainly wasn't about to let this guy charm me into losing my objectivity when it came to the case, even if he did make a damn good ham and Swiss sandwich. At least Max would be with me tomorrow when we drive back to Biscay to talk with the waitresses and Frankie, the cook.

It was four o'clock when I finally decided to give Lucas Rackner a call. I wasn't sure where to begin without mentioning Alice Davenport and that was the *last* thing I intended to do. Heck, that woman gave me the willies and I'd never seen her face-to-face. For all I knew, Lucas might not have gotten over his fifth grade experience with her. Talk about nightmares. This was a genuine terror. No need for me to go there.

I decided to use the same tactic I did with Skip Gunderson. Identify myself and tell Lucas it was brought to the attention of our investigative firm that he may know something about Billy's death. I wouldn't have to go any further than that.

Lucas picked up on the second ring. So far so good. Then, once I had taken care of the preliminaries, he took me completely off guard. Talk about bombshells.

"Hey, I was wondering when someone would call about Billy Hazlitt. I guess I was one of the last people to see him alive."

Was Alice Davenport psychic?

Cradling the phone under my ear and reaching for a pen, I couldn't speak fast enough. "At the brewery? You were at the Crooked Eye Brewery that Sunday night?"

"Oh, heck no. I ran into him the day before in Willmar. It was really weird. I hadn't seen Billy in years. Oh sure, we'd run into each other once in a while when I was in Glencoe visiting my folks, but that was years ago. Anyway, there I was at the Pump & Pantry on 1st Street when who should walk in but Billy. He said he had some business at the fabricating company on 6th. I figured it had to do with the brewery."

"Fabricating company?"

"Yeah, they make all sorts of metal storage units, things like that."

"Um… Did you know Billy well? I mean, were you friends?"

"We went to the same schools but no, we weren't exactly best buds if you know what I mean. Not that we had anything against each other, we just didn't hang around with the same crowds. I was on the wrestling team as well as football. Billy played basketball and lacrosse."

"What about the way he acted when you ran into him? Anything unusual?"

"No, not at all. We talked for a few minutes about our families and stuff and then Billy said he had to get going but was making one more stop—to the chocolate shop on Becker Ave. I figured he was getting something for a girlfriend but didn't ask. Now here's where it gets really freaky. That chocolate shop and the flower shop next door to it both burned down in a wicked fire late that afternoon."

I remembered something Hogan had mentioned about a fire. His nephew's baseball game had to be postponed to Sunday because of all the smoke in the air.

"Hmm," I muttered, trying to conceal any hints of surprise in my voice, "That really is odd. So, uh, Billy was acting normal and all that when you spoke to him."

"Yeah, sure. Say, you're not hinting he might've had anything to do with that fire, are you?"

"Me? No. Of course not."

"Like I said, Billy and I talked about the usual stuff and we went about our business. He seemed as normal as the next guy."

"That's good to know. Listen, if you can think of anything else that might help us with this investigation, please give me a call, okay?"

"Sure thing. And I'm sorry about Billy. We might not have been friends so to speak, but he was a decent guy."

I thanked Lucas and hung up the phone. There was no way I was going to mention duking it out in the fifth grade at lunch. Whatever their issue had been as kids, at least Lucas had gotten over it and I'm sure Billy did as well. Yet, if it wasn't for Alice Davenport remembering that event, I never would have found out Billy had been in Willmar a few hours before a major fire. Did that have something to do with his murder? The questions were beginning to pile up and the answers seemed out of reach.

Everything was growing tentacles with this investigation. Tentacles and stingers if you count my mother and Alice Davenport.

There was one more thing I wanted to do before shooting off a report to Alice and heading home. I needed to outline a profile of Billy Hazlitt on the white-board—his family, friends, etc. I figured it would give me a better picture of whom I was dealing with and why someone might have wanted to kill him. Besides, I was familiar with the process. I had watched enough episodes of *Elementary* and *NCIS* to come to the con-clusion that every decent investigator sticks a picture of the victim on the board and jots down notes.

Then I realized something. We didn't have a picture of Billy. The sheriff's report didn't include one. But I was certain the internet would. I had Angie do a quick newspaper search of any promos that might have been in the papers regarding the Crooked Eye Brewery. Sure enough, she turned up a fairly decent picture of Billy, Tom and Hogan standing in front of the tasting room counter with a beer flight in front of them and the big brewery sign on the wall behind them. It must have been taken a few years back when they first opened.

I had just started to draw a red circle around Billy's face in preparation for taping it to the whiteboard when Angie announced that "Max was on line one" for me.

"How's it going, kid? Hopefully better than my day. My testimony's been postponed until tomorrow. Mu-riel Klemmer broke down on the stand, hyperventilat-ing until she fainted. They had to call in the paramedics and take her to the hospital. A precaution. Anyway, the judge is reconvening the trial for tomorrow at ten. I'm stuck here another night. Good thing my wife's in Roch-ester for a few days visiting with her sister otherwise she'd be pitching a fit. Hope this doesn't throw you off course because there's no way I'll be back in time to interview those waitresses like we had planned. Guess you'll be on your own for that one."

"No problem. I already interviewed Trisha. The skinny one with the ponytail."

"Huh? When? I thought you were staying in the office, going over the notes."

I explained about the late night call from Trisha, my encounter with Skip Gunderson, and my interview with the Barton sisters. I also mentioned running into Hogan when he saw me on the street. I gave Max every single detail with the exception of the beer tasting. Not that I thought he'd be upset, because after all, I was still gathering information. But, I could have gathered it while drinking bottled water instead.

"You're way ahead of the game on this one. Look, we'll compare notes once I get back. There's one more thing I need to do while I'm in Minneapolis and I'm hoping I can take care of it tomorrow afternoon if they call me to the stand in the morning."

"What's that?" I asked.

"I plan on paying a little visit to Longfellow Brewery. Billy worked for them before he opened up the Crooked Eye. I need to find out if anyone there might have an idea of who might have had it in for the guy."

"Longfellow Brewery? That's a huge company. Never tried their beers but I love their commercials. Especially the dancing cats. Honestly, Max, I never thought of asking around at his former workplace. It's going to take me forever till I get the gist of this."

"Stop beating yourself up. You're doing great. Catch you later!"

I went back to the whiteboard, taped Billy's photo on the left hand corner and jotted down the snippets of information I had managed to garner. The list was longer than I realized and nothing seemed to be connected. Lack of sleep and new hunger pangs were interfering with my brain. It was almost five and Angie would be heading home for the day. I planned on walking out the door with her. I could always finish Billy's profile in the morning. Plenty of time before I had to drive to Biscay.

Without Max, I had no plans to walk into the Crooked Eye. I'd wait until both of us could interview Tom. Besides, there was no guarantee that the poor guy would even be in. According to Hogan, he was taking it really hard. I mean, who wouldn't? Imagine finding out that your younger brother was shot in the head with a .357… OH MY GOSH! WHAT THE HECK PLANET HAVE I BEEN ON? The gun. The gun. I never asked anyone about the gun.

ELEVEN

My PHONE WENT off like a cannon the next morning and I dropped my eyeliner in the sink. I was applying makeup with the finesse of Rembrandt and dabbing just enough mousse on my hair to fight off the Minnesota summer humidity. I raced back to the bedroom and picked up the receiver. Maybe Max had a change of plans for me.

"Dammit Marcie. Will you get a boyfriend already! Mom is driving me insane."

"Gee, nice talking to you, too, Jonathan. Especially when I'm in a hurry to get to work."

"I'm serious. She woke me up. Gale, too. At least the baby sleeps through anything."

I didn't know what to say and waited for my brother to continue. "She played bridge last night with some of her friends and apparently one of them mentioned a niece who never married and was now living with eleven cats. That's when Mom got the idea I needed to do something about your social life."

"She's certifiable! I have one cat. O-n-e. Holy crap. What does she expect you to do? Conjure up a guy for me?"

"Conjure's a good word. She's insistent I introduce you to one of the single men who work in the research lab."

"Yeesh."

"Wouldn't believe me when I told her they were either married, gay or ancient. Said to pick one."

"Figures."

"Look, I know you haven't been divorced all that long so I understand if you're not ready to dip your feet in the water, but…"

"What? What were you going to say?"

"Make up something. Anything. Just get her off my back. The conversation I had with her this morning was nerve wracking. I swore if she said 'poor Marcie' one more time I was going to lose it."

"Did you tell her I was doing fine? I *am* doing fine, you know."

"As far as she's concerned, you're one step away from buying bulk litter. I mean it, Marcie. Do something."

I told my brother not to let Mom get to him but who was I kidding? I was convinced Iris Krum could get the most seasoned intelligence agent to crack in a matter of minutes. Retrieving my eyeliner, I was thankful I had applied it before the phone rang.

"Do you have to make an appearance in court, too?" Angie asked when I walked into the office an hour later. "That must explain why you went for the uniformed look—navy twills and a white top."

I furrowed my brow and shook my head. "I went for the 'uniformed look' because everything else is waiting to be washed. And no, not court, I have more interviews this afternoon in Biscay."

"Oh, I see. I hope it's all right but I made four appointments for you next week with prospective clients. One lady recently found out she has a sister and wants an investigator to track down that sibling. Then there was an elderly lady looking for her roommate… Oh, and a man who wanted us to locate his wife so he could expedite their divorce. Not sure about the fourth call. They didn't say much. Anyhow, I set up the appointments for you and not Mr. Blake since I didn't know how dragged out his court appearances would be for that other case."

"That's fine, Angie. Max…I mean, Mr. Blake…and I share all the information anyway. If I'm not at my desk I'll be hovering over the whiteboard in the workroom."

Angie nodded and went back to whatever paperwork she was doing while I was trying to decide if I should continue filling in Billy's profile on the whiteboard or review the sheriff's notes again. I decided on the notes.

The gun had been plaguing me all night. First of all, I couldn't believe I hadn't asked anyone about it. And secondly, I wasn't exactly sure how to approach it. I couldn't very well blurt out, "By the way, do you happen to own a .357 Magnum?" I would have to take an indirect approach to see if anyone laid claim to the revolver cartridge made famous by Smith & Wesson and Winchester back in the 1930s. Oddly enough, its styling still looked the same and always reminded me of the guns I used to see on those old cowboy movies, certainly a far cry from a safe action pistol like a Glock.

It wasn't as if the .357 had been located. That would have pushed the investigation straight to the finish line. Serial number. Point of purchase. Done deal. No, there was no gun. Only the coroner's report and initial findings that indicated it was a .357. To make matters worse, the forensic crew couldn't find a single decent fingerprint on the scene. Smudged prints were all over the

front door of the brewery and the back door, the one
that the killer most probably used, was wiped clean.

According to the crime scene notes, there were
no useable prints anywhere. The counters had been
scoured clean along with the sink in the kitchen and
the restroom. Even the handle to the toilet was clean.
It wouldn't have made sense for Billy to do such a thorough job after closing up. I mean, why do something
like that when you've got a paid cleaning service coming in the next morning? It had to be the murderer.
Whoever it was, they weren't about to leave any clues.
That meant tracking down the killer with sleuthing as
opposed to forensics. Too bad my comfort zone rested
with statistics and analyzes. Still, I had a penchant for
puzzle solving and that, combined with the questioning
skills I was learning from Max, would have to suffice.

I put the file down and headed to the workroom when
Angie announced I had another "call on line one."

It was Rose Barton. She had remembered something
and wanted to know when I was going to be back in Biscay. With a full diner line-up in the afternoon, I really
didn't want to add one more thing to my day so I asked
her to tell me what it was. She refused. Vehemently.

"I can't tell you over the phone. This line could be
tapped. They do that, you know. Tap the line and listen in."

I couldn't believe what I was hearing. It sounded
like my mother and her friends. Was this age related
or what? I tried not to laugh. "Who does that? Who's
listening in?"

"Why, the government, dear. They tap your phone
line and listen to everything you say. Then they raise

your taxes. That's why we need to speak privately. When can I expect you?"

As much as I wanted to tell Rose Barton that the government couldn't possibly care less about what was going on in her life, let alone move her into another tax bracket, I chose not to. No sense in alienating a possible source of information. Especially one who can bake such good chocolate chip cookies. I acquiesced and decided to head out for Biscay earlier in the day, figuring I could make Rose Barton my first stop. I still had plenty of time to finish Billy Hazlitt's profile and grab some lunch.

Listed under Billy's photo, in no particular order, were the following:

> *Age: Forty-five*
> *Divorced twice, no children*
> *First wife: Jennifer Midland, now living in Seattle*
> *Second wife: school teacher in Minneapolis (Get her name!)*
> *Older brother Tom Hazlitt, co-owner in brewery along with friend Hogan Austin*
> *Retired from the military*
> *Worked for Longfellow Brewery in Minneapolis*
> *Lived alone*
> *Shot in head with a .357 Magnum*
> *Body found at scene of death in brewery*

Then, I started two new columns—Possible Suspects and Contacts. I only had one name under "Suspects"— Skip Gunderson. It was followed by a question mark. "Contacts" was another story. The list seemed to be growing: Hogan Austin, Tyler, the Barton Sisters, Trudy,

Trisha, Frankie the cook, George Bowman, Kaye Bowman, Marisa, Marisa's family and Lucas Rackner. I left enough space on this column because I was certain, after my meeting with Rose Barton, that I'd have another name to add.

At the top of the right hand corner I wrote the word motive in capital letters as if that would somehow compel what little knowledge I had to suddenly spew out a revelation. It didn't. The sheriff's department had ruled out burglary but what if something had been taken that they didn't know about? Revenge came next. Only because revenge is usually a motive when the act of murder is personal and committed in close range. The sheriff's department drew a blank on that one, too. That left a wide range of topics including personal vendettas, narcotics, secrets, and jealously. Until I could get more information from my contacts list, I chose not to speculate.

It was late morning when I decided to go out and get something to eat. No way was I going to have a repetition of yesterday with a grumbling stomach. I also thought it wouldn't look too professional sitting at the Triangle Diner stuffing my face when I was supposed to be interviewing their employees. Sipping on coffee was one thing. It was almost expected. Indulging in food was not.

I told Angie I would be heading back to Biscay after lunch and would check in later on. "At least you'll have both of us in the office all day tomorrow," I said as I flung my bag over my shoulder. "I'm afraid you'll start talking to yourself out of sheer boredom."

"Don't worry about that. I've got enough to keep me occupied. I plan to go over the accounts, pay some bills and finalize a few reports from last month. Plus the phone calls are a constant source of entertainment. Enough to keep me busy all afternoon and then some. Rest assured, if something comes up, I'll keep trying you until I get through."

I had no doubt about that. "Thanks, Angie. See you in the morning!"

She'd get calls all right. I only prayed they'd be from normal clients. I opted for a grilled cheese and bacon sandwich from a new shop that had opened a few blocks from the office. One bite and I knew I'd be back. They used Havarti cheese and apple-smoked bacon. My stomach wouldn't be rumbling at the Triangle Diner in Biscay.

TWELVE

MY FIRST STOP once I got off the highway was to Rose and Lila Barton's house. This time they were expecting me and had set up a small table with a teapot and some tiny scones in their dining room. Small white doilies atop the light blue tablecloth completed the tableau. The wall was painted a dark burgundy and showed off their collection of framed rustic paintings. The focal point, dead center among the artwork, was an old double-barreled shotgun that once belonged to their grandfather. I had remembered them telling me something about him on my initial visit to their house.

After they had ushered me into one of the cushiony chairs and handed me a cup of tea, Rose shifted the conversation from pleasantries to the real reason she had called me.

"I knew we had forgotten something about that awful night. But it seemed so inconsequential at the time. In fact, Lila said not to bother you at all with it but I thought it might matter."

"What might matter?" I asked, setting my cup on the table as I waited for Rose's response.

"The baby crying. That's what."

"Huh? What baby? I'm not sure I understand."

Then Lila chirped in. "It happened before that whole nonsense with the car muffler. And by the way, she *still* hasn't gotten it fixed. It's like an explosion in one's ears.

She should be arrested for disturbing the peace. So, like I was saying, it was still daylight. Rose and I were putting some of the zucchini loaves that we baked into the freezer when we heard a cat yowling. It was about an hour before *Masterpiece Theater*."

"It was a baby crying, Lila. Not a yowling cat. I can tell the difference."

"I'm *telling* you, Rose. It was a cat. Someone's cat in heat, that's what."

"You're wrong, Lila. We had this discussion before. I remember distinctly telling you that I wanted to finish up in the kitchen and take a nice soothing bath before we sat down to watch the television and you said that it wasn't going to be all that soothing with all that cater-wauling going on. And I said, 'Who's baby could that be?' and you said 'Get your ears fixed, it's a cat,' and then we both went over to the window to take a look."

I glanced at the window and then back to the two sisters. "Did you see anything?"

"We most certainly did," Lila said, glaring at her sister. "It was a cat all right, running across the street to the vacant lot."

"Tell her the rest of it, Lila. You're leaving out the most important part."

"Rose thought she saw someone running across the street into the Juniper bushes next to the brewery but I didn't see anything and I told her as much."

"Then how do you explain the baby crying and don't give me that bit about the cat, Lila, because the cat was long gone when the crying noise continued."

"There's more than one cat in the neighborhood, Rose."

"Well," I said, trying not to sound too patronizing,

"All of this information is very helpful. Very helpful indeed. And if you remember anything else, be sure to let me know."

I stood up and started for the door and that's when the most important bit of information dropped from Rose's mouth like a bowling ball hitting the alley.

"We both saw a flash of light coming from that direction. Poof! Just like that!"

"Is that true, Lila? You saw a flash of light?"

"It could have been anything. A cluster of fireflies. A reflection from the brewery…"

"Not in broad daylight, Lila," Rose said. "And a cluster of fireflies doesn't turn on and off like a wall switch!"

I couldn't bear spending another minute with the Barton sisters but if it wasn't for them, I wouldn't have known about the change in the timeline. Maybe someone was sneaking into the brewery around seven that night. But why use a flashlight? It wasn't even close to dusk.

"Did either of you hear anything that could have sounded like a gunshot?" I asked.

Both of them shook their heads and Rose spoke. "The only thing we heard was an hour later and that was the muffler."

I thanked them again and closed the door behind me. I could hear the two of them, still arguing over whether or not it was a baby or a cat. Laughing to myself, I started toward the diner. With the diner closed during the night in question, I didn't hold out any great hopes that anyone there would have firsthand knowledge pertaining to the events. What I counted on was finding out a bit more about Billy Hazlitt and any of his relationships. Relationships that could have gotten him killed.

Trisha waved and motioned me over to a table in the back when I walked through the door. The lunch hour was long over and only three or four customers were in the diner. None of them was Hogan Austin. I could see Frankie behind the grill and another older waitress folding napkins with silverware tucked inside. I figured that had to be Kaye, the owner's sister.

"I'll tell George you're here," Trisha said. Then, she leaned over and whispered, "I'll call you tonight," before standing up and announcing, "I'll get you that coffee right away."

Wonderful. Another late night call. Maybe she can time it in-between my runs to the bathroom with all this tea and coffee.

"Trisha, not too late, okay? I'm already sleep deprived."

"Uh huh. I'll hurry up with that coffee."

George Bowman took a seat across from me, rubbed his double chin and cleared his throat. "I already spoke with the other investigator the other day. Not much more to tell you except I'm getting sick and tired of how skittish the waitresses are getting. One little noise and they're jumping out of their skins. I swear, whoever killed Billy Hazlitt is killing my business. I hope to God you find the SOB who did this before I have to file for bankruptcy."

I gave him a quick nod. "Mr. Bowman, the sheriff's report indicated that Billy was shot with a .357 Magnum. Do you know anyone who would have such a gun?"

The guy looked at me as if I had asked him if he

knew anyone who could command a lunar spaceship. "Hell no! The folks who come in and out of here are regular citizens, not snipers. And the ones who do have guns are hunters. You know, wild turkey, deer… I don't know anyone who would own such a weapon. And this is small 'townsville.' People don't need to arm themselves like they do in the big cities. No…if you ask me, it had to be someone who wasn't from around here."

As it turned out, George Bowman couldn't tell me too much about Billy other than the fact the two of them exchanged cursory greetings and the usual small talk when Billy came into the diner.

"Listen, if anyone knows anything at all about Billy, I wager my sister does. Her nose isn't too far away from the rumor mill. Hold on and I'll get her for you."

As soon as George Bowman stood up, Trisha came back to re-fill my coffee. "Tell me what you find out when we talk tonight."

"I, er…" By the time I could say anything, Trisha had left and Kaye Bowman reached out her hand and introduced herself. It was the strongest handshake I ever felt. Maybe because it was so unexpected. Kaye Bowman was a petite gray-haired woman who looked as if she'd collapse if she was asked to lift a five pound bag of flour.

"Kaye Bowman. Pleasure to meet you. Heard you were investigating the murder across the street. Nice guy, too. Always polite. We thought it might have been a burglary gone bad but that's not what the scuttlebutt says."

George was right. This was one lady who wouldn't miss much.

"The scuttlebutt?"

"I don't know how you professional detectives conduct your investigations but I've learned to pick up every little thing that comes wafting under my nose."

A comically grotesque image came to mind so I bit my lip in order to stop myself from laughing. The pain actually made me wince and at that very moment, Hogan Austin strolled into the diner looking straight ahead at me.

THIRTEEN

I GAVE HOGAN a wave and turned my attention back to Kaye. He took a seat at the counter and waved back. Then, when Kaye wasn't looking, he made one of those funny talking signs with his hand.

"As I was saying," Kaye went on, "I make it a point to keep my ears open around here. If someone's talking about it at the diner, I'll be sure to find out."

Naturally I asked her the same question I asked her brother. Did she know anyone who owned a .357? Her answer was straight to the point.

"You're kidding me, right? A .357? Half the people would shoot their toes off and the other half would shoot off a different appendage."

Again I tried not to laugh. I asked her three questions on the off chance that she'd be able to answer at least one of them.

"Do you know anything about Billy that would have gotten him killed?"

"Do you know anyone who had anything against him?"

"Do you have any information about the night he was murdered?"

Kaye had no idea what happened the night Billy Hazlitt was murdered and she hadn't heard of anyone who might have wanted to kill him. But she did have some ideas about what might have *gotten* him killed.

"From what I've gathered," she said, propping her elbows on the table and inching her head toward me, "Billy might have been having an affair with a married woman."

"A married woman? Who? Where?"

"I don't know her name but I do know she and her husband own a chocolate shop and a flower shop in Willmar. The same two stores that burned down in that fire the day before Billy's murder. Now if that's not a coincidence then I don't know what is."

"Did you tell this to the sheriff? What did they think?"

Kaye grimaced. "That it was a coincidence."

"I see. Can you tell me where you heard this information? I mean, about the affair? I mean, about the *alleged* affair."

"I didn't hear it. I saw it! With my own eyes."

"Huh?"

"My dermatologist's office is in Willmar and the only good thing about driving that far away is to stop in the chocolate shop on Becker Avenue and buy their homemade truffles. Now I'll have to settle for month old M & M's from the grocery. Anyway, when I was last in their shop, who do you think I saw but Billy Hazlitt! Coming out of the back room with the owner, a cutesy-tootsie thirtyish woman who was fawning all over him. Reminded me of Pippi Longstocking only the hair was a different color. They didn't see me because I turned the other way to rummage through the assorted chocolate bins."

"How long ago was this?"

"Maybe two months ago. I'd have to check my calendar. I write down every single doctor's appointment and keep track of the mileage for taxes."

"Uh-huh. That makes sense. But how do you know they were having an affair?"

"Like I said, she was all over him and he didn't seem to mind."

"That doesn't necessarily mean that they were having an affair."

Kaye flashed me a pained look. "I know an affair when I see one. Not only that, but I overheard her say 'I don't want him to find out. It will upset him to the breaking point.' And then I heard Billy say 'Don't you think he'll find out one way or another?' And then *she* said, 'Not unless you say anything.' If that's not enough to convince me they were having an affair, I cannot imagine what would."

I made a mental note not to have any personal conversations with anyone if Kaye was within earshot. And while her evidence was far from ironclad, it was the stuff that murders are made of—rumor and innuendo. Maybe Kaye wasn't so far off the mark. I thanked her and stood up.

"With all this coffee, I need to visit your restroom."

"Sure, sure. I'll tell Frankie to hightail it over to your table as soon as he's done with the next order. George can take over the grill from there."

I passed Hogan on my way to the ladies' room and whispered, "No ham and cheese today at the brewery?"

"Nah. Sometimes I get in the mood for one of Frankie's hamburgers and nothing else will do."

Just then Frankie spoke up. "Looks like it'll be one of George's hamburgers because I'm supposed to talk with the lady investigator."

I whipped my head around. "My name's Marcie and I'll be back in a few minutes."

"You heard her," Hogan said. "Plenty of time to get my burger going!"

I was only in the ladies' room for a few minutes but when I got back Frankie was already seated at my table and George had taken over the grill.

Frankie had his elbows propped and his head resting on the backs of his hands. He lifted his eyebrows when I sat down. "I won't take much of your time," I said, reaching into my bag for my small notebook.

"Take as much time as you want. It's not every day I get an extra break from the grill."

I asked Frankie the same three questions that I had asked Kaye. Plus the one about the gun.

"Sorry," he said. "Don't know anyone around here who would have a handgun. I know a few people who wouldn't think twice about blowing your head off with a shotgun, but a handgun? Nah."

I put my pen down. It was the first time I had taken a really good look at Frankie. He appeared to be in his late twenties, about five foot eight or nine, slender, with that "Brad Pitt shadow" on his face. Either Frankie didn't feel like shaving or it was the style he was going for. His wavy dark hair was slicked back and I imagined it was because he didn't want to wear a hairnet. Judging from his bare arms, he was certainly toned, but I wouldn't go as far as to use the word "buff." There was also something oddly familiar about him but I couldn't place it.

"Um, about these people who would blow off your head, who are you talking about?"

"Aw, just the local hotheads who get riled up about anything—the government, taxes, that kind of crap."

"Anyone in particular? Anyone who might have had it in for Billy?"

"Not that I know of. Billy got along okay with everyone. And even if someone were to piss him off, he wouldn't make a big deal of it. Didn't want to lose any customers for the brewery."

Frankie had a point. When you're in business you need to let a lot of those little things slide and it sounded like Billy was pretty good at that. I was still struggling with motive. Someone had to have a reason for killing him like that. Maybe Trudy would be able to fill in the blanks for me.

"Thanks Frankie," I said. "I appreciate your time. Can you find Trudy and send her over?"

"Didn't my boss say anything? Trudy called in sick. You'll have to catch her another day."

Now that I thought about it, I didn't see Trudy when I walked in. "Oh. Well. Thanks."

I stood up, grabbed my bag and headed toward the door but not before thanking George Bowman for letting me speak with his employees. He groaned and began to rub his temples.

"Yeah. Don't know what's going on with Trudy. Like I said, the waitresses are really jittery. Looking over their shoulders all the time. Expecting to be gunned down. How can you run a business with all that going on?"

"Hopefully my partner and I will be able to get this case solved," I said, trying to sound as professional as possible. "I'll call the diner and set up another time to see Trudy, unless you don't mind giving me her phone number. That may be easier."

George nodded and headed back to the grill. While

I was talking with Frankie, a few more customers had come in. I needed to move closer to the counter so I wouldn't bump into their tables. Instead, I actually bumped Hogan's chair.

He turned his head and lightly touched my arm. "All done with your interviews?"

"Yeah. Trudy called in sick but I was able to speak with everyone else."

"Any revelations?"

"One."

Hogan looked surprised. "One?"

"Yep," I said. "The coffee's really good."

He laughed. "That's a diplomatic way of telling me to mind my own business. Do you have to rush back to work? I can order you one of these great burgers if you want to stick around for a while."

I didn't know if it was the aroma from the grill or Hogan's invitation but I wanted to sink my teeth into a juicy hamburger with all the fixings. So much for the grilled cheese and bacon lunch I ate earlier.

"You know, that does sound awfully good. Sure, I'd love a burger—medium with lettuce, tomato—"

Without warning, I felt the sharp vibration of my cell phone. I had put it in my side pocket and it was going off.

"Hold on a second, Hogan. I've got to take this call."

It was the office. I moved a few feet away so I wouldn't disturb anyone.

"Hi Angie. What's up?"

"Oh thank goodness the call went through. This is the third time I've tried you. You were right about the sporadic service. You'd think with the cost of cell phone plans they could install a better tower or something."

"Uh-huh. So, what's going on? Is Max all right?"

Angie lowered her voice and I had to strain in order to hear her.

"Two US Marshals are sitting in the office. They said it was important. They had to speak with you. I told them you wouldn't be back until tomorrow but they insisted I contact you. Said they'd wait until you got here. Something about a national threat. What's going on, Marcie?"

"What's going on?" *I'll tell you what's going on. My mother! That's what's going on! I can't believe this! The only reason United States Marshals would be sitting in our office was because my mother contacted them. Or the Federal Bureau of Investigation. Or Homeland Security. Or whatever national response team she thought should be involved. Unbelievable!*

I passed Hogan again at the counter and tried not to show any signs of distress. I kept calm and made sure my voice was low.

"Angie, please tell them I'm driving straight back from Biscay. It shouldn't take me more than an hour or so. Offer them some coffee or something and if Max calls, please, under no circumstances, tell him there are US Marshals in his office. I'll take care of this."

"Okay. Got it. Are you or Mr. Blake in any trouble? Is someone after you?"

"No, no. Everything's fine. Make a fresh pot of coffee. I won't be too long."

Turning to Hogan, I slipped the cell phone back in my pocket and held up my hand. "Hold off on that hamburger order. Something's come up and I've got to race back to my office."

My face was beginning to warm and it was impossible to hide it. I was upset but I didn't need the entire diner to find out just how looney my mother was.

Hogan gave me a quizzical stare. "You look as if all hell broke loose back in New Ulm. Anything I can do?"

"No, I'll be fine. I mean, it'll be fine. Thanks anyway."

By now I was at the door, reaching for the handle. Hogan stood up and was a few feet from me. "Lucky I give rain checks. I'll reserve one for you."

Then he held the door open for me as I hurried toward my car. It was only a few yards away in front of Rose and Lila's house but it seemed like a mile. I couldn't move fast enough. The thought of having to deal with two US Marshals was enough to give me heartburn. I had no idea how I could possibly explain my mother's irrational fears.

I was furious. Not only had she butted into this investigation but she had managed to deprive me of a juicy hamburger and lunch with Hogan. It wasn't until I had gotten into my car and turned onto the highway when I realized I had forgotten to get Trudy's phone number from George Bowman. I would have to call him later.

Thank you, Iris Krum!

FOURTEEN

THE TWO US MARSHALS were sitting stone-faced in the office when I arrived. They made Sergeant Joe Friday and Officer Bill Gannon from *Dragnet* look like Jerry Lewis and Dean Martin. I don't recall ever seeing such stern and dour expressions on anyone. It took me over twenty minutes to convince them that there was no threat, that I had nothing to hide, and that the source of their information was about as reliable as Holden Caulfield.

"I'm really, really sorry to have wasted your entire afternoon," I said, "but when it comes to my mother,... well, she tends to go overboard first without checking to see if she brought a life jacket, if you know what I mean."

One of the marshals, the tall one with a buzz cut, asked where my mother would have gotten the idea in the first place that the killer could have been a sniper or, at the very least, the kind of marksman who doesn't miss.

My stomach was tightening up. "I'm not sure where she got that idea in the first place but you can see for yourself on the sheriff's report why someone might have thought it was a professional hit. It was a clean shot to the right temple."

I was about to hand him the folder when I had a better idea. I had Angie make them a copy of the report.

"So you see," I said, "most likely my mother heard something on a news report and filled in the details to suit herself. In her mind, it would have to be a terrorist or someone along those lines in order to get a shot off like that."

The marshal shook his head. "Hate to break it to you, or her, but according to what I'm reading, the victim was shot with a .357 approximately six feet away. That's like hitting the side of a barn from ten paces. No, nothing spells out an alert for Homeland Security. Well, we'd better get going."

Like a carefully rehearsed routine, both marshals stood up and started toward the door. I held up my palm as if I were a crossing guard. "Wait a second. I was wondering… Since you've got a full copy of the report, would you mind giving it a good going over? You know, in case anything jumps out at you that we might have missed."

The men looked at each other until one of them finally spoke. "I seriously doubt we'll pick up anything you haven't but we'll keep it on file as evidence of our response to this call."

I knew what that meant. It would be filed and forgotten. I apologized again for wasting their time and walked them to the door. Then I apologized to Angie. "Sorry for keeping you here so late. We'll make it up to you."

"Not to worry. It isn't every day I get to share coffee with two burly US Marshals."

"Yeah, well, maybe tomorrow will be a little more normal. Max will be back and—"

Angie let out a sigh and cut right in. "Oh my. With all of this going on, I completely forgot. Max called a few minutes before you walked in. Said that everything was all right but that you needed to give him a call."

I envisioned the worst—that he was stuck another day in Minneapolis with the Klemmer trial.

"Don't worry about it, Angie. I'll call him and lock up the place. You go on home and have a good evening."

Once Angie was out the door, I shut the lights in the front office and turned the deadbolt before retreating back into my own office. I figured I'd call Max, find out what was so urgent, and then I'd give the diner a call to get Trudy's number. Fortunately, I had managed to subdue the screaming voice inside of me that wanted to call my mother and rant about her intrusion into this investigation. She had literally and figuratively "made a federal case" out of something and as a result, I was stuck in the office working when I should have been home kicking up my feet and indulging in the latest flavor of gelato. Not to mention the burger I could have shared with Hogan.

As I reached for the phone, my elbow slid a pile of papers off to the side of the desk and I groaned. My desk was starting to resemble something out of *Hoarders*. There were papers everywhere—legal size, letter size, scrap and a special variety of "wadded up." I would need to go through all of them before calling it a night. Not only that but I needed to give Angie all of the receipts I had acquired the past few days.

Maybe I could do two things at once. I un-snapped my bag and reached inside to remove the stash of receipts. Most were on small snips of paper and I had to strain to read them. *I am NOT ready for bifocals.* Gas, the diner, the donut shop… And suddenly I froze. There was another slip of paper inside my handbag and it wasn't a receipt.

It was about the same size as a receipt but folded over. I could see the angry black letters leaking through to the other side of the paper. My fingers unfolded it carefully as if it was about to disintegrate.

STOP! YOU'RE SNIFFING THE WRONG BUSH!

The paper dropped from my fingers. Letters staring up at me as if they were waiting for me to say something. Instead, I took a deep breath and tried to recall all the places I had been where someone could have slipped it into my bag.

Other than our office and my house, there was the brewery, the diner, the feed and grain store, the donut shop in Glencoe, Rose and Lila's house and the house with the young woman and her kids. What was her name? Oh yeah, Marisa. Over half a dozen places where someone could have snuck the note into my bag.

I'm not a big fan of cryptic notes. Or any anonymous notes for that matter. Ever since the sixth grade when I found a note in my locker telling me Robbie McGowen liked me, I've had a certain disdain for information I'm not given directly. For a kid who supposedly "liked me," he went out of his way to avoid me and would run like hell if he saw me coming. I found out later that the note landed in the wrong locker.

This time I was certain the one in my bag was meant for me. Whoever wrote it either thought I might be getting really close to finding out who killed Billy Hazlitt, which would have been news to me, or they knew something they couldn't tell me face to face. I folded it back up, paper clipped it to the file with the rest of the information on the case, and dialed Max's phone. I sure had a lot to catch him up on including my latest find—the cryptic note.

FIFTEEN

"YOU WON'T BELIEVE the whackadoodle day I've had, Max! Hope everything's going okay at your end. Angie said you wanted me to call you."

"Yeah. I did. I don't know what's on your docket tomorrow, but any chance you could drive to Minneapolis and do some homework on Billy Hazlitt's employment at Longfellow Brewery? I know I told you I'd do it but I'm dead beat."

"Sure. No problem. I'll leave a message for Angie on her desk."

"Thanks, kid. I finally gave my testimony on the Klemmer case but didn't get out of there until after five. Then the drive home. Thank God for leftovers in the freezer. What a day. Eight hours of sitting on a hard chair. Well, seven and a half if you count lunch. Anyway, I was whipped by the time I got through. Had all I could do to get into the car and head for home. I would have stayed another night in order to speak with Billy's former employer but I've got a full schedule tomorrow—the missing property case, another possible infidelity and some potential clients."

"It'll be fine," I said. "I've got to let the information from Billy's contacts marinate around my mind for a while anyhow. Besides, Longfellow Brewery might shed some light on Billy that no one else could."

"Absolutely. What do you say we meet for an hour

or so the day after tomorrow so we can catch up? I'm
already feeling way behind on this case thanks to the
Klemmers."

I was dying to tell him how my investigation in Biscay was going and show him the note but I knew how
whipped he was from the Klemmer testimony and I
didn't want to pile on more stuff that could wait. Especially my wonderful encounter with two government
agents. If nothing else, he'd get a good laugh. We agreed
to meet for a late breakfast near our office on Saturday.
Max stressed the word *late*.

"I must be getting old, Marcie. I'll need all the beauty
sleep I can get."

When I hung up, I immediately dialed the diner to
get Trudy's number. I was sure George Bowman must
have thought I was a blithering idiot for charging out
of there without as much as securing the information I
needed. Then again, maybe Hogan told him I had gotten an important call and had to leave immediately.

When the phone rang at the diner, it was Kaye. She
told me Trudy had "some sort of a bug" and would be
out for a few days. She also added that it was a good
idea for me to call instead of arranging to meet with
the waitress.

"You can't be too careful these days. If I were you,
I'd wait awhile before breathing the same air as Trudy.
I told my brother to have her stay out the entire week.
Don't need to contaminate the customers. Did you know
some viruses can linger on a surface or in the air for
hours or even days at a time?"

"I, uh, no. It never crossed my mind."

"That's because you're not in the restaurant business.
Those inspectors can shut down a place at the drop of

a hat. Don't need to tempt fate with a waitress who's coughing, sneezing or wheezing."

"Um, yeah. I suppose you're right."

I thanked her for giving me Trudy's number and hung up. I had already planned on getting the information over the phone. And frankly, I didn't think Trudy could add a whole lot more than Trisha but as things turned out, I was wrong.

My call to Trudy went to voice mail. I figured she was too sick to bother taking the call. Or maybe she had her phone turned off. I seriously doubted she used a landline. It was the cut-off that separated the early twenty-somethings from us later ones.

Grabbing a sheet of paper from the copier, I wrote a large note for Angie and put it on her desk. Then I went back to my office to turn off the lights and get my bag when I felt an awful pit in my stomach—Alice Davenport would be expecting her "it-doesn't-necessarily-have-to-be-in-chronological-order" end-of-the-week report.

"Aargh." My groan ripped through the room. If I was going to be in Minneapolis tomorrow, I'd need to write the darn thing tonight or somehow squeeze it in when I got back late in day. Late in the day would be Friday night and I knew I'd have absolutely no desire to sit down and write a thesis for Alice Davenport when I could be doing more enjoyable things.

I forced myself to take a seat, boot up my computer and pen my rendition of the "investigative progress" we were making. I filled it with names, places, and times but left out any inferences or pertinent details. Lucas Rackner notwithstanding, the last thing I needed was for Alice Davenport to tell me how to go about my business. As it was, my mother was doing a fairly good job of that.

When I was satisfied my report was grammatically correct and organized in a succinct and sequential order, I printed it out and put in an envelope for Angie to mail to Alice. Alice insisted that all correspondence be mailed. Loud and clear. Since the original was in a Word document, I emailed Max a copy and one to Angie for her files. As old school as Max was, at least the guy utilized electronic mail. The same could not be said for Alice.

"I'm not about to leave my life wide open for any cyber hacker or lunatic. No siree! Use priority mail, Marcie."

Gathering up everything I thought I might need for tomorrow's visit to Longfellow Brewery, I gave the office a quick once-over before turning off the lights and locking up. My legs felt like lead as I trudged over to my car and headed home. I was so exhausted that night I fell asleep long before the evening news came on and didn't bother to shove Byron off my chest where he decided to stay for the night.

SIXTEEN

THE VOICE AT the other end of the phone was husky and hoarse. All I kept hearing was someone asking for Marcie Rayner. It was some godforsaken hour in the middle of the night and my mind was fuzzy and dazed. Then, as if a shot of adrenaline hit my veins, I sat up in bed, tossing Byron on his side. *Oh my God! Did something happen to my mother? A heart attack? A stroke? Who the heck is calling me?*

"It's Trudy. Trudy from the Triangle Diner. Is this Marcie Rayner, the investigator?"

Trudy. Not my mother. Not a heart attack. Trudy. It took me a minute or two to process what was going on while Trudy kept asking if it was me. My eyeballs felt as if they had been glued together and I struggled to see the time on my digital clock. Six. In the morning! It might as well have been the middle of the night. The sun hadn't even come up yet but that didn't stop Trudy.

"I hope I didn't wake you up and I figured your office would be really busy and I didn't want to be put on hold, so I got your home number from Trisha and decided to call you since I wasn't at work yesterday. I've got a cold and feel lousy but I could have gone to work if it wasn't for Kaye thinking I'd cause an epidemic or something."

"Um...yeah, well, she's probably right. Customers

really don't want their waitresses sneezing on the food or…anyway, getting back to your call…"

I was trying to focus so that I could ask her the same things I asked everyone else about Billy Hazlitt. She beat me to it.

"Look, I'm sorry but I can't give you any information about Billy Hazlitt's murder. Your guess is as good as mine. There's one thing though. Maybe it's nothing but you never know."

I tried to subdue the enthusiasm in my voice. "What? What thing?"

"Once in a while he and his brother would get into it, but I mean, what family members don't? I had a fight once with my sister and it lasted for a month. You don't go taking someone else's makeup and using it, if you know what I mean. What did she think? That I wasn't going to notice?"

Again, I was struggling to comprehend what on earth she was saying. I swear, between both waitresses calling me at ridiculous hours, it was a wonder I wasn't totally sleep deprived.

"Is that what happened? Billy took something of Tom's?" *And please don't tell me it was makeup. This case is already complicated.*

"No. Who said *that*? The only thing I ever heard them argue about was the brewery. And let me tell you, I kept my distance."

"Trudy," I said, taking a slow breath, "Can you remember exactly what the argument was about? Or when it took place?"

"Not argument. Arguments. Plural. It was always taking place. The same thing over and over again. Just like Pam and me. First my clothes. Then my makeup."

I tried not to sound exasperated. "I get it. I do. But what about Billy and his brother? What was their problem?"

"Billy wanted to add more unique beers and Tom said it was getting too expensive and that they should concentrate on a handful. And Billy said that it was specialized beers that were going to make the brewery well-known, not the stuff you could find in any old microbrewery."

"How do you know this?"

"Heck. Everyone did. Whenever the two of them would come in here and order breakfast or lunch, it was all they would talk about."

"What about Hogan? Did he ever get involved?"

"You know, I'm not sure. If he did, it wasn't here in the diner. Hey, you don't think Tom would have done anything to his brother over that, do you?"

The whole Cain and Abel thing flashed through my mind. It had been a long time since I sat in a Sunday school class. Something about anger and jealousy. Yeah, I was sure of it—anger and jealousy, not whether or not to keep producing specialized beers. In my mind, that was hardly a reason to kill. Still, I couldn't ignore it.

"Yeah, about that…did you ever hear them threaten each other?"

"Like physically or something?"

"Any kind of threats, really."

"Nope. No threats. Only long winded discussions about beers. And money. And how if you're going to make money, you have to invest it in your product. All that stuff. But threats? Nah. And even if they did threaten each other, they wouldn't have meant it. I always threatened Pam I was going to donate her good sweaters to charity when she wasn't looking but she knew I was just pissed at her."

"Okay, then. Thanks for calling me, even though it was really early. I hope you feel better soon."

"Even though I'm missing out on my pay, I'm kind of glad I'm home."

"What do you mean?"

"I'm on the girls swim team at my school and we have a meet in a few days. I don't want to miss it by being sick. But that's not the real reason. Truth is, it's getting to be a pain in the butt working there. My boss is getting really crotchety and Kaye gets more unbearable by the hour. And I don't want to go into that walk-in fridge and told George that. I said, 'If there's a killer around and he starts running scared, he could take it out on the rest of us.'"

"What did Mr. Bowman say?"

"Humpf! Quit coming up with excuses to avoid going into the walk-in!"

I tried not to laugh and thanked her again. She had made my job a tad easier when it comes down to talking with Tom Hazlitt, something I needed to do as soon as possible.

It was now six thirty. Plenty of time for me to feed Byron, jump into the shower, make a cup of coffee and head toward Minneapolis. I decided to take my large portfolio bag so that I would look "more the part" of a private investigator. Then again, the dark circles under my eyes from lack of sleep were a dead giveaway. I was beginning to resemble Philip Marlowe, and I didn't like it one bit.

SEVENTEEN

IF I THOUGHT the entrance to Longfellow Brewery was imposing, with its glassed-in pyramid and fountains, the waiting room was downright palatial. I doubted it was designed to intimidate visitors but that's exactly the reaction I had.

High beamed ceilings with modernistic chandeliers made the place look larger than it actually was. The walls had framed posters of all the brewery ads since they opened sometime in the late 1800s. I clutched my portfolio close to my side and approached the reception desk. Three impeccably dressed employees, two women and one man, were on duty as I waited my turn in the single line that branched out to the different receptionists.

Scouring the room, I could see at least seven or eight people seated in comfortable armchairs waiting to be helped or escorted elsewhere. The line moved quickly. In a matter of minutes I had explained to the tall blond woman that I was a private investigator and needed to meet with someone in Human Resources.

The woman looked at my card, nodded and asked me to be seated. "I'll call you as soon as someone is available, Miss Rayner. Please make yourself comfortable. We have a coffee machine and water to the left, near the restrooms."

I was about to say, "What? No beer tasting?" but I

held back. I was, after all, a professional and not some college kid. Besides, I already knew that beer tasting was included with the brewery tours, but that was a separate entrance and the lines were staggering.

Noticing an available chair with a view of the fountains, I walked over and sat down, leaning my portfolio against the side of the seat. Both chairs on either side of me were occupied and judging from the stylish wardrobes that its occupants were wearing, I assumed they were here for job interviews. I was mistaken. The woman seated on my right, who appeared to be in her late thirties or early forties, turned to me and spoke.

"Forgive me if you think I'm being rude, but you look as exhausted as I do. I had to take the redeye out of New York last night and drove straight over here from the airport. What about you? Did you have a long flight?"

"Um. No. I—"

She continued before I had a chance to explain. "I know we're all competitors but frankly it feels nice to be able to talk with someone who doesn't look as arrogant as that crew over there."

The woman pointed to a cluster of men and women who resembled high paid models as she went on. "I bet they've got their pitch worked out to the final syllable. Honestly, I don't know why I'm so nervous about this. It's not as if I haven't been pitching ads before, but this one, well, I don't have to tell you, this one will land the lucky winner quite the bonus, not to mention what it will do for their company."

I had no idea what she was talking about but it didn't matter. She kept on going. By the end of our conversation I had learned more about a possible motive for Billy

Hazlitt's death than anything I gleaned from Human Resources.

"As if the redeye wasn't bad enough. All of this came down to us last minute. Literally. We had to drop every project we were working on and come up with a campaign in record time. I blamed my boss and the other honchos for being asleep at the wheel and making us pay for it. How does that saying go? Oh yeah, *'Lack of planning on your part doesn't constitute an emergency on mine.'* Well, whoever coined that, didn't work for my company. I suppose you had more time to develop your platform and campaign."

"Actually, I—"

"You don't have to say anything. So where are you from? London? Toronto? Chicago?"

At last I was able to utter a complete sentence and it left her speechless. Even if it was only for a second or two.

"I'm from New Ulm, Minnesota. About an hour or so from here."

"New Ulm? Never heard of it. You must be with a very small agency. It was my understanding that Longfellow Brewery only considered proposals from the top ten."

"I'm sure you're right. About the top ten. I'm not with an advertising agency. I'm a private investigator doing a background check on someone."

The woman looked as if she had "literally stepped in it" and couldn't worm her way out fast enough.

"It's okay," I said. "It's my portfolio, isn't it? I bet everyone else thinks I'm here to pitch an ad, too."

Her demeanor changed instantly and she began to

relax. Then, leaning closer toward me she asked if I wouldn't mind listening to her proposal.

"Sure, until they call my name, I've got plenty of time."

"My agency has two proposals—one that I helped to develop and the other, well, you'll see for yourself."

As soon as the first slogan rolled off her lips, everything in my mind began to click like a pinball machine that was on fire with each ping. I was listening to everything she said but processing none of it. Instead, I was playing over the murder at the Crooked Eye Brewery. This time with a possible motive in mind.

"Miss Rayner?"

The voice came from the reception desk—loud and authoritative.

"That's me," I said, interrupting the woman's spiel. "Good luck with your pitch. It sounded fine. Sorry I didn't get to hear the other slogan."

Grasping the handle of my portfolio, I followed a tall, slender man through two large doors that led to an elevator.

"Take this to the third floor. That's Human Resources. They're expecting you."

I thanked him and watched as he headed back to the reception desk. Then, I stepped inside and pushed the button, grateful I didn't have to give a presentation in order to land an ad for my company.

The reception area for Human Resources paralleled the downstairs entry only on a slightly smaller scale. While it lacked a fountain, it compensated with overstuffed chairs, teak tables and chandeliers that could dazzle Hollywood. In lieu of framed brewery posters, the walls boasted abstract metal sculptures. I was ushered into one of the offices by a soft-spoken reception-ist who appeared to be my age.

Once inside, the middle-aged Human Resources of-ficer with short red hair and carefully plucked eyebrows provided me with dates of employment and a list of all the positions Billy Hazlitt held while working for Long-fellow Brewery—apprentice brewer, assistant brewer and a memo that he was being considered for brewing supervisor but had requested a transfer to the brew-ing lab. There were no disciplinary actions taken, no counseling memos, nothing of the sort. Billy appeared to have been a model worker on his way up the ladder for Longfellow Brewery when he decided to open his own beer business in Biscay.

Since it had been nearly a decade when Billy was an employee, few people would remember him, according to the woman in Human Resources.

"We have a large turnover in plant operations and most people who are serious about making this a ca-reer, have long moved out of the departments Billy was in. To thrive in this profession, one can't afford to re-main still."

She didn't believe there was anyone who would be able to provide me with more details but she did agree to send an email to the department supervisors asking them to canvass their employees to see if anyone re-membered Billy Hazlitt and if so, to notify her office.

She was quite cordial and assured me if anyone came forward she would notify our office.

It was a little past midday when I exited the build-ing and started for my car. A voice called out from be-hind me and I recognized it instantly. It was the lady from the advertising agency who had been sitting next to me in the lobby.

"Miss Rayner! Wait! If you're heading somewhere for lunch, perhaps I could join you. They're running late and I won't be able to give my presentation until three o'clock."

I hadn't really thought about eating. I just wanted to get on the road and get back to my office, but something about her request was so compelling. I figured she wanted to practice her pitch again.

"Sure," I said. "I saw a deli a block or two from here. Walking distance."

"Sounds great. By the way, I'm Addison. Addison Markham."

"I'm Marcie."

"Thanks, Marcie. You're the first person who's smiled at me all day."

EIGHTEEN

"SHOOT THE TASTE buds off your tongue with Wild Turkey Bourbon Beer from Longfellow Brewery, purveyor of quality lagers and ales."

"Well, what do you think of that slogan, Marcie?" Addison said as we made ourselves comfortable in a booth at the deli. "It's the one the head honchos want me to use. Frankly, I'm having a hard time coming up with an image for that one. Let me go ahead with my proposal."

I knew Addison was looking for some feedback on the ad proposals but it was the premise behind the proposals that set me on edge. It was the product itself—Wild Turkey Bourbon Beer. Wasn't that the special flavor Billy Hazlitt developed? The pride of the Crooked Eye Brewery? And didn't Hogan say those formulas weren't common knowledge? That every brewmaster really worked hard to tweak the combination of malts and extracts? Like a veritable chemistry lab...

"Marcie, are you listening? You look like you're miles away."

Got that right. I didn't even process the ad you came up with.

"I'm sorry, Addison. Your proposals got me thinking about something, that's all."

"I know. How do you shoot someone's taste buds? It

would either have to be the goriest commercial or some bizarre cartoon. So, which one do you prefer?"

"Honestly, they're both good. *Even the one that blew by me.* Pitch both of them and see what happens."

We placed our drink orders with the waiter and looked at the menus. Then Addison plopped her elbows on the table sending the silverware into the water glasses.

"You know how I was going on about my company waiting for the last minute to get this project going? Well, guess what? After you left, two men from a Toronto agency and a lady from one in Chicago joined me and said the same thing. That their companies waited for the last minute, too, before giving them the assignment. Seems the culprit in all of this was Longfellow Brewery. They sent out the call for proposals with very little lead time and they want the product rolled out in time for the holidays. That's only a few months away. It's as if they just found out they were going to make that Turkey Bourbon beer. Jeez. Talk about rushed timing. Well, everyone's in the same boat as far as the proposals go."

Before I could say a word, the waiter returned and took our orders.

I tried hard to concentrate on my conversation with Addison but my mind kept circling back to that new beer. It had to have been Billy's formula. Had someone from Longfellow tasted it at the Crooked Eye and approached Billy for the recipe? And when he said no, would that person have killed to steal the formula? After all, the beer was, as Hogan put it, "truly unique." Heck, even I've heard of industrial espionage and that was long before I started to work with Max. I took a sip of my soft drink. This wasn't industrial espionage. It was murder.

Addison's voice knocked me out of my stupor and I pretended to pay attention. The rest of our conversations that afternoon dealt with small stuff—families, hobbies and things like that. Addison had gotten into the ad business after her twin sons headed for college so she always felt as if she was catching up. I told her about my background in campus security, leaving out the "failed marriage" addendum. I also neglected to tell her this was my first year at Blake Investigations and that technically, I wasn't an investigator. Only an investigative assistant.

We exchanged business cards and promised to keep in touch. Again, I wished her good luck on her proposal. Then, I walked to my car as quickly as possible and phoned the Human Resources office at Longfellow. Luckily the woman I had met with earlier was available to take my call. I asked her if she could please track down the last supervisor Billy Hazlitt had when Billy was an assistant brewer; and to let me know if that person was still working for Longfellow.

She agreed to go through the files and get back to me within a few days. It was the best I could hope for—a real lead. Not wanting to wait until I got back to the office to talk with Max, I dialed his cell phone as soon as I got into my car. He picked it up on the second ring.

"Everything okay in Minneapolis? I wasn't expecting to hear from you until much later today."

"You're not going to believe this, Max, but I think I've got a clue, well, not exactly a clue, but a motive. An actual motive."

Before he had a chance to comment, I went on to tell

him about Addison, the ad agencies and the last minute campaign they were all given. The words were flying out my mouth. Especially my theory about someone from Longfellow killing Billy in order to steal the Wild Turkey Bourbon formula. Too bad Max didn't share my enthusiasm or my opinion.

"Take a breath, would you? And listen. It might be the opposite way around. Maybe it was Billy who stole the Longfellow Brewery formula and his killer was getting even."

"But the timeline for the ads. It was so sudden…"

"Marcie, Billy Hazlitt might not be the person we thought he was."

"What do you mean? What are you saying?"

"I got a call a few minutes ago from the police department in Willmar. They collaborate extensively with the county sheriffs' departments. Most recently on a major fire that took place the last weekend Billy was seen alive. The cause of the fire, which was under investigation, was deemed arson. Worse yet, the police department uncovered evidence that points directly to the Crooked Eye Brewery and more specifically, to Billy. They notified their Kandiyohi County Sheriff, who in turn notified the McLeod office."

"Oh my gosh. They think *Billy* started that fire and that's what got him killed? Is that what you think, too?"

"It's way too soon to speculate but I have to admit, the evidence is compelling."

My mouth was suddenly dry and there was a frog in my throat. I mean, it wasn't as if I had known Billy or felt one way or the other about him, but I knew that Hogan had cared about his friend, along with everyone else I spoke with in Biscay. Except maybe Skip Gunderson.

"What was the evidence? What did the fire department or police find?"

"They found remnants of Molotov cocktails that were thrown into the chocolate shop and the flower shop on Becker Avenue. The glass bottles used to make the incendiary devices were all from the Crooked Eye Brewery. Easily identifiable."

"That doesn't mean Billy was the one who did it."

I tried to sound emphatic but the words came out slow and whiney as Max continued to explain.

"Look Marcie, I know this is never what we want to hear, that the person we thought was the victim might well be the perpetrator in this case. And we still don't know but—"

"Those glass bottles or growlers don't mean anything. Anyone could have bought them at the brewery."

"That's what I thought at first, too. But not these. They had been specially made for an event and weren't available for the public to purchase."

The frog in my throat turned into a twist in my gut. If Billy wasn't the one who made those Molotov cocktails, then it left only three other people—his brother Tom, that kid Tyler who works part time and Hogan. *Please don't let it be Hogan. He's the one person I judged to be on the up and up.*

"Why do the police think it was Billy and not anyone else?"

"Because they were able to match a partial fingerprint with the one on file from Billy's service record."

I paused to let his words sink in.

"You all right, Marcie? Say something."

"Um, yeah... I'm fine. Just surprised, that's all. I'm heading back to New Ulm now. Will you still be at the office?"

"I'll make it a point to stay here until you arrive. I should have told you this before. You cannot let these cases wreak havoc on your emotions. Murder especially. Never get too close to the victim or the suspects. It will only come back to bite you. Got it?"

"Uh-huh."

"Good. See you soon."

I pushed the red end button and stared at the cell phone. *Oh, Max. It might already be too late for your advice.*

NINETEEN

MY HANDS MIGHT have been behind the wheel but my mind kept flipping back and forth between the arson investigation in Willmar and Longfellow Brewery's sudden pressure to come up with an advertising campaign at the last minute. I wanted desperately to believe Billy Hazlitt wasn't an arsonist and that his murder had nothing to do with that unfortunate event. I knew I would have to press harder on the information from Longfellow Brewery if I was to prove that Billy was innocent in all of this.

It was like I was at one end of a wishbone while the law enforcement agencies in Willmar were at the other. Each one of us pushing and lifting on our side of the bone until it would finally crack and break. And the worst part of it was the fact that Max wasn't taking either side. Not that I expected him to do so. He made it clear that solid investigations meant neutrality. We were private investigators, not lawyers.

I felt drained and exhausted when I got back to the office and the last thing I wanted to hear was that I had received three messages.

"You don't have to answer the first one, Marcie," Angie said as I picked up the slips of paper from her desk. "Alice Davenport called to ask if you had mailed out her report since it's the end of the week. I told her it was mailed and she said that was satisfactory."

"That's it? Just satisfactory? No smiley face?"

Angie could barely contain her laugh. "Maybe she'll give you one when she reads the report."

"I don't dare ask. Who else called?"

"A Rose Barton called and then a few minutes later, a Lila Barton called. Very strange. Anyway, it's all written down for you."

She handed me the slips of paper at the very second Max stepped out of his office.

"Hey Marcie! You made good time. Traffic must have been light."

"Yeah. I managed to beat the rush hour."

"Listen, I've got an appointment coming up in a few minutes with a new client. Something about a dog snatching. Anyway, what do you say we grab a pizza after work and fill each other in?"

"Sounds good," I said as I walked toward the workroom. "I need to add notes to the whiteboard and return some calls."

It only took me a few minutes to draw the wishbone image that was in my mind—the Biscay investigation with a tentacle leading to Willmar and the arson case and the new ad campaign for Longfellow Brewery. I put a question mark next to that one before returning to my desk to call the Barton sisters. I prayed they weren't going to relive their argument about the cat yowling.

Lila Barton must have been sitting inches away from the phone because she picked it up before it had even completed the first ring.

"Hello. This is Lila. Am I speaking with Miss Rayner?"

I assured her that indeed she was speaking with me

and then I had to listen very carefully because her voice was barely a whisper.

"Last night Rose thought she saw someone sneaking around the bushes near the brewery. It was almost dark. I told her she was imaging things and that it was probably a dog. You know, we have lots of strays around here. People drop them off thinking us country folks will take them in. But Rose insisted that it was a person. That's why she called you but I wanted to talk to you first because it had to be a dog. Why on earth would someone be rooting around those Juniper bushes at nightfall? Shh…here comes Rose. I'll put her on."

Lila must have dropped the receiver because the clunk reverberated in my ear, making it difficult to hear Rose at first.

"Miss Rayner? Is that you?"

"Yes, it's me; can you please speak a bit louder?"

"I most certainly can. I have nothing to hide from my sister who probably told you not to pay me any mind."

I could hear Lila's voice. Followed by Rose's.

"I didn't say anything of the kind, Rose. All I said was that—"

"Never mind what you said. I'm talking on the phone!"

"Um… Rose? What was it you wanted to tell me?"

Even though I knew what she was about to say, I let her explain.

"So there you have it. I walked over to the window to draw the curtains. It was getting on dark. And naturally, I looked up and down the block to make sure everything was as it should be. The brewery was closed and there were no cars. Then something caught my eye. It was a person, I tell you. A person. Someone was sneaking around those bushes. You know, the same bushes from the other time. But like I said, it was getting on dark and I didn't see them come out. Lila insisted it had to be a dog but that's just like her, refusing to believe that something suspicious is going on around here."

Maybe Rose was "getting on" and her faculties weren't quite what they used to be but twice now she mentioned those Juniper bushes. I figured I'd do a bit of sleuthing around there myself. I still had to interview Tom Hazlitt and I wanted to speak with Hogan about the arson evidence that the police in Willmar uncovered.

I thanked Rose and told her I would look into the matter. I also told her not to go over there on the off chance there really might be evidence of some sort and it shouldn't be tampered with. Or trampled, in her case.

"Don't you worry about me, Miss Rayner," she said. "I have no intentions of snooping in and out of bushes. Heaven knows what could be lurking in there."

Again I thanked her before hanging up. Max's client arrived while I was on the phone with the Barton sisters. Angie came into my office with the most recent fax from the McLeod County Sheriff's Department—a copy of the arson report in Willmar. While Max was busy with the dog-napping case, I used the time to re-read all of the reports and look for any possible threads that could lead to something. So far lots of strings and they were all "loose ends." The remainder of the work day flew by.

Max and I grabbed a pizza at Pagliai's, a neat little family restaurant that had been around for decades, and washed it down with ice cold beers. There was no reason to meet the next day since we had reviewed everything on the Hazlitt investigation, including the bizarre note I found in my bag.

Max considered the note more of a clue than a threat and told me to "work it into my investigation". He even had his own name for that sort of thing.

"Yep, I call it 'working the sidelines,'" he said. "Sometime witnesses don't want to come forth or family friends and acquaintances don't want to stick their necks out, especially if they think there's the slightest chance they could be wrong. So, what do they do? They leave us little crumbs like the one you found in your handbag."

"It seems more than a little crumb."

"Maybe. Maybe not. Follow up on it and see where it goes but don't make it your number one focus."

"Understood."

Max reached for another slice of pizza. "So, you think those Barton sisters are just plain looney or are they on to something?"

"They're the proverbial spinster sisters and Kaye Bowman's not far behind. I figure I'll drive to Biscay midday tomorrow so I can try to catch Tom Hazlitt at the brewery. I also want to ask Hogan Austin a few questions about the glass container that was found at the arson site."

"I have to say, 'you're really on top of things.' You know, you don't have to work on a Saturday."

"I know. I know. But it's not like other jobs where you can put stuff in a neat pile and get back to it a few days later. Besides, I don't have anything else pressing to do. Byron usually sleeps all day, and other than meowing for food, he isn't all that active until dark. Not as if I had to deal with a dog."

"That reminds me. This weekend I'll be working the dog case. Shouldn't be all that challenging. The owner's got a pretty good idea of who took off with her precious canine. I really want to wrap that up so we can concentrate on the murder. Sure you're okay with stopping by the brewery tomorrow?"

"Honestly. I'm fine with it. By the way, what about talking with the owners of the chocolate and flower shops in Willmar? I mean, I know the police did, but maybe the owners will tell us something they didn't share with the authorities."

"Whoa, kid! You're one step ahead of me. I figured that's something we'd both do on Monday."

"Good. You know, I can't seem to shake the feeling that Longfellow Brewery had something to do with Billy's death. It's like having an itch I can't seem to scratch."

"Means you're beginning to think like a detective but don't get too rooted in one scenario. Let the evidence lead you to a conclusion. Even though you may not be happy with the result. And watch the way in which the witnesses and contacts respond to your questioning. Our best hope is that they'll be lousy poker players."

I looked directly at my boss. "It was easier with crime statistics. It's tough reading people. What do you think? Do you believe Billy could've been the one to set that fire?"

"I try to visualize the situation from all angles before I favor one theory over another. Just as many innocent people out there getting framed as guilty ones walking away scout free. Our job is to make sure we get it right."

TWENTY

Not surprising, the US Marshals Service, on behalf of Homeland Security, informed my mother that "given the information received and reviewed," they did not deem the matter to be one involving a governmental agency. They had no reason to believe this was the act of a terrorist, domestic or otherwise, and informed her that the case should remain as is, under the investigation of local authorities.

They were timely, appropriate and all business. Had they been dealing with anyone other than Iris Krum, the matter would have been resolved. Not so, as far as my mother was concerned. The thought occurred to her that if it wasn't a sniper or terrorist who killed Billy Hazlitt, then it had to be someone from organized crime. Worse yet, the thought came to her late at night and roused me from a sound sleep as I reached for the phone. At least it wasn't an early morning wake-up call. I could still manage another few hours of sleep.

"Marcie? Were you sleeping? Wake up and listen."

"What? What's going on? Are you okay?"

"Yes, of course I'm all right. I was worried about you. I got to thinking about that awful murder and now that we know it wasn't some crazy terrorist, the only thing that makes sense is a mob hit!"

"A WHAT???"

"You heard me. A mob hit! You know, gangsters.

Crime bosses. There's no denying it, Billy Hazlitt was in the business."

Holding the receiver in one hand against my ear, I found myself pounding my forehead with the palm of my free hand.

"What business? Billy wasn't involved in organized crime."

"He was running a brewery, wasn't he? The mobs are always up to their necks with the production of alcohol and liquor."

"Good God, Mother! This isn't prohibition! It's the twenty-first century and believe me when I tell you, NO crime boss is the least bit interested in a microbrewery located in the middle of Minnesota. And it's not alcohol and liquor anymore. These days it's illicit drugs and sex trafficking."

"Good heavens, Marcie. What was that man into? Whatever you do, don't refer to those things when you communicate with Alice Davenport. The phrase 'illicit activities' should be enough. And I still think it had to do with those mobs. I'm not telling you how to go about your investigation, but if I were you, I'd be looking into those syndicated crime families. And do it from a distance."

A chill ran through me and I couldn't get the words out of my mouth fast enough.

"Whatever you do, Mother. Do not, I repeat, DO NOT, call the FBI. You're only slowing down our investigation." Then I stretched the truth. Like trouser socks that had been in the dryer. The words I used were familiar to anyone who watched as many TV dramas as my mother. "Max and I are closing in on the case."

There was a long pause on the line before my mother

finally spoke. "I see. That should make Alice Davenport extremely happy."

"Mother, don't say anything to her. Not until we're sure. Understand? Not a word."

"You know, honey, I'm only trying to be helpful."

"I know. I know. Right now the best help you can give me is to let me go back to sleep. I'll call you this week. Promise."

My head fell back against the pillow and I pulled the sheet up to my neck. Even in the heat of the summer I still had to have some sort of blanket or covering. For some reason, Byron decided to plop himself at the foot of the bed for a change. Just as well. I was so restless I would have tossed him off of me.

Mob bosses. Crime families. What next? Was someone going to "make me an offer I couldn't refuse?" Images of the Corleone Family danced through my head as I finally got back to sleep.

The next morning I threw in a load of laundry and made myself toast and coffee. I wavered between calling and not calling the Crooked Eye Brewery to let them know I was coming. I finally decided not to call, figuring that if Tom Hazlitt was going to be there, warning of my visit would scare him away, given his fragile state of mind according to Hogan.

In addition, I really needed to broach the subject of guns with Hogan. Maybe with any luck, he'd offer to buy me a burger again, the closest I thought I'd get to a date with him. It was barely noon when I left my house and approximately a quarter past one when I pulled into the parking lot in front of the Crooked Eye.

It was busy. I should have realized. A microbrewery on a Saturday afternoon was bound to have customers.

There were at least five cars and some motorcycles. The patio was filled, too. Families and couples. Not a great time to take Tom or Hogan away from their patrons.

Across the street I could see the diner was pretty active, too. I was about to stop in and order a coffee while I waited for the crowd to thin out at the brewery when I realized it was the perfect time to follow up on Rose Barton's phone call. The Juniper bushes. She insisted she had seen someone there on two separate occasions. The first being the night of the murder. The night she thought she saw a flash of light.

I pulled my car over to the far end of the lot and got out. The row of Junipers was actually two rows of giant bushes that someone probably planted at least a decade ago to offer some privacy between the house on one side and what used to be a garage, now the brewery, on the other.

Thankfully the grass was thin surrounding the bushes. Not enough sunlight to cause a whole lot of growth. It was also dry. We hadn't had rain in the past few weeks causing some talk about an early drought in the area. I walked slowly around the perimeter, heading to the street first before doubling back on the other side. With my head down, I looked for anything unusual or out of the ordinary on the ground. Nothing. Pine needles. Animal scat. Lila had been right. Probably stray dogs or cats. I kept walking.

Rounding the line of bushes and back to the spot where I started, nothing caught my eye. Not at first anyway. I had walked past my first piece of solid evidence and didn't even realize it until I stumbled on a rock and caught myself in the branches. When I looked down I saw a spec of blue. Maybe a piece of trash that had blown under the bushes in the wind.

Oh my God! I can't grab this with my bare hands. I need an evidence bag. Or any bag for that matter as long as it says "Ziploc." What was I thinking?

The only plastic bag I had wasn't even plastic. It was an old potato chip bag that had been sitting on the floor of my car. A very small bag, I might add, but a potato chip bag, nonetheless. A tribute to my failed attempt at eating healthy. Still, it was better than nothing. I walked back to the car, retrieved the bag and bent down to pick up the item in question, greasy chip bag covering my hand.

Reaching my arm through the brush I tried not to concentrate on how scratched up I was getting. Whatever the thing was, I had only seen a glimpse of it. Pine needles covered the rest. I could hear the bag crunching as I honed in on my prize. It wasn't a piece of litter after all. When I picked it up, one thing became crystal clear—Marisa, the young woman who had recently moved into the house across the street, had lied to me.

I was staring at a blue and white binky. It looked exactly like the one that was in her baby's mouth when I first knocked on her door. One of my girlfriends, who recently had a baby, referred to those pacifiers as "sanity keepers." And my brother and his wife had said the same thing. Now, this piece of evidence was standing between me and a possible murderer. It also validated Rose's story and I hoped she wouldn't pass the information on to anyone else. One murder in a small town is more than enough.

TWENTY-ONE

TORN BETWEEN RACING across the street to Marisa's house and demanding to be told the truth, or heading back to the brewery to speak with Tom Hazlitt, I opted for the brewery. I needed time to figure out how I was going to approach Marisa without bumbling into her house and ruining my chances of finding out the truth.

In the short time I had been working with Max, I realized one thing. There was a "fine art" of getting people to give you the information you needed and that included confessions. I wasn't even close to mastering that talent. I also needed more information about the night in question and it appeared as if the only witnesses were two eccentric sisters who couldn't agree on the time of day. Maybe I could glean a bit more from Hogan and then reach out to Marisa.

The parking lot had started to clear out. Only two cars remained, not counting the truck off to the side of the building that probably belonged to Tom or Hogan. Maybe even Tyler. A middle-aged couple was seated on the patio with a small growler of beer and a bowl of pretzels. I nodded to them as I opened the door.

Tyler was wiping down the counter as I approached. The only other person in the room was an elderly gentleman who had just finished his beer tasting. He thanked the kid and headed out of the building.

"Hey, Tyler, nice to see you again. I was hoping Tom and Hogan would be here. I need to speak with them."

"Tom's in back, checking the tanks and Hogan won't be in till tomorrow. He's got the day off."

I tried not to show my disappointment but it was too late. Tyler saw the expression on my face. "Maybe Tom can give you the information you need but if not, I've got Hogan's cell number if you want it. Not that it'll be much help. It can be a dead zone around here as far as cell service is concerned. Real iffy."

"Um…that's okay. I'll catch him another time. Meanwhile, will you let Tom know who I am and that I need to speak with him?"

"Sure thing."

Tyler opened the door to the walk-in while I turned toward the parking lot. The elderly man had gotten into his car and was pulling out when I heard a voice behind me.

"Hi. I'm Tom Hazlitt. I understand you wanted to speak with me."

His voice was almost robotic. I could understand what Hogan meant when he said that Tom was merely "going through the motions."

"Marcie Rayner with Blake Investigations. Maybe we can talk on the patio if you don't mind."

"Sure, sure. I don't know what I'm thinking. Come on, let's go sit down."

Tom lumbered toward one of the tables and chairs, pausing to wipe his brow with a white cloth. He was fortyish, overweight but not what I would call obese. His dark brown hair looked as if it could use a trim but other than that, he gave no indication that he was struggling. He was clean shaven and his Crooked Eye

Brewery T-shirt and jeans looked as if they had been washed recently.

I gave him some background about our company and the investigation before asking him the same general questions I had asked everyone else. His answers didn't come as any surprise. No enemies. No threats. Tom was home the night of the murder and was called to the brewery the morning the cleaning crew discovered his brother's body.

"It's like I can't get that image out of my mind. All that blood. And why someone tried to slide him out of the way, who knows... None of this makes any sense."

"Tom," I said, pausing for a second or two, "Do you have any idea why your brother would have been in Willmar the day before his murder?"

"No. And that's another thing. The sheriff came to my house last night asking the same question. There was that big fire over in Willmar and they think Billy might have had something to do with it. The only reason any of us... Billy, Hogan, me...go to Willmar is for stuff we need done to the tanks. Our fabricating company is there. But it's nowhere near where the fire was and Billy would have told me if he was having something special done to the equipment."

"I hate to bring this up, but you probably know that the police in Willmar have evidence that points to your brother for starting that fire."

"Yeah. So I've been told. It's not much evidence and it's not good. What's the word? Oh yeah. Circumstantial. The sheriff said they found my brother's fingerprint on a piece of glass from one of our growlers and that the growlers were used to start the fire—Molotov cocktails. Those bottles are sterilized before we add the beer to them and we use rubber gloves for handling. But once the beer is bottled, we can hand pack them into cases of four. That's probably how Billy's prints got on the bottles. And whoever started that fire must have known that."

"Tom, who buys those cases of four?"

"Lots of customers."

"Do you keep track? You must keep track."

"Yeah. Of course we do. It's on our copy of the register tape. But that doesn't tell us who bought the beer. Only if they used a credit card."

I remembered something Max had said. The growlers that were found on the scene of the fire were made for a special brewery event and weren't available for the public to purchase.

"Wait a second, Tom. I'm sorry. I forgot. I thought I heard somewhere that those particular growlers were for some sort of event and weren't available for the public to purchase."

"The Oktoberfest. We have one every year. But someone screwed up when we were bottling the growlers and used some of the special ones. We couldn't leave the beer sitting around for months so we did sell some with the specialty bottles."

"Okay. That's good. It narrows down the timeframe. Can you get me copies of the register tapes from the time you bottled beer in those special growlers up until the day of the fire in Willmar?"

"I'll have to wait until we close the brewery so that I can run a targeted report."

"How about I pick it up on Monday? My partner and I have to drive to Willmar that day and we'll be passing by here. Oh, and Tom, please don't say anything to anyone about what I'm asking you to do."

"I don't like keeping things from Hogan or Bi—" He stopped short and corrected himself.

"If it makes you feel any better, I'll tell Hogan myself when I see him, but for now, just keep it between the two of us."

"Do you think whoever set that fire killed my brother?"

"I have no idea. That's what we need to find out. By the way, it's okay to let Hogan know you talked with me today. Besides, Tyler would've probably told him. That kid seems pretty sharp."

"Uh-huh. He really has had to step up to the plate these past few weeks. I… I haven't been myself. The kid's a quick study. This is all he's ever wanted to do. Learn how to become a master brewer. Too bad his dad is such a jerk. The guy equates beer making with low level grunt work. If he knew what went into it he might think differently but he's one of those elitist types who thinks his own crap doesn't stink. Wants his son to be a professional. Suit and all. Oh gee, I shouldn't be going on about this. It's just that Tyler gets ragged all the time from his dad."

"That's really too bad. At least he's got two good mentors with you and Hogan."

"Billy was the one who spent most of the time teaching him. Said Tyler was like a sponge, soaking up everything and waiting for the right moment to wring it out."

I nodded and mumbled "uh-huh." I really wanted to ask Tom about his disagreements with his brother over the signature beers but that would be hearsay from Trudy and I wasn't sure how to approach it. Plus, looking at the guy's face, I could tell I had pushed the interview as far as it was going to go. It was bad enough Tom had to mull over the possibility that his brother could have started that fire, the last thing I needed to do was to press him about Billy's formulas.

Did someone steal Billy's recipe for that Wild Turkey Bourbon Beer or was it the other way around and Billy paid the price? If I could get the answer to that nagging question, everything else would fall into place.

I thanked Tom and got back in my car. There was still one more stop I wanted to make and that was the diner. I'd be buying my own burger today.

TWENTY-TWO

EVEN THOUGH IT was a quick walk across the street, I didn't want my car to take up space that could be used for the brewery customers. Not that throngs of people were flocking over there, but there was always that possibility. I found a parking spot a few yards past the diner and pulled in. I was so deep in thought about Tom and the brewery that I nearly collided with Trisha who was on her way out of the place and charging down the front steps.

"Marcie! Are you here to make an arrest? Can you do that? Arrest someone?"

"Arrest who? What? What's going on, Trisha?"

"That jerk, Skip Gunderson, is here with some of his buddies. Yucking it up and making wise cracks about blowing people's heads off. Guess he got tired bragging about the new truck he bought."

"Is that why you walked out? Because of Skip?"

She shook her head and looked down before glancing back up at the diner door. "No, my shift's over. Kaye's here. Believe me, I would have liked to. Walk out like that, I mean. Anyway, was I right about Skip? Did you find out anything?"

"I'm sorry, Trisha. There's no evidence that points to him but we're not done investigating. You told me a while back that Skip is George Bowman's brother-in-law. I thought Kaye was single."

"Oh, she's single all right. All but got that plastered across her forehead if you know what I mean. George and Kaye have a younger sister, Corrine, and she's the one who got stuck married to that Neanderthal."

"Ah, that explains it. I thought maybe Kaye was a nickname for Skip's wife. Frankly, I was really having quite a time wrapping my head around the idea it might be her. I mean, the age difference and all. Hey, before you take off, do you know anything about that young couple who bought the house across from the brewery?"

"You mean the frazzled woman with the zillion kids?"

"Yeah, I suppose that describes her."

"They come in here once in a while. Usually Trudy waits on them. She's got more patience than I do. And that one kid, the baby, geez, the minute he drops his pacifier it's like a scene from *The Exorcist*. You've heard of that movie, right? It's a real, real old one. I saw it once on late night TV and it really creeped me out."

"Um, yeah. Sure. Is there anything else you can tell me about that family? I'm looking into all possible witnesses."

"They didn't move in until after Billy got killed. But they were around here *way* before that. I was working the week they moved in and the guy was in and out of here every other minute to get sandwiches and stuff."

"Hold on a minute, Trisha. Do you remember how long ago you noticed them?"

"Gosh. It had to be at least a week or two before the murder. They had the key to the place but weren't allowed to move in until the official bank closing. That's what the guy said when he first came into the diner."

Maybe the Barton sisters were a bit odd, but they

were right about someone being in those Juniper bushes the night Billy got shot, and…given what Trisha was saying, I was placing my bet on someone in Marisa's family. Maybe they weren't moved in, but they had the key to that house and their baby's pacifier sure looked like the one I found.

"You've been a great help, Trisha. I promise we'll figure this out."

"You don't think that family has anything to do with this, do you? It's not like they're related or anything. Well, at least not that I know of…anyway, I've got to get going. And if you can arrest Skip Gunderson, do it!"

I watched as Trisha raced down the steps and laughed at the thought of the Barton sisters fuming when they got to hear the noise from her muffler again. Evidence on the Biscay side of the wishbone was piling up, even if it was unsubstantiated. However, I couldn't lose that nagging feeling that Billy's murder had more to do with Longfellow Brewery than it did with anyone in this little hick town.

Kaye greeted me the minute I stepped inside. I took a small booth facing the front of the street. Skip Gunderson was seated a few booths away with his back toward me. Just as well. Maybe he wouldn't notice me given the other customers in-between us.

I glanced at the brewery parking lot on the off chance that Hogan would show up. If so, I'd be able to ask him about that cryptic note and see what else he knew about Billy's formulas. When Kaye came to take my order, I stuck to the safety zone, ordering a burger and fries even though The Triangle Diner had an extensive menu. She had just written down my selection when I cleared my throat. "Do you have a minute or two to chat while Frankie gets my meal going?"

She shrugged. "Don't see why not. No one's yelling for me, yet, and my brother's busy re-arranging the freezer. Got a delivery coming first thing Monday."

"Listen Kaye, I got a copy of the arson report from the Willmar Police Department and I was wondering if you could tell me anything else you might remember that day you saw Billy at the chocolate shop."

"Nothing else to tell. That hussy was leaning all over him and he wasn't complaining."

"Who left the store first? You or Billy?"

"Billy did. I waited till he was gone before I bought my truffles. I'm not one for awkward situations."

"What about the other store that burned down? The flower shop next door. Did you happen to go in there?"

"What on earth for? I don't need any flowers. Waste of money if you ask me. Sure, sure, everyone thinks they're romantic but it's like giving the gift of death. Two or three days later those things shrivel up and die. Why pay good money for that?"

For a second I didn't know how to respond. Finally, I said something about people enjoying the scent the flowers gave off.

Kaye shrugged. "Like I said, no reason for me to go in there. Besides, that guy looked like he was busy enough. It was prom night according to the sign in front. Figured he had enough to do making up corsages."

Prom night. She had to be right. I mean, it was a couple of months before Memorial Day. Typical time for school proms. If nothing else, Kaye was one to pay attention. Then my imagination went really loco. What if some disgruntled adolescent who wasn't invited to the prom decided to set fire to the flower shop? But why would they wait two months?

Terrific. I can now sign up to work with Stephen King.

Wacky theories may be great for television drama but I knew that in order to draw a decent inference I would need strong background information and appropriate evidence. I had one more question before I let Kaye go.

"I know Skip Gunderson is your brother-in-law so I can understand if you don't want to say anything, but… I know he loaned Billy money and…"

"You can stop right there. Skip Gunderson has the manners of a mule and the personality to go with it. I told that idiot sister of mine not to get involved with him, but she did. Corrine never did have good taste in men and she sure proved it when Skip put that wedding ring on her finger. Her problem. Anyway, Skip's not your killer. He may act all rough and tough but he wouldn't kill anyone. Especially over money. Then he'd have nothing to hold over them if you catch my drift. It's the soft-spoken well-mannered ones you've got to be on the look-out for. They'll surprise you every time. Them and jealous husbands."

Kaye didn't have to take it any further. She had already accused, tried, and convicted the woman's husband from the chocolate shop in Willmar. And for all I knew, she might have been on to something. It would just have to wait until Monday.

TWENTY-THREE

LUANNE AND GARY SAUNDERS leased the property for their chocolate and flower shops from a real estate company in Hutchinson. I spent most of Sunday morning reading over the reports from the Willmar Police Department and the sheriffs' departments from both counties, not to mention the notes that Max had added. In my prior job, I'd spend countless hours poring over crime statistics with a special focus on type, location, and time. The community college had to be sure it was utilizing its security resources effectively and they had come to trust my predictions when it came to staffing. Reading the police reports, although not statistical, was a similar process for me, but instead of predicting what might occur, my focus was on what did occur and what led up to it.

The anecdotal reports were different. They gave me the "filler" that helped to put everything in perspective. Kind of like the flipside of statistics, if I thought about it as a coin. Max had always said I was a "quick study" but the truth of the matter was that he spent a heck of a lot of time showing me what he looked for in those types of reports and why. I made it a point to learn fast. Frankly, it was the puzzle that intrigued me and doing detective work had become more and more appealing each day.

According to my information, the Saunders had paid

their rents on time and there was nothing suspicious about either of their businesses. The real estate company was one of those mega companies with properties all over the state. It wasn't as if the Saunders were leasing from some Mom and Pop operation where things were more personal. Then, there was Billy. For the life of me, I couldn't find any reason why he would have started that fire.

Max and I had spoken early that morning. He was still busy with the dog-napping case and was certain he'd have it solved by the end of the day. That meant he wasn't available for me to toss ideas back and forth until Monday when we'd take the drive to Willmar.

Up until now I'd been working by the seat of my pants when it came to questioning people. With an entire day to myself, I thought it might be prudent to actually write down some of the questions I wanted to ask Luanne and Gary. The good news was that I wouldn't be working alone. Max could question Gary while I could ask Luanne about her relationship with Billy. That is, if we could manage to speak to them individually. If Luanne was romantically involved with the victim/suspect as Kaye suggested, she certainly wasn't about to blurt it out in front of her husband. *Gee, honey, all those dying flowers remind me of our dying marriage...* Nope, it wasn't going to be an easy interview. Not face to face with both of them at the Caribou Coffee in Willmar. Still, it was the best we could do.

Angie set up the meeting for us. She was able to locate Gary Saunders via his phone number on the Willmar Police Department report. I had less than twenty-four hours to come up with a plan to speak privately with Luanne. If she was really having an affair, which I highly doubted, there was no way she'd reveal it in front of her husband. If I didn't unearth the truth, Kaye's rumor would go viral.

While Sunday morning got off to a productive start, the afternoon turned out to be a disaster. First, my mother called and I picked up the phone without bothering to check the caller ID. *Calamity Jane* was at it again.

"I am so glad I caught you at home, Marcie. Dee-Dee, Maybelle and I may have come up with something to help you find that killer. You remember my friends from Mah Jong, Dee-Dee and Maybelle? Actually, it's Deirdre but everyone's called her Dee-Dee since she was a child."

"Yes, of course, Mom."

"Well, good. Because this is what we think— someone must have hired that killer off of Craigslist."

"What? You can't hire assassins off of Craigslist!"

"According to Dee-Dee and Maybelle, you can hire anyone off of that thing. Why, in Marin County, California, you can hire someone for seventy-five dollars an hour to tickle your back with a peacock feather. Dee-Dee saw the ad herself."

"Oh dear God, Mother. Who cares about peacock feathers and crazy people in California? And Craigslist does not have a column entitled 'Murder for Hire.'"

"I was only trying to help you, Marcie."

"Well, don't! Each time you call with some lunatic idea it drives me nuts!"

"Fine. Fine. One of these days you'll be sorry you didn't take my advice."

"Um, about that… Jonathan called me the other day. Quit pestering him to find me a boyfriend. I'm doing perfectly fine meeting men on my own." *Granted, they're murder suspects but they are men.*

I could hear the sigh in my mother's voice and I knew where the call was headed.

"I worry about you, Marcie. You're my only daughter. I'm only trying to make life easier for you but if that's too much to ask—"

"No one's asking. Especially me."

The line went silent. I knew my mother well enough to know she'd remain with dead air space until I caved. I figured why prolong the agony. And by agony, I meant mine.

"Sorry Mom. I know you mean to help and I do appreciate it. But Max and I can handle this investigation and I can manage my social life. Really. So, don't worry. I'll keep you posted."

I was able to end the call without my mother reiterating how concerned she was about me and all the baggage that went with it. As annoying and time consuming as that call was, the next one was far worse.

It was the alarm system company our office used calling to let me know that there was a break-in. That call was immediately followed by one from the New Ulm Police Department.

"Am I speaking with Marcie Rayner? This is Officer Delaney from the New Ulm Police Department. We have you and a Mister Blake listed as the contacts for Blake Investigations."

I figured Officer Delaney must be new since the entire staff at the police department was familiar with Max, as he had worked directly with most of them.

"Um, yes. This is Marcie Rayner."

"The police department received a call from your

alarm company. We've dispatched a unit to that address."

Twenty minutes later, I was standing in front of our office looking at the broken glass from our front window. The shards were all over the sidewalk. I guess whoever decided to break in didn't want to deal with the deadbolt lock and decided to opt for the old-fashioned way—breaking a window. The good news was they smashed the small panel window and not the larger one.

I stared at the damage and caught my breath. Unlike break-ins at retail establishments, our office didn't have any cash or valuables that would scream "Smash the window and grab some loot." Whoever did this was either after information that they thought we had or they were trying to give us a message to steer clear. Hard to say. Other than Billy Hazlitt's murder, Max had other cases including dog-napping and infidelity. Maybe someone with a vested interest in one of those cases decided to pay us a visit. I figured I'd wait and see what the police had to offer.

The uniformed officers who were sent to investigate appeared to be my age. Both of them male with wedding bands. I figured my observation might come up on one of Iris Krum's quizzes later.

I could hear her now. "That's terrible news about the break-in. So, tell me. Were any of the police officers single?"

Yep, I was prepared. Years of warding off my mother's intrusions in my life had taught me to be observant, if nothing else. There was always an Iris Krum interrogation to look forward to following any social activity I'd ever engaged in. And while it was downright annoying when I was growing up, I had to admit, it came in handy in my new role as a detective. Without even thinking, I honed in on little things like the way someone's hair looked, especially if they told me they had been in their house all day and yet it looked damp at the base of their neck as if they had been out for a run.

The officers asked me to wait outside while they went into the office to make sure that whoever broke in wasn't still hanging around. I imagined the siren from our alarm system sent the culprits running but I was wrong. Whoever did this stayed around long enough to rummage through our desks and erase everything I had written on the whiteboard. All of my copious notes on the board were gone along with my timeline and miscellaneous information.

Damn.

"Are you all right?" one of the officers asked when he saw me gasp at the whiteboard.

"No. I mean, yes. Yes, I'm all right but all my notes on a homicide case were erased."

"All your notes?"

"Well, the thinking out-loud ones. At least the computers aren't turned on so our file notes are still safe. Either the person wasn't savvy enough to figure out our passwords or they didn't have enough time. Besides, I have all the information backed up on a flash drive."

"Looks like someone went to a lot of trouble to slow down your investigation more than anything else. Look around, will you? See if they've made off with anything. Meanwhile we'll dust for prints. My partner and I will be right over there by the door. Give a holler if you notice anything of concern."

"Anything of concern?" I'd seen fraternities looking

better than our office, and that was after Greek Week on campus.

"You may want to get your cleaning service in here," the officer said, "when you're done checking out the place."

Our cleaning service consisted of a sixty-year-old Lebanese woman and her on and off again daughter-in-law. And no, I wasn't about to call them.

"Um, yeah. It'll be fine. We'll take care of it."

I spent the rest of the afternoon sweeping up glass from the sidewalk, arranging for an emergency window repair, waiting while the new window pane was installed and double checking our files to make sure nothing was missing.

After a quick bite for dinner, I returned to re-do the whiteboard. I knew Max was busy with his canine case so I didn't bother to call him until later that evening. He was so busy tracking down that stolen dog, he never bothered to check his voice mail from the police. As promised, Max found and returned the pup to its rightful owner, who in turn, pressed charges against the dog-napper immediately. She also gave Max a fairly substantial bonus along with his regular fee. Probably enough to pay for our broken window. No sense contacting the insurance company since the deductible would be used anyway.

"Do you need me to come down to the office?" he asked. "I can be there in about a half-hour."

"No, nothing that can't wait until tomorrow. Unless of course you feel like coming down here to straighten out the mess on your desk and the drawers that were pulled out. The police need to know if any valuables were stolen. I didn't think so but I told them you'd give them a call once you checked out your office."

"Valuables? The only item worth stealing from my desk is an old calculator. No, we both know whoever did this was more interested in information and it doesn't take a genius to figure out that it has to do with the Hazlitt murder."

"That's what I thought, too. You think whoever broke in might have been the person who killed Billy?"

"It's a strong possibility. Say, did the police take any prints?"

"Actually, they did. They dusted for prints on the surfaces of our desks and if they match anyone in their database they'll let us know. Expect it to take a while."

"Ugh. It always does. Listen, kid, stay put for a few minutes. I'm not waiting until tomorrow. I'm on my way. And make sure the door's bolted."

Max must have raced through more than one red light and kept a heavy foot on the gas pedal. He was at the office in twenty minutes and assessed the place in a matter of seconds. "This wasn't a professional job, Marcie. A professional would have used lock-picking tools to get in. Whoever did this probably used a hammer, or any heavy object for that matter, to break the glass. I imagine you had quite a mess."

"The window company removed most of the debris but some of the larger jagged pieces of glass that were still stuck to the frame broke in the process."

"That would give whoever did this some nasty cuts if they weren't careful. Any blood on the floor?"

"None that I could see. That doesn't mean the suspect didn't wipe it up. Or if it was minor, wipe it off on his or her clothing."

It was after nine when we locked up the office and entered the security code for the alarm system. Both of us were too tired from cleaning up to go out for something to eat, but Max insisted he owed me a steak dinner for ruining my weekend.

"I'll take a rain check," I said as I got into my car. "But you'll owe Angie a whole lot more when she sees the mess on her desk."

"Uh-huh. Now that you mention it, I'd better give her a call when I get home and warn her. She's always the first one in and I don't need her to get into a panic."

"Somehow Angie doesn't strike me as that type. But yeah, you should probably call her."

I watched as Max got into his sedan. Even though the weekend was a bust, it was still more exciting than my job running stats at St. Paul Community College. Adrenaline rushes like this one coupled with reading people instead of statistics was fast drawing me into its web. And I had to admit, I liked it.

TWENTY-FOUR

MAX STOOD BY the coffeemaker in the workroom waiting for it to stop brewing. "Obviously whoever broke in wasn't looking to steal anything as much as they were intent on slowing down our investigation."

It was the following morning. Angie had already cleaned up her desk and had finished going through the files. I listened to what he was saying but I wasn't so sure I agreed.

"How can we be certain they didn't take anything?" I asked.

"Angie's been through all of our files and both of us had the Hazlitt information in our possession during the break-in. I seriously doubt whoever came in was looking for something else. Otherwise why would they bother to stop and erase the whiteboard? None of the other case notes were on it."

I shrugged. "To throw us off?"

"Nah, we give these criminals a lot more credit than they deserve."

"Max, do you think it could be the same person who slipped me that note the other day? The message that said we were sniffing the wrong bush. And by the way, what kind of expression is that? Usually it's the one about barking up the wrong tree."

"Bush. Tree. It doesn't matter. What matters is that

someone in the Biscay vicinity knows full and darn well what happened. We've just got to keep the pressure on."

"Speaking of pressure, how do you want to approach Marisa about the evidence I found in those Juniper bushes? I really wasn't sure how to go about it so I didn't."

"Full force, kid. Full force."

"Huh? What?"

"Calm down, Marcie. You look as if we were going to play storm trooper and barge right into her house."

"Then what did you mean, exactly?"

"On our way back from Willmar we'll stop by her house. We've got to be in Biscay anyway to pick up those register receipts from Tom Hazlitt, right?"

I nodded as Max continued. "Two investigators can be more intimidating than one. It's plain and simple. We show her that pacifier-binky thing and tell her we know she was there the night of the murder."

"But we don't know that! Especially about the night of the murder. She could have been walking around those bushes with the baby and he could have spit that thing out of his mouth at any time. Not necessarily that night."

"Ah-hah! Think back. Those Barton sisters thought they heard a baby crying from over in the bushes that night."

"Well, one of the Barton sisters. The other insisted it was a cat."

"I'll let you in on a secret, Marcie. Half of investigating is making the other person believe you have more evidence than you really do. If they're guilty, they sometimes admit it."

"Marisa? Billy's killer?"

Max let out a long sigh. "I don't believe she's the person who killed Billy Hazlitt any more than I believe she was the one trying to slow down our investigation. There's no motive. What I *do* believe is that she and/or her husband were there the night of the murder. And they may know something. Now we need to get her to admit it."

"It's a slow process, isn't it?" I asked. "I'm so used to pulling up facts and figures in a nanosecond for analysis that these one-to-one conversations are, well, for lack of a better word—glacial."

"Whoa. Never heard that term used in this context, but yeah, investigative work, especially when dealing with suspects and witnesses can be slow and tedious. Plus, it has to be exacting. Then again, nothing compensates for the look on someone's face when you've got them and there's not a thing they can say or do to wrangle out of it."

"So, lots of wrangling ahead, huh?"

"At least we're dealing with a small circle of townsfolk in Biscay and of course, the Willmar connection."

OUR MEETING WITH Luanne and Gary Saunders, the proprietors of the chocolate and flowers shops, was set for the early afternoon and it was approaching eleven. I wasn't sure what to expect when we met with them. After all, they might still be in shock over the loss of their businesses.

"Shouldn't both of you be on your way to Willmar?" Angie announced as Max and I stepped out of his office. "I set that meeting up and I wouldn't want you to be late."

"We're on our way out now," Max yelled. "Wouldn't want anyone to think you didn't keep your word."

He gave her a wink and told her to lock up the office at five. "It's at least two hours to Willmar and we've got other business on the way back. If we need anything, we'll call."

I made sure I had all of my files with me. Not that I thought there would be another break-in but why take a chance? Max drove us to Willmar stopping only once at a fast food place for a quick lunch. We arrived at Caribou Coffee at a little past one.

Luanne and Gary Saunders were sitting at a table by the front window. I imagined they were eyeballing the parking lot wondering what to expect. Luanne appeared to be in her early thirties with light blond hair tied in pigtails. Pigtails! With ribbons no less. Gary was about the same age. He had his long brown hair pulled into a ponytail. Both of them looked as if they spent all of their free time trying to save the whales or promote sustainable farming. Max introduced us and we took a seat.

"I don't know what we'll be able to tell you that we haven't already told the police," Gary said re-folding a napkin. "We didn't have a problem with anyone. We don't owe anyone anything."

For a brief second I was taken back. It was the same thing I had heard from the brewery. Max went on to question Gary, handing him the police photo of Billy. It was an old one that they had secured from the newspapers when Billy's photo appeared for the opening of the Crooked Eye Brewery.

"What about this guy? Our murder victim? Your arson suspect?"

Gary remained unmoved.

"Take another look," my boss said. "Do you recognize him?"

Gary shook his head. "Sorry. Same thing I told the police. I don't recognize him. It doesn't mean he never came in my shop or Luanne's but lots of people walk into, I mean...*walked into* 'Hearts & Flowers.'"

Luanne glanced away from the photo. Was I imaging things or was Kaye Bowman right about an affair? I took the photo and touched Luanne's hand with the edge of the paper.

"What about you? Have you seen him in your chocolate shop?"

Her voice was soft and tentative. I'm sure Max and her husband didn't notice, but her lower lip was starting to quiver and she was fiddling with one of her pigtails.

"I might have. I see lots of people. Especially around the holidays."

Max jumped back in. "I understand that you lease both store fronts. Do you know if the other stores on Becker Avenue are leased by the same company?"

"Only ours," Gary said. "They're the only ones in that building. The other buildings are owned by different companies. Luanne and I checked into all of that when we started our businesses. You know, now that I think of it, the leasing company offered us money a few months ago for an early termination. They wanted the lease to end in six months rather than the three years we have left on it."

It was as if a beacon of light flashed on my boss's face. "Did they say why they wanted an early termination?"

"No, no reason. Luanne and I figured they had another business lined up that was willing to pay more."

Oh my God! Not the brewery! Don't tell me Billy had this planned so that the Crooked Eye Brewery would move to a big city like Willmar.

Luanne got up and excused herself to go to the ladies' room. It was my one and only chance to learn the truth about her relationship with Billy Hazlitt.

"Um… I think I'll go, too. It's a long ride back."

Before anyone could say anything, Luanne and I walked to the rear of the room where the restrooms were located. I wasted no time pulling her aside as soon as we got into the ladies' room.

"Look, we don't have much time and I didn't want to say anything in front of your husband, but please… please tell me the truth. You *did* know Billy Hazlitt, didn't you? The truth's going to come out anyway so you might as well tell me."

"It's not what you think."

"What do you mean?"

"Billy's been a regular customer. Had a sweet spot for homemade chocolate. Stopping in here whenever he was in Willmar. We would always flirt with each other and well, you know what I'm saying."

"That you were having an affair?"

"What? Shh! No. What are you talking about? We weren't having an affair. Like I said, just some harmless flirtation. Billy would stop in whenever he was in town. He did business with the fabricating company, that's all. Look, I didn't want to say anything because it would only lead to more questions. He seemed like a really sweet guy and for the life of me, I can't imagine why he would do something like that. Destroy our business. It doesn't add up."

"I know. So, what do you do now? Now that your businesses are gone."

"We're looking at moving to a new location. Possibly the mall. Flower and candy shops do well in those malls. It won't be the same because Becker Avenue has this neat historic flavor to it, but what choice do we have? In the meantime, I can continue to produce some chocolate products from our home and get them to distributors. Anything from fudge and caramels to malts and syrups."

I wanted to believe everything that Luanne was saying but something was off. I couldn't quite figure it out but I had the feeling that she wasn't telling me everything. It was the little signs that led me to believe she was holding back. Like the fact she kept twirling the ends of those pigtails and looking down whenever Billy's name was mentioned.

We headed back to our seats as Max and Gary were finishing up their conversation. I could hear Max's voice as Luanne and I approached the table.

"Thanks for giving us your time. We want this solved as much as anyone. I'll be looking into that leasing company in case there's anything fishy going on. Guess that's about it."

The couple thanked us and we were on our way. I waited until I got into the car before saying anything. "So what do you think? I mean, they sound like they're on the 'up and up' but I have the feeling Luanne is hiding something. And not just because of what I heard from Kaye."

"We'll still keep at it. Got to admit, though, it

wouldn't surprise me one bit if that leasing company was the one responsible for setting the fire. I've got their information. Believe it or not, they're located closer to us—in Hutchinson. That'll be a quick drive this week. Probably tomorrow."

I tried to hide my disappointment. "Could Billy have been working for them? The leasing company?"

"Depends upon whether or not there was something in it for him. People have done worse."

I didn't want to believe Billy was an arsonist. I still held on to my belief he had been framed. Still, if he wanted to use that building in Willmar so badly for the brewery, it would be motive enough to start a fire. Becker Avenue was the center of the historic district and its quaint little shops attracted a whole lot of people. More than a tiny street in Biscay.

TWENTY-FIVE

"So, what do you want to do first, kid? Stop by the brewery for those receipts or play Twenty Questions with that young mother. Marisa, right?"

"Yeah. Marisa. Let's get that part over with first."

We were a few miles out of Biscay and both of us wanted to finish up the last two stops before heading back to New Ulm. There were a few cars parked in front of the diner and four or five vehicles in the brewery's parking lot.

Max turned to me and lifted an eyebrow. "Got that binky thing with you?"

I could tell this wasn't the typical evidence he'd been used to dealing with on the police force. Of course the same could be said for me, although that will probably change since I've recently become an aunt. And hopefully one who doesn't get asked to change too many diapers.

"Yep. It's in this sealed Ziploc bag. I even put on gloves to move it from the potato chip bag to something more professional. And look, I wrote the date and place of discovery on the label."

"Impressive. Who knows? Maybe that baby's DNA is on file."

"Very funny."

The usual amount of kids' toys and paraphernalia were stashed on the porch. Lots of plastic things in primary colors. Max stepped aside as I rang the bell. Marisa came to the door but this time without the baby in one of her arms. She recognized me immediately and ushered us inside.

"Shh. I finally got him to sleep. And my other kids are napping, too. Come on in but speak quietly. We can sit at the kitchen table."

I nodded. "I know we should have called you first to make sure that it would be all right to speak with you again but we really didn't know what time we'd be in Biscay. We had another appointment in Willmar. Anyway, Marisa, this is my boss, Max Blake, and we have some more questions for you if you don't mind."

"I won't mind the questions if you don't mind the mess. It's never-ending. The poop, the pee, the throw-up, the— Oh my God, look at the sink. I'm still dealing with last night's dinner dishes. Feel free to ask away."

Max gave me a quick look and I knew he wanted me to be the one to refute what Marisa had told me previously. Uh-huh. I was going to be the one to call her a "big liar." My brain worked frantically to figure out how I could say it diplomatically. Tactfully. Appropriately. What came out instead was blunt and to the point. Like everything that comes out of my mother's mouth.

Dear God, last thing I need is to become the next Iris Krum. I read somewhere that we all become our mothers in time. I can only pray whoever wrote that was delusional.

I took out the Ziploc bag and placed in on the table. "You didn't exactly tell me the truth, Marisa. About the night of the murder. You were there." I caught a quick breath and continued. "I doubt this is the only evidence we'll uncover by the Juniper bushes. Tell us, what were you doing there?"

Her eyes widened and her cheeks began to blush. "I was afraid something like this would happen. I know you're not going to believe me. We didn't have anything to do with that murder. Honestly. We didn't even know the people associated with the brewery until we moved in."

Oh my gosh, Max was right. She thinks we know more than we're letting on. They never taught me to bend the truth in my criminal justice classes.

I spoke slowly, enunciating every word. "Then what were you doing in those bushes that evening?"

I glanced to my right and could see Max giving me a subtle nod. I was doing okay with this. As long as I kept my hands in my lap so Marisa wouldn't see how nervous I was. It shouldn't have mattered. She wasn't exactly the epitome of calm, either. Her voice got wobbly and she had to stop to take some breaths.

"I told my husband it was a stupid idea but he wouldn't listen. The prior owner let us have the key to the house a few weeks before we moved in. He said we could store some stuff in the garage but not move in."

"Uh-huh. Keep going." I wasn't about to let up.

"So, that night…the night the man in the brewery was shot…well, that evening my husband got the bright idea to take a photograph of our new house from across the street. He wanted it to be at dusk so that it would look more dramatic. And um, well, let's just say the dim lighting covers some of the defects that we'll have to work on. No one would notice chipped paint or dented rain gutters."

"Why didn't he just go across the street by himself?"

"He started to. Almost made it out the door. That's when the two-year-old began screaming and my husband thought it would be easier if we all traipsed across the street. I wasn't one to argue since I would've been dealing with a temper tantrum instead. And my husband was hell bent for leather to take that picture of our first home."

"Sounds like it was really a big deal for him, huh?"

Marisa gave a quick nod. "I still can't believe we're living in our own home and not a lousy apartment. We were lucky to get the place for a price we could afford. Maybe other folks didn't want a location so close to a diner but we didn't care. It was such a great deal. I'm surprised the people who saw the ad posted on the feed and grain store bulletin board didn't jump on the chance to make an offer. Anyway, my husband was going to frame the picture and hang it up. Then, every few years, take another picture once we made improvements. We parked our car in the garage and walked across the street. We hadn't yet filled up the garage with our stuff."

"That makes sense," I said. "By the way, did your husband take the picture on his cell phone?"

"Cell phone? No. He used our old digital camera while I was holding the baby and trying to keep the other two from getting hurt in the bushes. It was a nightmare. Do you have any idea how bright that stupid camera flash is? As soon as it went off the baby dropped his pacifier and started screaming. I think sounds get amplified at night because his shrieking was so loud I thought it would disturb the neighbors. Oh, and if every nerve in my body wasn't already on edge, the older brothers ran around like nincompoops until we were able to corral them and walk back to the house. Why?"

She didn't have to say another word. Rose Barton was telling the truth. She did see a flash. A flash from that camera. And she did hear a baby crying. Or howling if Marisa wasn't exaggerating.

"Marisa, can your husband email us a copy of the photo?"

"Then you believe me?"

"Yeah, I do. You still have our business card?"

"Yes, I put it in my desk drawer."

"Good. Our email is on it. Send us a copy of that picture as soon as you can."

I couldn't believe it. I had handled the whole business with Marisa from start to finish without as much as a peep from Max. We thanked her and crossed the street to the brewery. A car was still in the lot plus two trucks off to the side.

"I don't suppose this will take us too long," Max said as we reached the entrance. "But if you don't mind, I've got some questions I'd like to ask the owners. By the way, great job back there with Marisa. You almost had me going. Especially the insinuation about other evidence."

"I kind of went by the seat of my pants on that one."

"Hmm. Always a good option."

Just then, someone opened the door from the brewery and walked out. It was a middle-aged man who headed directly for his car without saying a word to either of us. Max and I stepped inside to find Tyler behind the counter.

"Your last customer didn't look too happy, Tyler," I said.

"That's because my last customer was my father and he's not too happy. It isn't bad enough I've got my girlfriend on my back to quit my job and go work elsewhere because she thinks I'm going to be shot in the head like Billy, but now I've got my Dad on my case because he decided I should go work for him. In real estate. I hate real estate. All I ever wanted to do was to learn how to become a brewmaster like the guys I work for in this place. The last thing I want to do is show houses or draw up contracts. He just doesn't get it. And all I get is a ration of crap from him. Sorry about that. I suppose you're looking for Tom or Hogan."

"We are. Can you tell us—"

"Tom went home a few hours ago but left an envelope for you and Hogan should be back any second from the diner. Want me to call him and tell him you're here?"

Max spoke up. "No, that won't be necessary. We stopped by for the information Tom left us. You said Hogan's at the diner? Come to think of it, I could use a good cup of coffee. What about you, Marcie?"

"Uh, sure." *Coffee. Hogan. Whatever.*

I had to admit, Hogan was easy on the eyes and struck me as one of those down-to-earth men who didn't need to go to great lengths to impress anyone. Was I hoping to develop some sort of relationship with him? Frankly, I hadn't been interested in pursuing any kind of relationship with a guy since my divorce, but that was well over a year ago and yeah… Hogan *was* easy on the eyes. Then again, he, like everyone else in Biscay, was a murder suspect.

I glanced at the parking lot hoping Hogan was on his way back to the brewery so we could make this a quick conversation. No such luck. Max and I thanked Tyler and walked over to the diner, the parking lot gravel crunching under our feet. I was already wired from the coffee I had in Willmar but I could always order decaf. That, and let Max do the talking.

TWENTY-SIX

LIKE THE OTHER days I'd been there, the diner seemed to have a steady stream of traffic. Not overly crowded but enough customers going in and out to keep the place busy. Frankie and Kaye were the only ones working. I figured Trisha and Trudy were at their late day classes.

Hogan was sitting at the counter. Same spot as the last time. He acknowledged Max and me as we walked in, and then said something to the guy sitting next to him before standing up and walking toward us.

"Hey, I know it's no coincidence you're here. Tyler told you I was at the diner, right?"

"Yeah," Max said. "We've got a few more questions for you. Hope that's all right. We were on our way back from Willmar or we would've called."

"Not a problem. Why don't we grab that table in back?"

Hogan led the way as Max and I skirted around the tables and booths, careful not to jostle any of the customers. Kaye stopped wiping the counter and watched us. "I'll be right with you," she said.

"Okay, what's up?" Hogan asked, looking directly at me. He held out a chair and I sat down.

"Um…like my boss said, we were in Willmar. Looking into that arson. It doesn't look good as far as the evidence is concerned. I imagine Tom filled you in."

Hogan clenched his teeth and gave a quick nod as I

continued. "Look, we'll be going through the receipts for the growler purchases. Just because there's circumstantial evidence, it doesn't mean Billy was involved."

"Yeah, I know. So what was it you needed to speak with me about?"

His voice was monotone and direct. I figured that was because Max was with me. Still, it was a bit unnerving. I made it a point to respond the same way. "Willmar. Becker Avenue to be more precise."

Hogan shrugged. "I don't get it. What are you talking about?"

Just then Kaye walked over to take our orders. Three coffees. Two black and one decaf for me. As soon as she went back to the counter, Max spoke up. "I'll get right to the point. Were you or your partners looking into moving your brewery to Willmar? To Becker Avenue?"

"What? No. Becker Avenue?"

"Yeah. Becker Avenue. Billy Hazlitt was familiar with it. It's the new hotsy-totsy historic place that's bringing in tourists and, well, for lack of a better word—hipsters. The kind of people who would make your microbrewery well known."

"The Crooked Eye is doing fine right here. If Billy was thinking of moving it to Willmar, he would've shared that revelation with me and his brother. Cripes, we've got enough going on with keg production for the bars and restaurants. Plus our own little tastings. Small town. That's all any of us wanted."

"Are you sure?" I said, reaching to touch Hogan on his arm. As he moved his hand, I could see a large bandaid on the inside of his palm and I jerked my hand back. Hogan gave me a funny look.

"What? This cut on my palm? It's nothing. Stupidity really. I was making myself a tuna sandwich last night and dropped the jar of mayo when I was taking it out of the fridge. Talk about a mess. Anyway, I got cut on one of the shards and had to toss the whole jar away. New jar, too. I wound up making myself peanut butter and jelly."

I didn't say a word but I couldn't hide the look on my face.

"Hey. It's just a little cut. I'll live. So, was that all you needed to ask me? About relocating to Willmar? Look, I happen to like small towns like the ones in this area. The only thing Willmar's good for is the baseball games."

Then I remembered. Hogan had mentioned something about his nephew playing. I wanted to believe him. Believe that he, Tom and Billy had no intention of moving their business to Willmar. More than that, I wanted to believe the cut on his palm was from a mayonnaise jar and not our plate glass window. Was he the one trying to slow down our investigation? A zillion thoughts were clouding up my mind as I sat there. Was he the one who stuck that puzzling note in my bag? I was speechless but my mind was spinning. Max was saying something to Hogan but it wasn't sinking in. Then, he turned to me.

"Uh, Marcie...your coffee's going to get cold. You all right?"

"Yeah," Hogan added, "You look as if you're miles away."

"Oh. Sorry. It's already been a long day."

Hogan pushed the chair back from the table and it made a grating sound. "Well, if there's nothing else I can help you with, I've got to get back to the brewery.

Tyler's by himself and if we get busy, it wouldn't be fair to him. Give me a call if you find out anything. Okay?"

He stood up and stared directly into my eyes. My arctic blue eyes that were only a shade off from his. It was a long stare and I wasn't sure what it meant.

"Thanks for your time," Max said. "Hope that nasty little cut doesn't get too bothersome. It's in a bad place."

"Don't worry. I'll be more careful next time."

"Was that an innuendo or small talk?" I whispered to Max once Hogan reached the door.

"Both. Add Hogan to the list of people we need to be watching."

Wonderful. I meet a guy who seems like he could be decent dating material and boom! He becomes the prime suspect? Terrific. My track record was soaring. *First a philanderer, and now what? I didn't want to say the word out loud.*

TWENTY-SEVEN

"Okay. Okay. I had the same thought you did, Max, about that cut on Hogan's palm but he didn't act as if he had anything to hide. I mean, he came right out with that mayonnaise scenario. He didn't even pause to come up with a story."

"Maybe he's had practice with that sort of thing."

"Lying?" The word caught in my throat. "Because he doesn't strike me as a liar."

"The good ones don't."

"Let's give him the benefit of the doubt. I mean, it's not as if we have hard core evidence."

Max and I were in the car heading back to New Ulm. I hoped he didn't detect too much emotion in my voice. Last thing I needed was for him to think I wasn't going to be objective about the case.

One by one, I rolled the players over in my mind. So far, Marisa's story seemed to check out. Luanne and Gary were still a "loose end" but the possibility that Hogan was the one who broke into our office made me question everything. He was the last person I suspected of being involved in Billy Hazlitt's death. My own fault for letting my feelings cloud my vision. My boss, however, was more clearheaded.

"If Hogan was the one who broke into our office, what I want to know is why he would be trying to deter us, unless he was responsible for his partner's death or he was protecting someone who was. Either way, we're going to have a tough time proving anything right now."

"This is so darn frustrating." I could almost hear the exasperation in my own voice. "It's like we're chasing a million little clues hoping they'll all add up."

"Welcome to Investigating 101. Speaking of which, I'll do a little digging on that real estate company and try to find out exactly why they wanted the Saunders to terminate their lease."

"You think there could be a connection between that leasing company and the Crooked Eye?"

"Uh-huh. Let's just say for a minute that they wanted to oust the Saunders' little 'Hearts & Flowers' for a business that would be more lucrative. A brewery. Higher rents. And let's just say they asked Billy Haz-litt to move up the timeline…"

"Then why would they murder him?" I asked.

"Maybe they weren't the ones who did. Someone could have seen him, followed him back to Biscay and waited for an opportune time to shoot him. Someone who had something else at stake."

"Like what?" I held my breath waiting for Max to continue theorizing.

"Like committing the perfect crime and cover-up. Get Billy to do the dirty work, get rid of Billy and leave the place wide open for another business to move in. The quintessential double cross. I've seen it before. But hey, I'm only speculating."

"Two can play that game," I said. "I'm still pretty convinced Longfellow Brewery's latest product was stolen from Billy's formulas."

"Game on, kid. Let's see who gets to the finish line first."

Both of us started to laugh and then Max changed the subject. "By the way, that Alice Davenport was sure prompt with her payment. Forgot to tell you. Angie said it arrived by Express Mail in two days. Always a good thing to have a client who pays their bills on time."

"I suppose she'll be keeping her receipts in chronological order."

"Huh?"

"Never mind. I'm glad she sent the payment right away. But I'm getting worried we won't be able to solve this case fast enough for her."

"Don't tell me she gave you a deadline?"

"No. Not exactly. More like a recommendation."

Max let out another laugh. "Don't worry about it. Well, looks like we're back home. I don't know about you, but I'm pooped. It's going to be Doris' leftovers for me. Pray to God it's not something healthy. Her health foods are killing me. Lately if it doesn't have flax seed in it or spelt, she won't prepare it. Ugh. What do you say I just drop you off at your car? We've both had a long day. Nothing that can't wait till the morning."

"Um…actually, I did want to stop into the office for a few minutes. Maybe I'm being really OCD but I want to make sure everything's okay."

"Now you're making me feel bad. That should be my job. But fine—ten minutes and we're out of there. Understood?"

"Yep. Ten minutes."

Angie's desk was back to being carefully organized and everything in the front room looked exactly the way it should. Max went into his office and I quickly turned on the lights to mine. I could see Angie had placed a large priority mail envelope on the top of my desk.

It was from Alice Davenport. Now what? Grammatical rules for written reports? I shuddered as I fiddled with the tape and opened the tab. I could see a piece of paper wedged between two cardboard sheets. It was an old 8 x 10 photograph. A class picture. Billy's to be more exact. It had to be at least forty years old. A small note accompanied the photo.

Dear Miss Rayner,
I thought you would find this quite helpful. When you have completed the investigation, please be sure to return this photo to me and use the same cardboard sheets that I have enclosed. It's a much sturdier cardboard than the inexpensive kind that's sold today. Incidentally, I don't like wasting paper products.
I look forward to your next report and of course, your prompt resolution to the investigation.

Respectfully,
Alice Davenport

I let the note drop to my desk as I reached for the photo. Twenty plus fifth graders stood perfectly still on the steps of the school with Miss Davenport off to the right. Presumably to make sure they remained that way until the photographer was finished. On the back of the photo, Alice had written all of their names.

Billy was standing in the back row, fourth to the left, between a kid who looked as if he was about to be executed (probably got scolded by her seconds before) and another boy with curly hair and braces, smiling like the Cheshire cat.

Glancing at the names, I could see Lucas Rackner's. I immediately located him way off to the right in the last row. And there was a tall kid with a surly looking expression on his face who looked vaguely familiar. A kid named Stanley Evans. It didn't ring a bell.

"Hey Max!" I shouted. "You're not going to believe what came in with the mail! And whatever you do, don't toss that cardboard. Here, see for yourself."

I darted across the room to his office and handed him the photo. "Vintage school days. I think Alice Davenport must have a shrine somewhere in her house that's plastered with these."

Max adjusted his bifocals and squinted. "Not that I don't enjoy a good clue landing on my desk but I seriously doubt Billy Hazlitt's murder was the result of an old childhood grudge. Especially in elementary school. High school might be tempting. If it was over a girl or something. But these are little kids. Aargh. Look at their faces. Most of them are squirming to get out of there."

"I suppose if Miss Davenport was your teacher you'd be squirming, too."

"Nope, I'd be ditching school."

"Very funny. Anyway, this may come in handy. In these small towns everyone seems to have a connection with someone else."

"Good point. Look, tuck that picture in your desk and let's get going. We've dillydallied enough in here. Tomorrow's another day. Which reminds me, what does your schedule look like?"

"I've got two appointments with new clients and I thought I'd contact Longfellow Brewery for an update on Billy's supervisor. The person in human resources was supposed to look into it for me."

"Sounds good. I've got some odds and ends to take care of as well. No news from either sheriffs' departments or the Willmar Police means they haven't gotten too far on the case either."

"I know. And you know what the worst part is?"

"Knowing the killer is still on the loose?"

"No. Feeling the heat from Alice Davenport breathing down my neck. I could just strangle my mother for sending this case my way."

"Don't do that. I don't feel like breaking in another investigator."

TWENTY-EIGHT

I WOKE UP the next morning clutching my pillow and grinding my teeth, having narrowly escaped from one of the worst nightmares I'd had in years. In the foggy haze that only dreams can deliver, I was locked in a walk-in freezer with a faceless entity waving a gun in my face.

"It's just a dream," I kept telling myself yet I knew otherwise. Trisha and Trudy were right to be scared of retrieving things from the diner's freezer.

It took me two cups of coffee to shake away the visions from that bizarre night terror. When I got into the office, Max had already left for Hutchinson. Angie filled me in on the details.

"Mr. Blake certainly got an early start this morning. He was here before I got in. Said he wanted to get to Hutchinson right away. Something about a realty company."

"Yeah," I said, "all part of the Hazlitt case."

This was the first time I had actually sat down at my desk to work. Between road trips to Minneapolis, Biscay and Willmar, it was good to feel grounded. I booted up the computer and straightened out the piles of paper on my desk while I waited for my emails to appear. My first appointment wasn't for another hour.

The emails had the usual queries about our business, some solicitations from companies who offered to sell us anything from pencils to recording devices, and

one message that read "What you wanted." It was from
ogeewhiz30@yahoo with an attachment. My finger was
poised to delete it when I suddenly realized it could be
the photo from Marisa. Praying I wasn't about to open
some nefarious virus, I held my breath.

Sure enough, it was from her husband. The photo
was actually three photos, in the form of a slide show,
all taken within a few seconds of each other. The background lighting at sundown varied slightly. The message
in the email read "Sending you the pictures of our house.
My wife says she's sorry she wasn't upfront with the info.
Good luck with your investigation." Robert and Marisa.

I immediately printed out the copies but the screen
version was much clearer. The words "Starter Home"
came to mind as I stared at the little clapboard house
out in the middle of "Small town, USA." Front porch,
classic shutters on the windows, two stories, small garage. I clicked through all of the images and at first
everything looked the same. Then, something struck
me and I called out for Angie.

"Angie! Can you come in here and look at something?"

"On my way!"

I got out of my seat and made Angie sit in front of
the computer. "What do you see, Angie?"

"Is this some kind of a test or weird computer thing
where a monster pops out at you? It better not be, because I hate those."

"No, no. These are photos of the house across from
the Crooked Eye Brewery. Scroll through each of them
and tell me what you see."

"They all look alike. I mean, the sky in the background seems to vary but other than that, they look
the same. Darling little house. It really has a case of

the 'cutes.' Reminds me of my grandmother's house in Little Falls when I was growing up. Same shutters, too."

"Take a closer look. Notice anything peculiar about one of the pictures?"

"Hmm, now that you mention it, it looks like someone stepped in front of one of the upstairs windows in this particular photo. I wouldn't have noticed it if you didn't say anything."

"So it *does* look like a person to you? That shadowy thing."

"Yeah, it really does. Especially when you compare that picture with the others. Someone in the house decided to look outside just as the photographer snapped the shot. Why? Is that important?"

"Oh yeah. Because no one was in the house at the time."

"Ew, that's kind of creepy. I guess the homeowners will start locking their doors from now on. Unless it wasn't a person."

"Please don't tell me you think the shadowy thing was some sort of apparition."

"Of course not. It could have been a large dog. Do they own a large dog?"

"No. And dogs usually stand on all four feet. Take another look."

"It's a silhouette all right. And I'm sure there's a logical explanation. Why? What were you thinking?"

With Max out of the office, I had to bounce my ideas off of someone or I'd go nuts. Angie seemed more than willing to listen, or maybe she was being polite. Anyway, it didn't matter. I gave her the full-blown story about Marisa and her family. If that wasn't enough to make her yawn, I added the Barton sisters to the mix as well as the crew from the diner.

"Gee, that's quite a lot on your plate. No wonder you seem so frazzled. Maybe you ought to narrow down your suspicions."

"Okay, fine. Here goes: Scenario number one. Marisa and her husband lied. They were in their house and they weren't alone. Whoever was with them may have been Billy's killer."

Angie leaned her head on the palm of her hand and paused. "Sounds reasonable. What else have you got?"

"Scenario number two. Marisa and her husband had no idea someone was in their house. Someone who could have been scoping out the brewery from an upstairs window, waiting for the opportune time to shoot Billy Hazlitt in the head. Remember, they were across the street at the time."

"That sounds feasible. Of course it also sounds like the opening scene to every horror movie on the market. Got any other ideas?"

"Maybe. There's scenario number three. The image in that photo is some sort of printing fluke. Heck, that's not a scenario. It could be a dead end. Say, do you know if the clarity of the picture could be improved?"

Angie shook her head. "Gosh, I thought that's what you guys did."

"Not us. Tech support. Darn it. I wish Max were here. When did he say he'd be back?"

"He didn't. But I can look up our tech support files and see who we've got."

"Great. Meanwhile I'll start writing these theories on the whiteboard. Then I'll—"

"It'll have to wait. Look behind you. Your first appointment's about to walk through the front door."

TWENTY-NINE

My FIRST APPOINTMENT turned out to be an elderly woman in her eighties who wanted us to track down her college roommate. She explained that since she didn't know how to use a computer, and had no intentions of starting now, she wanted someone who "wasn't afraid of having one of those things in their house."

I took down all of the information including the college, the dates of attendance and anything else I deemed pertinent to the investigation. In the back of my mind, I wondered if I shouldn't be starting with the obituaries from her college but decided not to mention that. Not right away. It was a very pleasant meeting and I promised to get back to her by the start of the following week. As she left the office, I was thankful the case seemed fairly easy and relieved that the woman didn't demand a chronological report.

With an hour and a half before my next appointment, I took another look at the photos of Marisa's house and then pulled up her address on a Google Earth map. Max and I had used Google Earth before when we first started the investigation. Looking at the Crooked Eye Brewery in relation to its surroundings was a start. This time I was checking Marisa's place, directly across the street.

Like the brewery, it was surrounded by woods. Beyond that was the highway—Route 22. No one would be stupid enough to park a car on the side of a highway and traipse through the woods to get into that house. But that didn't mean they couldn't have parked elsewhere. I tried to imagine where I would have stashed *my* car if I didn't want to be seen. Certainly not in their parking lot or right in front on the street, even though it was a Sunday night and the diner was closed. But what about the small driveway to the left of the diner? Delivery trucks used that driveway. It led straight to the diner's back door. Could one of the diner's vendors have had it in for Billy Hazlitt? I doubted the two businesses used the same suppliers. Still, it was a possibility. Especially if...

The phone rang, interrupting my thoughts as Angie called out to me. "Iris Krum is on line one for you."

Oh no. Now what? More snipers? Mob bosses? Lunatic terrorists? That woman needs to find a hobby or something.

"Hi Marcie. I thought you'd call me last night."

"Mom, I'm at work. Can this wait?"

"I wanted you to know that Maybelle, Dee-Dee and I saw the movie *The Girl on the Train* yesterday. We went to the afternoon matinee at our recreation center."

"That's why you're calling me at work? To tell me you went to the movies?"

"Don't be ridiculous. I'm calling because watching that movie gave me another idea about that awful brewery murder."

Before I had a chance to stop her from yet another bizarre revelation, my mother continued. "It was probably a psychotic ex-girlfriend of his. Or maybe a psychotic ex-wife with a drinking problem. Be careful,

Marcie. Unbalanced people will do anything. They have no sense of propriety."

"I'll, uh…keep that in mind, Mom. Look, I've got to get back to work. I promise. I'll call you later."

This time I was the one who didn't give her a chance to say anything before I hung up. My mother's "epiphanies" were beginning to wear me down.

Just then, Max breezed through the door to my office.

"Whoa," I said. "You're back in record time from Hutchinson. What did you find out?"

"I talked to a guy by the name of Harold Evans. He's one of the owners of that building. Late fifties. Been in real estate all his life. Anyway, he said they didn't pressure 'Hearts & Flowers' to end their lease early and has no recollection of anything of the kind."

"Did you believe him?"

"No. And it wasn't based on any character traits either. When I was waiting in their office to speak with Mr. Evans, I happened to walk past their conference room and did a little side step inside. Guess what I saw? A map of the entire Becker Avenue on the wall with plans to turn it into some sort of high end entertainment center—fancy restaurants, bars, you name it."

"And cute little 'Hearts & Flowers' along with the other small businesses in that district wouldn't fit in."

"More than likely, wouldn't cash in."

"So, you think the realty company resorted to arson? And what did Billy Hazlitt have to do with this, if anything? I mean, other than his fingerprints showing up on the arson evidence."

"I think you need to present some of these recent

findings to Billy's co-owners and go from there. I'll do a little probing too, but it'll have to wait."

"Wait? Why?"

"That's the other part of what I wanted to tell you. I've been called to testify on a case that I handled a few years ago for the police department. Apparently, the case has been moved to appeals so who knows how long I'll be stuck in another courtroom. At least this one is right here in New Ulm. They'll let me know later today if I have to report tomorrow or the next day. So, looks like it's *you* for the next day or so."

"Okay. I suppose I can drive back to Biscay and dig for more information from Hogan and Tom, although I'm not really counting on Tom for much. Besides, I'd like to do a little snooping around myself."

I proceeded to show Max the photos that Marisa's husband emailed us and he agreed the shadow in the upstairs window sure looked like a person.

"Look Max, if I can narrow down a timeline, a real timeline, it may lead us closer to finding out who shot Billy. Let's face it. We don't need tech support to tell us what we already know. That's no shadow in the window. I'm convinced whoever killed him was the same person standing in front of that upstairs window. I have a hunch they parked their car behind the diner and from there, walked to the back of Marisa's house."

No sooner did I finish my sentence when Angie appeared at my door. "Your next appointment is here, Marcie. She's a bit early."

"I'll take that as my cue to leave," Max said as he stood up and stretched. "Let's catch up over a late lunch. I've got a pretty busy schedule until then."

I followed Angie and Max to the front office and

introduced myself to the client who was seated near the window. She was a young woman, maybe early twenties, with naturally blond hair and a figure that would rival a supermodel. As it turned out, she wanted a woman investigator to handle her case since it was somewhat "delicate." Apparently she had let an old boyfriend take some compromising photos of her when they were younger and wanted to make sure those photos didn't turn up anywhere.

I figured unless she was planning to run for political office or get a job with a government agency, she was probably worried for nothing. Then again, I thought about my own ex-husband and cringed. For all I knew, her former boyfriend might still be holding a grudge. I would need to track him down and arrange for both of them to meet. Preferably chaperoned.

The woman listened intently when I explained I would be tied up for the next few days but could begin shortly after that. She left a deposit with Angie along with her contact information. I walked her to the door, thanked her and headed straight for my desk.

As I passed Max's office, I peered in to see if he was available. He wasn't. It looked as if he was meeting with one of his clients. That meant I could tackle a chore I was putting off—the grunt work of sorting through the register tapes from the brewery. Tom had given me all of the tapes from the time the specialty growlers were produced until the date of the fire in Willmar. Our next step was to contact a friend of Max's who was still in the detective division at the police department and who had agreed to use his resources to link credit card numbers with actual names and addresses. Thank goodness Max had a never-ending cadre of people who "owed him one."

If I knew who had purchased those specially marked beer growlers I might be able to find a connection between the buyer and Billy Hazlitt. A connection that might very well prove someone set Billy up.

THIRTY

A WAD OF register tapes had been stuffed into the manila envelope along with a note from Tom that read, "I do remember one cash purchase for the specialty growlers. Lila Barton, who lives across the street with her sister, stopped by and bought the four-pack carton. Not sure exactly when. She said something about a gift for someone but I wasn't really paying attention. I had Tyler carry it over to their house when he came in later that day. That's all I remember. Sorry. Best I can do. Tom"

Lila Barton. Of all people. She was the last person I expected to be purchasing beer. Sweet boysenberry wine, maybe, but not beer. At least her purchase narrowed the search down by one, but the job was tedious. Tedious and time consuming. I had to locate the code for the growlers and separate those purchases. Then, I had to do it again, this time separating the cash purchases from the credit card ones. My eyes were bugging out by the time I had written down all of the credit card information for Max's contact.

As it turned out, there were only four purchases for the specialty growlers and one of them was Lila's. There was another cash purchase, made on the same day and made within minutes of Lila's. Would she remember anything about the person who bought those growlers? I could always ask her.

The other two were by credit cards which meant we

could get contact information. I picked up the phone, called Max's detective at the police station and he, in turn, gave me his email address so I could forward him the numbers. Detective Zach Melbourne. Spelled like the city. I felt as if I had accomplished a major feat but I was miles away from finding an answer.

"Hey, Marcie! You ready to get a bite to eat?" Max's voice bellowed across the office. It was one forty-five and I was ravenous. Angie had taken her break an hour before and put the phone on voice mail so my boss and I wouldn't be interrupted.

"So, what will it be? Deli? Burgers? Pizza?"

I grabbed my bag and headed out the door with Max. We opted for sandwiches from a small mom and pop shop a few blocks away. Both of us wanted to take advantage of a decent summer day and get some fresh air.

In between mouthfuls of food, Max and I caught up on all of the details for the Hazlitt case. We agreed I would go to Biscay the next day to press Tom or Hogan further regarding a possible motive. I also needed to speak with Lila Barton about her growler purchase and find out who the recipient was. Not to mention I was anxious to snoop around the back of the diner.

I was certain the killer parked his or her vehicle behind the diner and walked the few yards to the back of Marisa's house to sneak inside. They must have looked down the driveway to see the family crossing the street to take pictures. All it would have taken was one open window or an unlocked door and they would be in the house. What they had to do was hide and wait for the family to leave for a while that night.

Maybe the killer worked for one of the banks. Or a loan company. Heck, for all I know, he or she could've been friends with the seller. I remembered something one of the waitresses told me. Marisa and her husband pretty much informed the diner personnel of their arrangement. They could move their things inside the house but not sleep or eat there. Not until the house closing. If Trisha, Trudy and Kaye knew that, it meant everyone in a five mile radius of Biscay knew it as well. Including Billy's assassin.

"I imagine Zach Melbourne will get that info on the growlers back to you in a day or so," Max said as we returned to the office. "He's pretty quick."

"If we didn't have your contacts I don't know what we'd do."

"Yeah, well…it works both ways. It has to in this business or we wouldn't be able to solve a darn thing. Hey, don't look so down. The clues will start to come together. At least you get a nice drive tomorrow while I'll be cooped up in a courtroom."

"I suppose. Meanwhile I'll get going on those other clients. Small cases. No deaths. Not yet. I mean, not that I want one. Although I might have to break the news to some elderly woman that her college roommate is deceased."

"That's never fun. Listen, are you having second thoughts about leaving your job in campus security?"

Max's question took me completely off guard. I hadn't decided yet and tried not to think about it until the time came when I would have no choice.

"Um…no. Things are fine. Honest."

"Would you tell me if they weren't?"

"Yeah Max. I would."

Angie was on the phone when we walked back into

the office and quickly wrote a name on a piece of paper and held it up for us to see.

Alice Davenport.

I quickly slid my thumb across my neck to indicate I didn't want to speak with her. Not right at the moment.

"As I was saying, Miss Davenport," Angie went on, "Miss Rayner is due back within the hour. I'll let her know you called."

"Whew. Thanks Angie," I said as Max tried not to laugh.

He raised an eyebrow. "Seems our new investigative assistant has learned the fine art of avoidance and has managed to share that skill."

"That's not funny," I whined. "I just need time to prepare for her calls."

Angie slid the phone a few inches away from her hand. "Time and an entire case of those growlers."

THIRTY-ONE

I WAS FEELING the pressure of trying to catch a killer. On top of that, I had those ridiculous end-of-the-week report deadlines for Alice Davenport. Not to mention the daily musings and phone calls that never stopped. Every time the phone rang I cringed. It felt like being in seventh grade all over again, only instead of book reports, I had updates. Updates that had to be mailed.

What's wrong with these people? Don't they know it's the twenty-first century and mailing a letter is like hitching a horse and buggy?

I took a quick shower and towel dried my hair before reaching into my closet for a pair of form-fitting slacks in lieu of my usual twills. Then a V-neck top instead of a button down one. Who was I kidding? The clincher was when I applied the tiniest bit of mascara to offset the eyeliner. I was attracted to Hogan Austin before I knew he could quite possibly be tied into the murder. So much for listening to Max's sage wisdom. I wasn't sure what I felt about Hogan or how it would affect my work. It was something I was going to have figure out if I could trust my initial impressions of people I would meet in this job.

I left for Biscay around nine, having called Lila Barton the night before to arrange for a quick little chat with her in the morning. Then I figured I could saunter into the brewery and speak with Hogan. I wasn't necessarily counting on Tom to be there.

Lila and Rose were expecting me, chocolate chip cookies and all. I was ushered into the living room and given the seat of honor in a comfortable captain's chair by the couch. Rose was seated across from me in a smaller armchair.

"Would you care for something to drink?" Lila said, leaning over the couch. "We can offer you tea or milk if you would prefer."

"Thanks but no, I've had plenty of coffee this morning. I won't keep you long. I was hoping you might remember someone who was at the brewery the same time you were there, purchasing a four-bottle carton of their specialty growlers."

Lila and Rose stared at each other as if I had accused them of high treason. Then Rose raised her voice at Lila as if her sister were five years old.

"I told you someone would find out about those bottles of beer. Didn't I? Well, didn't I? Don't bother to answer because you know I did."

"There's nothing wrong with drinking beer, Rose. We've gone over this time and time again. And I, personally, enjoy a glass of beer with my homemade sausages and sauerkraut."

Before either of them could say another word, I jumped in. "So, um…that carton of growlers was for you, Lila, not for a gift?"

Rose immediately began to question her sister. "Is that what you told the people at the brewery, Lila? That it was for a gift?"

Lila nodded as Rose continued. "Well thank goodness for that. At least we won't have the entire town thinking we're a couple of lushes."

"It's only a glass of beer with dinner, Rose," Lila replied, "and contrary to what *you* may think, it will not make me fall over drunk!"

"One glass no. But you bought a whole carton of them. A whole gosh-darned carton of them!"

"And what did you think I was going to do? Drink all those bottles at once?"

"How am I supposed to know what gets into the head of a drunkard?"

"Oh, so now I'm a drunkard, am I? Well I've got news for you—"

"Ladies! Enough!" I shouted. It was like a tennis match gone bad. "This isn't helping. I really need you, Lila, to concentrate. Okay?"

Like a petulant child, she took a step back from the couch but not before glaring at her sister. I moved closer to them and gently put my hand on Lila's wrist. "This is really, really important. Do you remember the other customer who was in the brewery the same time you were? That other customer also purchased a carton of the specialty growlers and paid cash."

Lila pursed her lips and took a deep breath. "Of course I do. I have a photographic memory."

Then Rose cut in. "Too bad the same cannot be said about your hearing."

"There is nothing wrong with my hearing, Rose. You're the one who can't tell the difference between a baby's cries and a cat in heat. And last night you thought you heard a scritching noise!"

"I absolutely did. Like static or mice scritching and scratching about in the attic."

"We do *not* have mice, Rose. The exterminator checked the house last month. You're imaging things. And anyone can tell the difference between a baby and a cat!"

I froze. *Please, dear God, do not let them have that conversation again.*

"Forget about the cat and the baby," I pleaded. "Please, Lila. Tell me who that other customer was. It's very important."

Lila moved to the front of the couch, took a seat and leaned toward me. "It was a man in his late forties or maybe fifties. So hard to tell these days."

"I thought you said you had a photographic memory, Lila," Rose chimed in. "Well, was he forty or fifty?"

"I don't work at a carnival sideshow, guessing people's ages. For crying out loud, the man was about six feet tall, medium weight, brown hair. Thin mustache. He was wearing light beige slacks, a blue button-down shirt, and no tie. How's that for my memory?"

Rose didn't say a word and I used the opportunity to question Lila further.

"Did the man say anything about where he was from, where he worked, did he say anything at all?"

Lila shook her head. "No. In fact, he didn't even taste the beer. He was more interested in the room where they kept the tanks. Honestly, who wouldn't sample the beer? They give free samples, you know. He didn't even do that. Why I—"

Rose was beside herself. "You what? Say it, Lila. Say it! You went over there to drink yourself silly on that beer. Didn't you?"

Lila gave her sister a stare that could scare small children. "I most certainly did not. I wanted to purchase some beer to enjoy with my meals. And to the best of my knowledge, unless you are aware of some laws prohibiting it, keep quiet Rose! Now then, regarding Miss Rayner's question, no, the man didn't say anything. Came in. Wanted the specialty beer in those growlers, paid cash and left. I had already made my purchase and was having a nice conversation with Tom about having someone take the carton to my house. I certainly couldn't carry anything that heavy. Or fragile, for that matter."

"Lila," I said. "Did you happen to notice what that man was driving?"

"You'd have to be blind not to. No one here owns one of those expensive fancy-dancy cars. You know, the ones with those cute little mountain lions on the hood."

"A jaguar? He was driving a jaguar?"

"If that's what you call them, then yes. It was black and read '338 WPX.' Now how's that for my photographic memory, Rose?"

I didn't give Rose a chance to respond. "Lila, I could hug you. I could hug both of you!"

I grabbed my purse, wrote the number down and thanked both of them profusely.

"This was a great help. More than you can imagine. I've got to head over to the brewery to finish up. Thank you so much!"

Both of the sisters stood up to walk me to their door. As I reached for the knob, Lila whispered, "Was that the murderer? Was I standing next to a murderer? Oh dear God."

"I'm sure he wasn't," I said. "We're just hoping he may have some information for us."

Lila let out a slow breath. "That's a relief. I would hate to think I stood within inches of a killer."

"It would serve you right," Rose said, "for sneaking off to drink beer."

I closed the door quickly and scurried across the street. I never expected my sleuthing to open the Barton sisters' "can of worms" regarding the consumption of alcohol. Then again, they probably argued about everything.

Ducking into my car, which I had conveniently parked on the street, I phoned Max's detective contact, Zach Melbourne, and asked if he would do one more "tiny little favor" for us.

"These tiny favors are adding up, you know. Tell Max I'll add it to the tab."

Then he laughed and I knew without question Zach would track down the owner of that black jaguar. Thank you, Lila Barton, for your photographic memory!

"Nah. I'll take a break myself when you get back. Thanks anyway."

I hoped with Angie out of the office for the next half hour or so I'd be able to get some work done. Her voice mail would catch the phone calls and with any luck, lose the ones from my family members. I did, however, make sure my door was open so I could see anyone who came through the door.

Then as I sat back down to begin a computer search, the phone rang and like a moron, I instinctively picked it up.

"Miss Rayner! Marcie! It's me! Trisha!"

"Trisha. I didn't expect you to call until later this afternoon. It's lunch hour. Shouldn't you be waiting on customers?"

"I told Trudy I needed to step outside for a minute. I'm out back by the garbage bins. Your text sounded really important. Did they arrest Skip Gunderson? Is that why you called?"

"No. Sorry to disappoint you but I needed to ask you something."

I paused long enough to let Trisha process the fact that Skip Gunderson was still a free man. "Trisha, listen. Do you remember Tyler from the brewery bringing over a carton of growlers? You know, those glass containers they make for beer? These were specialty ones filled with the aged brown ale. It would have been before Billy's murder."

"Yeah. Sure I remember. Cute roundish bottles. Four of them with a cool Oktoberfest design. We all tasted the stuff and thought it was pretty neat. It was a slow afternoon and George opened two of the bottles right before Trudy, Frankie and I left. Kaye was there, too.

We all went into the kitchen and tasted it. Why? Was something wrong with it?"

"No. Nothing like that. You said George opened two bottles. The carton holds four bottles. What happened to the empty bottles and to the rest of the box?"

"The empties went into the re-cycling and got picked up that week and Frankie put the carton with the un-used ones in the walk-in behind the cases of bread."

"Trisha, this is really, really important. Can you check to see if the carton is still in there?"

"I don't need to check. It's not. We had to make more room for the bakery delivery a few days ago and the carton wasn't there. I hate going in that walk-in. I still keep thinking someone is going to shoot me in the back of my head or worse yet, lock me in there. Anyway, Trudy and I had to go in. I remember asking her if she thought that maybe the carton with the other two bottles got moved somewhere else in the walk-in so we looked. It was gone. I figured George or Kaye took those bottles home. Not really my business. Trudy's either. Um… what does that have to do with Billy's murder?"

"I'm not sure yet but it may hold a clue. Please do NOT say a word to anyone. Okay?"

"Okay. But I'm telling you, it was Skip Gunderson. It had to be. Listen, I've got to run. George will be screaming for me any minute."

"Thanks a million. Remember, not a word."

Like that, the call ended and my search narrowed.

THIRTY-FIVE

COOKS AND FOOD prep workers use food handling gloves. No surprise there. George or Kaye could have donned those gloves to remove the bottles and still keep Billy's fingerprints on them. Another no-brainer. Billy was the one who packaged the cartons. Tyler had told me that Billy was totally in charge of those specialty growlers and didn't want to risk anyone breaking them. And not only did he tell me, he also shared that information with the diner employees. They had to know the only fingerprints on those bottles would be Billy's.

I took a slow breath and bit my lower lip. If I couldn't prove that someone other than Billy started that fire, then Billy's estate would be responsible and that could have serious repercussions for the Crooked Eye. According to Max, the sheriff's department hadn't filed an official report of its findings yet. I still had time. That meant confronting Kaye and George and I wasn't so sure I could pull that off. Sure, I was okay with the basic run-of-the-mill questioning but as far as pointed accusations go, I was *way* out of my league and thought it better to wait for Max.

Then, as much as I hated to admit it, there was one more piece of evidence I needed to see—Billy's formula book that they kept on a hook near the brite tank. On my first visit to the brewery in Biscay, Hogan had given the notebook a cursory look and told me everything was fine. And me, being too new at the job, didn't bother to check it out myself. That notebook of Billy's could hold the very clues I needed.

How could I be so naïve and stupid not to look at it myself?

I spent the next five minutes with my palms clasped together and my head resting between them. If Max were here, he would've told me to cut myself some slack. It didn't matter. It would mean another trek to Biscay and I didn't want to wait until the next day. In fact, I didn't even want to wait until Angie got back from lunch but twenty more minutes wasn't going to make a big difference.

I picked up the phone and dialed the Crooked Eye Brewery. This time I was going to be polite enough to let Hogan know I needed to make another visit. If he was surprised to hear my voice again, he didn't sound like it.

"Okay. Sure. So…uh…you're heading over now?"

"In about ten or fifteen minutes. Will you still be there?"

"Tom and I will be here until closing today. Tyler's got the afternoon off but I can give him a call if you need to speak with him, too."

"No, no need to call him. I'll see you in a bit. Thanks, Hogan."

I hung up before he had a chance to add anything. I didn't want to risk mentioning the notebook. For the next fifteen minutes I focused on the shutter bug ex-boyfriend case. It appeared to be a pretty routine computer search and I figured I'd be able to locate the jerk in a few days. I was so engrossed on my computer screen that I didn't even hear Angie walk in.

"I'm back, Marcie. Any calls I missed?"

Shoving the chair out from my desk, I walked to the front office. "No calls. No drop-ins but something's come up and I need to drive back to Biscay. Now. Can you handle the place?"

"Sure. What should I tell Mr. Blake if he makes it in this afternoon?"

"Tell him I needed to check on something at the Crooked Eye and I couldn't do it over the phone. I'll call him later anyway."

"You should get paid by the mile. You'd make more money."

I laughed as I grabbed my bag and headed out the door. "Lock-up if I'm not back by five."

Like a plane on automatic pilot, I drove to Biscay hardly noticing anything. The ride was becoming so routine I actually considered getting one of those language learning tapes so I could teach myself French in case the opportunity to visit Paris ever came along. I decided against it. Not Paris. The tape. I had enough on my mind without adding new unpronounceable vocabulary to the mix.

Tom and Hogan were both at the counter when I walked in.

"Whoa! That was record time," Hogan said as Tom gave a wave in my direction. He had two customers in front of him, both young men in their late twenties or early thirties and it looked as if they were midway through a flight of beers.

"Good timing," Hogan went on. "You just missed the bridal shower."

"The what?"

"Yeah, you heard right. The bridal shower. Seems

this is the new way to celebrate bridal showers—go on beer and wine tastings in the area."

"Ugh. I feel bad for the designated driver."

"Don't. It's a paid limo company. Uh, you weren't too specific on the phone. What brings you back here so soon? Not that I'm complaining…"

"I forgot something. I'm still kind of new at this."

"That's okay, I think you're past on-the-job training."

"Some days I'm not so sure. Anyway, I should have looked at Billy's formula logbook when I first came here but I didn't. Do you mind showing it to me again?"

"I can do that, Hogan," Tom said. Then, as if realizing he still had customers in front of him, he added, "If you don't mind waiting until these gentlemen finish their tasting."

"Sure. I don't mind—"

Hogan cut me off with a quick response to Tom and a nod at the two men. "You go ahead and show Marcie the notebook. I'll finish up for you if these guys don't mind."

The men shook their heads and kept drinking as Tom ushered me toward the walk-in. His voice was as monotone and flat as the last time we spoke. "Billy's notebook… I mean, our formula logbook is on the hook by the brite tank. Hold on, I'll get it for you."

He walked over and removed the notebook. It was one of those marbled school notebooks complete with frayed edges and watermarks making it appear as if it came out of the 1950s. Tom held it as if it would shatter should it hit the floor. For a brief moment it made me think of my father's old pinochle deck. It was the only thing of his I really wanted to keep when he passed away. It's sitting on my bookshelf next to *The Castle in the Attic*, the first book we ever read together.

"I haven't been able to touch this since Billy's murder," Tom said. "Good thing the recipes were already cooking in the tanks. Here, take a look."

He handed me the notebook as if it were the Holy Grail itself, and actually, for the brewery, it was.

I reached for it carefully and spoke softly. "Is there any place I can sit down and take a good look?"

"I'm sorry. I'm not even thinking. Let me grab you a chair and you can look at it back here in the alcove without going into the walk-in."

"I'll be careful with it, Tom. I promise. You can get back to the customers if you want. It looks as if a few more just walked in."

"Okay. Fine. Let me know if I can explain anything."

Tom appeared to be relieved he didn't have to walk me through the formulas. I watched as he took his place behind the counter. Hogan was focused on the customers and hadn't turned around to see if I had the notebook.

With a flick of the wrist I flipped the cover open and one by one checked all the pages to make sure nothing had been ripped out. I even studied the binding. The notebook was completely intact. If someone did enter the brewery that night to steal the formulas, wouldn't they have taken the entire book or at least pulled out a page or two?

Whoever committed the murder didn't want to make it appear as if it was a robbery. A quick jolt on my leg and I realized my phone was vibrating. *My mother!* I waited it out until it went to voice mail. Then, like a sign from the gods, it hit me. Whoever did this didn't need to steal anything. All they had to do was take a picture of the formulas with their smartphone. Duh. *It's about time I wake up. This isn't the Middle Ages. Everyone's got a smartphone. Well, most everyone...*

Slowly, I went through each of the pages noting the names of the beers and the ratio of ingredients. There were side notes as well. Mostly numbers and doodles. Nothing unusual with the exception of a plus sign followed by a series of letters that appeared off to the side on the page with the Wild Turkey Bourbon Beer. When no one was looking I snapped a photo and quickly put the phone back in my pocket. Then I stood up and walked the notebook back to Tom. A few of the customers had left but others had taken their place at the counter.

"I don't want to interrupt either of you," I said as I handed the notebook to him, "but I do have one question about it."

Tom stepped away from the counter and we headed back to the walk-in. I turned to the page with the scribbly notes and asked him if he knew what they meant. He scratched his head and repeated my question. "Letters? Like A, B, C?"

"Yeah. In lowercase."

He shook his head. "Maybe Hogan knows. Hey, Hogan, can you check this out?"

Hogan turned his head in our direction as Tom made his way back to the counter.

I pointed to the page with the markings and waited for a response. Instead, I got a shoulder shrug and a shake of the head. "No clue. Honestly. Looks like one of those word games or an anagram. Then again, it could be nothing at all."

"Was Billy cryptic enough to be using anagrams?" I asked.

Hogan let out a laugh. "Not at all. Everything he did was straightforward. Chances are he started writing a note to himself and decided he didn't need it after all. So…what did you find out about those specialty growlers? Are you thinking someone from the diner is involved? Holy crap. Pardon me, but I'd hate to think it was someone I knew."

"Yeah, well…me, too. Listen, thanks, I—"

The sound of screeching tires on asphalt tore through the place before I could finish my sentence. Hogan and Tom seemed nonplussed but I couldn't imagine what had happened on the street.

"What the heck was that?" I said rushing to the front window.

"*That* would be Frankie," Hogan said. "Someone must have ticked him off and he takes it out on the road when his shift is over. That whole family is wacko if you ask me. Must be something in their well water. And they're not the only ones."

I gave Hogan a perplexed look and waited for him to continue. "Some of the folks around here are overly emotional. That's a nice way of saying moody and unpredictable. The one I feel sorry for is Tyler."

"Tyler? What do you mean?"

"You've met his girlfriend Kimmie, haven't you? If she doesn't have a meltdown a week then something must be wrong with the calendar. I once heard her flip out because someone on *Dancing with the Stars* got axed."

"Yeesh. What about Frankie? He didn't appear to be volatile at all when I spoke with him at the diner."

"He's not. Only when something really pisses him off. Um, er…sorry Marcie. I should have said *annoyed him*. Guess you're getting to see my true colors. Lousy language and all."

"I've heard worse." *And said worse. Really worse.*

"Anyway," Hogan went on, "Frankie's never walked off on the job as far as I know but he's not too keen on it. The few times we've spoken he mentioned wanting to work in a more upscale place. He went to culinary school for a year but had to drop out to take care of his mother. Anyway, I'm sure it's nothing. Someone just ruffled his feathers, that's all."

"Kaye or George, you think?"

Hogan shrugged. "Who knows. But it wasn't Trisha or Trudy because they're off work by now. Hey, don't worry about it. He'll get over it. It's the other drivers on the road who should be on guard."

I stared out the front window looking at the diner. Now would be a perfect time to press Kaye and George about the two missing growlers from their walk-in refrigerator. I hated to have Max drag himself back here for something I should be able to do.

Interrogation is simply pointed questioning. I have to stop being a wimp.

I turned my head to face Hogan and Tom. "Listen. I really appreciate your help. Thanks for showing me that notebook. I haven't eaten lunch yet today so I'll probably find out firsthand what the blow-up was with Frankie. I'm headed over there to get something to eat."

I didn't mean that as an invitation for Hogan to take me up on that hamburger but that's exactly what he did. "Hey, I owe you a burger, don't I?" Then, turning to Tom, he continued. "Can you hold down the fort for a half hour?"

Tom was about to reply when the door flew open and five or six somewhat elderly women charged in. They looked like the ladies from my mother's condo association in King's Point. Bright red lipstick and enough jewelry to blind someone. A few of them were giggling as they stepped inside.

"We were on our way to Glencoe for a book club meeting when Verna over here got the idea that we should be tasting one-of-a-kind beers. We can do that here, can't we?"

"Sure," Hogan said as he gave me one of those looks that I took to mean, *"Hey, I'm trapped here. Hope you understand."*

I was actually relieved. I mean, as much as I wanted to get to know this guy over a burger and fries, I was here on business, not my social life. And with Hogan at the diner, I'd be unable to ask about the growlers.

"Let's you and I do those burgers another time, okay?" I said as Hogan stood between the women and the door. "I can see that you're busy."

"You sure?"

"Absolutely."

I smiled at the women and told them that they were in for a treat. "Enjoy your beer flights, ladies. They're wonderful. Once the rest of your book club finds out, they'll all want to visit the Crooked Eye."

Hogan gave me a wink and I headed across the street to the diner.

THIRTY-SIX

THERE WERE A handful of customers seated throughout the place as I took a spot at the counter. I figured it was more private for a chat with either Kaye or George since no one was seated there. George had his back to me, preparing what looked like a club sandwich and Kaye greeted me as she returned from taking someone's order at one of the tables.

"Miss Rayner. Hello. We weren't expecting you. You didn't drive all this way from New Ulm just for our fine food."

Then George turned around, said hi, and went back to his sandwich making. I put my elbows on the counter and leaned forward. "I hadn't finished speaking with the owners of the brewery so I made another trip. Since I didn't want to drive back on an empty stomach and I enjoyed your food the last time I was in, I thought I'd grab a late, late lunch here."

"Great," Kaye said pointing to the chalkboard on the side wall. "Our specials are listed but we're out of the meatloaf."

"No problem. I'll try a bowl of your chili and a Coke."

As Kaye wrote the order on a small slip of paper, I propped my head on one of my arms.

"You know what would be terrific with that chili? A beer. An ice cold beer. Too bad the diner can't serve them. By the way, I understand that you all were able to taste their latest feature, that Turkey Bourbon beer. What did you think?"

I wanted to ease Kaye into responding so she'd answer without realizing what I was really up to so when George answered my question, I was completely taken off guard.

"Too heavy for my taste but I'll say one thing about it—it's not a flavor you taste every day."

"I kind of liked it, George," Kaye said. "In fact, I wouldn't mind trying it again."

"Knock yourself out, but on your own time. Didn't we put those extra bottles in the walk-in fridge? I almost forgot all about them."

Kaye grabbed a bowl and began to ladle out the chili from a big pot on the stove. "Someone did. But if you're not going to drink them, I'll take them home with me later when I get a chance. That okay with you?"

George handed her the plate with the club sandwich and started to put the sliced meats away. Then he picked up a newspaper and headed toward one of the tables where I imagined he was going to take a break.

"Yeah. Sure. Knock yourself out."

Without saying another word, Kaye handed me a glass filled with ice and a bottled Coke. Either she was lying and knew full and darn well the growlers weren't in there or she would be in for a surprise when she went to look. I watched her carefully to see what she would do next. Unfortunately, all she did was empty the dishwasher and tidy up behind the counter. I wasn't about to waste another trip to Biscay so I pressed the issue.

"You know, Kaye, if those growler containers aren't back there, then they might be the ones used in that arson over in Willmar."

"WHAT?" Kaye spun around as if her clothing had caught fire. "What are you talking about?"

"The growlers that were used to make the Molotov cocktails that started the Willmar fire came from the Crooked Eye and were specialty growlers for an event. All of them were accounted for except the ones that Tyler brought over here."

Kaye's face turned ashen. "You're not accusing one of us, are you?"

"I'm not saying anything, but you may want to scope out your fridge and see if they're still there."

Kaye immediately headed for the walk-in while I dipped my bread into the chili. In less than five minutes she was back. Only instead of heading my way, she went straight to her brother. I couldn't hear what they were saying but seconds later she was standing behind the counter in front of me.

"George seems to remember having some cartons tossed out to make room for a bread delivery. Happens all the time. The growlers were probably in one of those cartons. So… I'm out a good drink with dinner and that's that. I can assure you, those growlers weren't the ones from the fire."

I spoke slowly, articulating every word. I saw that once on a TV show and it made the detective look really intimidating.

"How can you be sure?"

"We have no reason to do something like that. Not like that little hussy from the chocolate shop. She might have gotten Billy to give her some growlers and then used them to set the place on fire for insurance. That kind of scam goes on all the time. I thought you'd be investigating her."

"We're investigating everyone and anyone connected with this case. So if my questions seem accusatory, it's—"

"Yeah, yeah, I know. It's part of the job."

"Um…speaking of jobs, is Frankie having any trouble with his? Not that it's my business but I think the entire street heard him screech out of here before I arrived."

"Arrgh. Frankie runs hot and cold if you know what I mean. Sometimes it doesn't take much to set him off. Today it was Skip Gunderson, who left before Frankie's shift was over. I don't know what the two of them were yammering about, but whatever it was, it hit a nerve with Frankie. Like I told you before, Skip's a regular Neanderthal and I guess Frankie wasn't in the mood to put up with that moron."

"I can understand that."

An elderly lady a few feet away walked over to us and whispered. "I think they were fighting over a broken promise or something like that. I wasn't snooping. Nothing like that. I was sitting at my booth doing my crossword puzzle and I overheard them. They were very annoying if you ask me. Well, anyway, that dreadful man, Skip something-or-other, told the cook in no uncertain terms, to give him his *payola*. That was the word he used—*payola*. Isn't that a word gangsters use?"

I started to open my mouth but thought better of it and let her keep talking. Kaye apparently felt the same way. The lady went on as if she was testifying for a grand jury.

"So…to make a long story short, the rude man said that it was time for a pay-up or pay-off."

"Humpf," Kaye muttered. "Frankie probably borrowed money from Skip and didn't pay it off. I intend to have a long conversation with that lousy brother-in-law of mine. This place isn't a community bank and we don't need our cook to be threatened. I don't care how much he owes to whom!"

"Oh dear," the elderly lady said. "I didn't mean to make trouble for anyone."

"You're not," I blurted out. "I mean, it wasn't your fault about their business."

Kaye gave the woman a pat on the arm and nodded. "Certainly not. And please accept my apologies for their rudeness. Hope we see you again soon."

"Oh, you will. I stop by on my way back from the hairdresser's in Glencoe once a month."

The lady headed to the door as I finished my meal. I thanked Kaye for the chili, told her it was good, which it was, paid her, left a decent tip, and headed toward my car. I was back at the office ninety minutes later in time to watch Angie lock-up the place.

"Did Max ever make it in?" I asked.

"No. He called. He also said he left you a message on your cell."

"Oh rats! Stupid cell service in Biscay. Did he say what he wanted?"

"Sorry, Marcie. But he'll be in first thing in the morning. He did say that. Oh, before I forget, Addison Markham called. She said to tell you there was some sort of snafu. That's the word she used—snafu. Anyway, the Bourbon beer campaign will take longer than expected so she won't be in Minnesota next month. Maybe by the holidays. I had just started to write it down when Max called. Sorry."

"No problem. Have a good evening. I'll lock the door behind you."

Back at my desk, I played "phone tag" with Max before clicking on the icon for photos and scanning to find the ones I had taken of Billy's notebook. In the back of my mind, I wondered what was up with Addison and Longfellow Brewery. Grabbing a pen, I left myself a note to give her a call at some point. Then, I focused on Billy's log page with his formulas and letters.

I was hoping to get an epiphany and figure it out. Unfortunately, the more I pushed, the more my brain shut down. None of it made sense. Ratios, ingredients and lowercase letters going nowhere. I was about to put the phone away when I remembered my mother's call. The one I let go to voice mail.

"Are you ignoring me, Marcie? I expected to hear from you. Call me."

My stomach tightened. I was in no mood to speak with her. Especially since she'd been nagging my brother to the point where he called me about my social life. And then, that business with Lance Presley over the phone. None of that would have happened in the first place if my family had kept their butting little heads to themselves. Irritated, I tried a new tactic. I placed the call and pretended I was losing the connection. Holding my breath, I waited for her response.

"This is awful. Like talking in a tunnel. I'll call you tonight on your home phone. You'll be home won't you?"

"Yes, Mot er I'll e home."

I hoped it was convincing. Of course all I really did was put off the inevitable. At that moment the only thing I wanted to do was bite into a giant chocolate bar and down it with a Coke. Thank goodness I take after my father and inherited the skinny genes in the family, unlike Jonathan, who wound up with my mother's Slavic ones. I fumbled around my desk drawers for the secret stash of candy bars I kept for emergencies. Tearing off a label that read "Dark Chocolate," my eyes immediately went to the letters *lat*. That was the instant I grabbed my smartphone and went back to the photo. Those three letters made up the latter part of Billy's notation—*ls c lat*. I should have figured it out on the spot but I was no Nancy Drew. It took my brain a good fifteen minutes to realize *ls c lat* wasn't part of the formula—it was the distributor.

THIRTY-SEVEN

THE NEXT MORNING, I couldn't seem to find Luanne Saunders' phone number fast enough. It was in the case folder that Max and I shared. Taking a deep breath, I placed the call from the phone on my desk. Cell phones may be convenient but landlines are a hundred times clearer.

"Luanne, is that you? This is Marcie Rayner from Blake Investigations. Is this a good time to talk?"

"As good as any, I suppose. I was about to start making something for breakfast but it can wait."

"Actually, what I meant was, are you alone? I need to speak with you privately."

I wasn't sure what her reaction was going to be. First I cornered her in the ladies' room back in Willmar. Now this.

"Gary will be home any minute. He had a very early meeting with the company that runs the mall, hoping to get us a new spot. What's this about?"

"Luanne, I have reason to believe your relationship with Billy Hazlitt was more than that of a customer who came in to buy chocolate."

"If you're insinuating that we were having an affair or something, I'm cutting you off right now. I already told you that all I did was some harmless flirtation."

"No, Luanne. I'm not accusing you of having an affair. But there was something going on, wasn't there? Something you were hiding from your husband."

The silence at the other end of the line answered my question before she did.

"I'll figure it out, Luanne, so please, save us both the time and be honest. It has something to do with his brewery, doesn't it?"

"It's not, I mean…it wasn't such a big deal. Look, like I told you before, Billy had a real sweet tooth. He thought if he could add dark Belgian chocolate syrup to his malt mix for that new Turkey Bourbon beer, it would give it a one-of-a-kind flavor. So I developed a unique syrup for him and that's what he used. It can't be duplicated for two reasons—no one else knows it and no one else has my special chocolate concoction even if they found the recipe. Does that answer your question?"

"Maybe. If I understand you correctly, that specialty beer has your chocolate mixture in it."

"Uh-huh. That's right."

"Luanne, did anyone else know you developed a special chocolate for Billy?"

"No. No one knew. Especially my husband. And the reason I didn't tell him was because he would have turned this whole thing into some cumbersome business deal when all I wanted to do was help out a friend of mine. Gary and I didn't need to be involved with Billy's brewery. We had enough on our plates running Hearts & Flowers. Billy would have been more than generous regarding my contribution to his formula. I didn't need a written contract. But there's something else, Marcie. Something I didn't want my husband to find out."

I all but stopped breathing in order to listen.

"The last time Billy was in the store, he could see

I had been crying. Sure, I tried to cover it up with my usual flirting but it didn't work. He knew something was wrong so I told him. And I made him swear he wouldn't tell my husband. I figured Gary had enough to worry about running two businesses."

"I'm listening. Please go on."

"You know how Gary told you that the owner of the building asked us to shorten our lease?"

"Yeah, I remember."

"Well, that's not all. That same day when Billy came in, another man approached me about the building. Only he wasn't making any offers. He pulled me aside from some customers and said that it would be in our best interest if my husband and I accepted the offer from the landlord, Harold Evans."

"That's it? That's all he said? Did he do anything else?"

"No. That's it. Look, it wasn't *what* he said. Gary and I knew that Harold Evans wanted us out. It was the *way* he said it. Not quite a threat. More like menacing. Before I could say anything, the man hightailed it and was out the door. I didn't have time to see where he went or what kind of a car he got into. I had customers waiting to buy candies."

"Luanne, why didn't you call the police?"

"What was I going to tell them? That some guy thought we should end our lease early? I didn't want the police to think I was wasting their time. Then, after the fire, I felt really, really idiotic for not saying anything, but by then it was too late. I would have been the one to blame about not reporting it, so I kept my mouth shut. Gee, I hope you can understand. Really."

"I do, Luanne. Honestly, I do. Listen, can you tell me what that guy looked like? Young? Old? Anything."

"Thirty or fortyish maybe. I'm not great with ages. Anyway, he looked like he worked out. You know, the kind of guy who hangs around a gym all the time. Not bad looking. Button down shirt and jeans. Taller than me and I'm 5'5" without heels. He had light brown hair and absolutely nothing that stood out. I mean, no tattoos, nothing."

"Okay then, what about the way he talked? You said it was menacing. What did you mean?"

"I can't explain it. It was just a feeling I got. Like talking to a real thug, only a *polished* thug. Boy, that doesn't help at all, does it?"

"It might, Luanne. It might. If you can think of anything else, please call me. You've got the number to this office, right?"

"Yeah, Gary wrote it down from the card you and your partner gave us."

"Good. Call me, even if it's for the slightest little thing, okay?"

"Sure. And please don't be mad at me for not telling you everything."

"No worries. Thanks Luanne."

I hung up the phone and leaned back in my chair, thankful I kept chocolate bars in my desk. If it wasn't for that sneaky habit, I never would have figured out such an important clue. Then I thought about Luanne's words. Thirty or forty. Normal looking. Decent physique…

There were three men who sort of fit that description— Skip Gunderson and Tyler's father, the man I presumed to be Stanley Evans. I had only seen Tyler's father once and he fit the description—late forties or early fifties and normal looking. I wondered if I could add the word *murderer* to complete the profile. Skip Gunderson fit it as well, only I'd add the word *miserable* to the mix. And as for the third guy, my throat tightened. I refused to even think about him.

THIRTY-EIGHT

THE LAST THING I felt like doing was placing a call to Alice Davenport but that's exactly what I did. The woman jumped on the phone as if she had been expecting it to ring.

"Miss Rayner. Is the case solved? That would be excellent news."

"Er...no. Not yet. I was calling because I thought you might be able to give me some information about another one of Billy Hazlitt's former classmates—Stanley Evans."

"Stanley."

She spoke the name once and then enumerated. "Stanley Evans. Quite a tiresome boy. I do believe he was born old."

"Huh? What do you mean?"

"It was as if that child carried the weight of the world on him. I taught his older brother, too. Harold. Not the friendliest child but Harold had a certain stick-to-it-ness I knew would pay off. Stanley seemed to follow in his brother's footsteps. Same clubs in high school. I kept track, you know. Let's see—Future Business Leaders of America and Chess Club. I happen to have an eidetic as well as semantic memory, you know. Their mother got divorced when Stanley was in high school. Harold had already graduated and was attending Business College by then. I heard the mother remarried a few years later

and had another child. Name started with an *H*. That
I do remember quite well because I recalled thinking
to myself that with twenty-six letters in the alphabet,
the woman could have found a name that started with
a different letter other than the one she had already
used on Harold."

"I see, um, well…"

"You know, Miss Rayner, that for some inane reason,
certain people seem to name *all* of their children with
the same first letter. Especially movie stars. And pop
singers. Tell me, why the interest in the Evans brothers?
Are they—"

"Um, oh. No. I mean, I don't know yet. This has been
very helpful, Miss Davenport. Very helpful. Thank you
so much. I'll keep in touch."

"Yes. You do that. In your next report."

*My next report… I've been writing so many reports
for that woman, I swear I'm doing them in my sleep.
Chronological, orderly, sequential, thematic…whatever.*

I don't remember saying good-bye to Alice but I must
have. Those kinds of things are automatic. As soon as
she mentioned another child whose name started with
an H, I froze. Hogan? He'd be the right age for their
sibling. And the last name, Austin, could be the new
husband's name. Was Hogan hiding this from me all
along? The fact he was Tyler's uncle?

What if the older brothers had a better deal for him?
Open a new brewery in a fantastic hotspot. He'd have
a motive all right. And what if Billy found out? It was
almost too much for me to think about with regard to
Hogan. Above all else, I had to be objective and that
meant weighing the information gleaned against intu-

ition and instinct. No an easy choice. Especially since I liked the guy.

I could almost hear Max admonishing me. *"That's why you don't get involved with clients or victims. You never know."*

Well, I knew one thing. I would have to speak with Hogan and ask him about his relationship to Harold and Stanley Evans. Explain that their real estate company most likely had some sort of a deal with Longfellow Brewery to build a satellite spot in Willmar. After all, those realtors owned the buildings. Addison Markham wasted no time telling me that Longfellow Brewery was about to embark on a satellite brewery business. Not a big leap for those guys to threaten Luanne Saunders.

Like a toboggan on a long slick hill, I was racing ahead without fully processing all of the details. Unfortunately, I sidestepped the one pivotal piece of information that would have prevented me from crashing headfirst into a wall. I must have overlooked it while I concentrated on the smaller cases that were piling up on my desk. The day vanished.

It was six thirty. Angie was long gone. If I hurried, I could be back in Biscay before eight. I didn't want to wait until the next day when Max got in. I was so close to solving this case that I was afraid I'd lose my momentum and most of all, my guts. I turned off the lights, locked the door and headed for my car. Hogan had mentioned having to stay late that night to pump the wort and hit it with oxygen. Something I figured had to do with fermenting and yeast.

I had to find out the truth about Hogan's relationship with Harold and Stanley and it couldn't wait. Oddly enough, I wasn't the only one who needed to ask Hogan a direct question. Apparently the Barton sisters did and their timing collided with mine.

I arrived at the brewery shortly before eight and walked quickly to the back entrance only to find Rosa and Lila at the door. They were wearing matching aprons with embroidered hens on the front and Rose was holding a large slotted spoon. Lila had a wooden spatula in her grip as if it was a javelin. Rose reached to turn the knob.

"What are you doing here?" I asked.

"We were invited to help brew the beer," Lila said. "I need to ask Hogan how that's done."

For the life of me, I couldn't imagine why on earth Hogan would ask those two for assistance. They had to have gotten it wrong. Before I could say a word, Rose opened the door and walked in. Either Hogan wasn't afraid of being caught off guard like his partner was, or he had simply forgotten to lock the door behind him.

"WHAT THE…" Hogan spun around from the brite tank where he was checking the carbonation and looked as if he had seen the ghost of Christmas past. "Rose? Lila? What are you doing here?" Then he stared at me. "What the heck?"

"Why, we've come to help you make the beer, dear," Lila said. "We got your phone message."

Hogan was wide-eyed and more than a little taken back. "Phone message? I never left a phone message."

Rose gave her sister a nudge. "I asked you three times, Lila, if that's what the message said. You need hearing aids."

"I most certainly do not. The message was loud and clear. And I recognized Hogan's voice. He said 'Brew beer with me at eight.' Anyway, it doesn't matter. We might as well get started. Rose, you're good at stirring, why don't you see if you can lean into that big pot over there and give it a good stir."

"WHAT??? NO!!!" Hogan yelled. "No stirring. No helping. Stay right where you are. PLEASE!"

Lila and Rose looked as if they might cry. They turned their heads toward me and I could see Lila's lip quivering.

"I don't think there's any harm done," I said. "Only a misunderstanding."

"It's a misunderstanding all right," Rose replied. "Lila's been misunderstanding things for years."

"Can't we at least stay and watch?" Lila asked.

Hogan groaned, stepped away from the tanks and walked toward the counter. His hand reached for a drawer. "I suppose, but if you get in the way, I'll have to scoot you out of here, understand?"

"Shoot?" Lila exclaimed. "You're going to shoot us?"

Hogan looked as if he had reached his breaking point. His jaw was clenched and I could see beads of sweat on his brow. "I'M NOT ABOUT TO SHOOT ANYONE. I'M REACHING FOR A ROLAIDS. SEE FOR YOURSELF! I HAVE INDIGESTION, NOT A GUN!"

"A gun!" Rose screamed.

Hogan immediately held up the jar of Rolaids and waved it in the air. "Rolaids, see for yourself."

Then, it was as if he finally noticed me. "Don't tell me you got a phone message, too?" he said.

I shook my head. "No, I had to ask you something and it couldn't wait."

Hogan turned to the Barton sisters and pointed to the chairs in the front of the brewery. "I need to have a word with Marcie. Why don't you help yourselves to the pretzels on the counter. We'll only be a minute."

Next, he ushered me to the front door and turned on the patio's outside light. "Grab a seat and tell me what couldn't wait. It must be urgent or you wouldn't have driven here in the evening."

"I need to know the truth," I said. "I have reason to believe you're Tyler's uncle. Given the family connection and their future brewery plans, that would've given you a motive to—"

"Don't say it, Marcie."

"But you *are* Tyler's uncle, aren't you?"

"Tyler's uncle? What gave you *that* idea? I'm not Tyler's uncle. As far as I know, and believe me, I'm no expert on the kid's lineage, but as far as I know, he only has one uncle—Harold. The other half of Evans real estate. Look, what's going on? I think I have a right to know considering you walked into the brewery unannounced. Of course, so did the Barton sisters but their quirkiness is something I've learned to expect. Boy, if this isn't turning out to be a three banner evening!"

Just then Lila Barton stepped onto the porch and asked Hogan if he had any dip to go with the pretzels.

"Just flavored mustard. It's in the small refrigerator under the counter. Help yourself."

Lila went back inside after informing me that she and Rose "didn't have all night to lollygag around."

I told her I'd only be a minute and that I would walk her and Rose back across the street. Meanwhile, Hogan leaned his elbows on the table, made two fists and propped his head on top of them. "You started to say something about motive. Am I right? Well, I'm not Tyler's uncle and while I may have had opportunity, I certainly didn't have a motive or the means to kill Billy Hazlitt. Hey, I don't own a gun like the other yahoos around here. Heck, I don't even own a water pistol."

I read the expression on his face loud and clear—hurt. I trusted my instincts and knew in that moment, the guy was no killer. When I worked for campus security, I always provided lucid, coherent explanations regarding any and all incidents. Sadly, I couldn't seem to tap into those skills at that moment. I muttered a series of words including, but not limited to: glass, palm, cut, break-in, satellite, hotspot, and formula. Then, as if that wasn't bad enough, I could feel tears welling up in my eyes and my voice got all choppy and hoarse.

"I… That is to say… I…um…"

"Whatever it is you're trying to say, I can see that this isn't the right moment. Look, I don't know about you but I haven't had anything much to eat today and I'm one step away from gnawing off my own arm, so how about if you walk the Barton sisters back home and we grab a pizza in Glencoe. They stay open late. It's on your way back to New Ulm and I'll follow you in my truck. The brite tank will be fine until I get back. Give me a few minutes to get everything set up and I'll pull out in front of you. I take it you're parked across the street?"

I nodded as he continued. "Good. Just follow me to the pizzeria. Beats the heck out of a hamburger any day. So, you're okay with this?"

"Yeah. I'm okay."

Regrettably, that wasn't the case with the Barton sisters. I didn't think they'd ever recuperate from the mix-up with the phone message or the fact that they had offered culinary services to Hogan and were turned down.

Lila grabbed me by the arm as we walked across the street and said, "We were thrown out of the place like common bums."

"You weren't exactly thrown out," I said as we reached their front door. "You were asked to sit at the counter and munch on some pretzels. Anyway, it was just a mix-up. Those things happen."

"Oh, we're not upset," Rose said. "But if I were you, I'd tactfully tell Mr. Austin that *he* needs to get his hearing checked. That poor man thought someone had a gun."

I mumbled something and headed straight to my car. Within minutes, Hogan's truck pulled up in front of me and I followed him to Glencoe. For the next twenty minutes or so I wondered how I'd be able to squirm my way out of this mess. If I ever did have a chance at a relationship with this guy, I undoubtedly blew it. I only hoped I didn't blow my chances at solving Billy's murder.

THIRTY-NINE

LIKE PAGLIAI'S PIZZA in New Ulm, the restaurant in Glencoe was also a small family owned place, small being an understatement. Hogan and I were seated at a table near the kitchen and it was such a tight fit that our knees were touching. All the more reason for me to feel uncomfortable. No matter how I moved, I managed to brush against his legs. He didn't say a word, nor did he try to back away. Either he was being nice or he was enjoying it. I didn't say anything either. We sat quietly for a few minutes, looking over our menus as if they were train schedules. Finally the waitress appeared to take our order and one sausage and green pepper pizza was on its way. Then Hogan broached the subject of tonight's fiasco. "Did you really think I could have been responsible for murdering my friend?"

"Hey, I jumped to a conclusion that obviously wasn't substantiated. I don't blame you if you're really ticked off. But hey, you have to laugh about Lila and Rose walking in with spatulas and slotted spoons."

Hogan burst out laughing and shook his head. "I don't know what was worse—those two poised to wreak havoc on the fermentation process or you pegging me for a killer."

I was forced to explain my last minute thinking which resulted in even more gales of laughter.

"I shouldn't be laughing, Marcie. Yet honestly, this

is the first time I've had a belly laugh since Billy was killed. And listening to those Barton sisters. On a good day it's a challenge."

He took a long breath, leaned over and grabbed me by the wrist. "Okay. So it turns out I'm not Tyler's uncle and I don't have a reason to put the Crooked Eye out of business. That doesn't mean you were totally off with your investigation or your reasoning. It wouldn't surprise me at all if a conglomerate like Longfellow Brewery wanted us out of the picture so they could set up their satellite breweries. Heck, we've got a Starbucks and a McDonalds on every corner, why not a microbrewery? Still, they could have done that without committing a murder. No, someone wanted something else."

"That's what I thought, too, but you and Tom said that nothing was taken from the brewery. Plus, both of us looked over Billy's notebook and everything seemed to be intact. No pages were torn out. Nothing was missing."

"Yeah, the sheriff's office thought the same thing but—"

"There's more, Hogan. There's more I need to tell you."

It was time he knew I had deciphered the letters in Tom's notebook. Deciphered and de-coded. They stood for a specialty chocolate that Luanne Saunders had prepared as part of the formula for the Turkey Bourbon Beer.

"What? What aren't you telling me?"

I reached in my bag to pull out my phone. "It's easier to show you. It's on my smartphone right— Oh my God! The phone is back at the brewery. I took it out when Lila, Rose and I came in and I was holding it. Just in case… Oh my God! I must have put it down somewhere in all of the fuss. OH NO!"

"Hey, calm down. It's not the end of the world. When we're done eating I'll drive you back to the Crooked Eye and you can get it. No sense taking both cars."

"Will my car be safe here?"

"It should be fine. And speaking of fine, here comes our pizza and it smells fantastic. Promise me that for the next five minutes all we hear is the sound of food being consumed. Deal?"

I shook my head and reached for a slice, careful not to let the grease from the sausage drip all over me. Hogan and I were both so famished that the subject of what I had on my phone didn't come up until much later. We devoured the entire pie before either of us realized it and by then we were back on the road to Biscay.

"I'm sorry this turned out to be such a long night for you, Marcie," Hogan said as we approached the exit to the small hamlet.

"It's my own fault. Frankly, I'm the one who should feel sorry for you. I mean, having to make another trek to Glencoe and back for my car, not to mention what happened during the earlier part of the evening."

"Hey, water under the bridge. I wouldn't waste another second on it."

Hogan's truck moved slowly down the main street. Off to the left, I could barely make out Marisa's house. It was totally dark. I figured with all those kids, she and her husband were fast asleep for the night. The Triangle Diner was pitch black, too, all closed up tight until morning. The only sign of life came from the Barton place. The lights were on upstairs. Rose and Lila were probably reading in their bedrooms or maybe even watching television. I was about to say something when Hogan suddenly gasped.

"What the heck! Look to your right at the brewery, Marcie!"

I quickly turned my head around but everything seemed normal to me. "What? What's going on?"

Hogan slowed the truck down a few yards from the brewery and turned off the headlights. "When I left the brewery, I shut off all the lights. *All* the lights. The only illumination would be from the small nightlights on the floor in the front room. Take a good look at the side window. The work lights are on in the walk-in fridge where the tanks are. The light is visible through the door to the walk-in. Someone's inside."

"Maybe it's Tom," I said, but there was no conviction in my voice.

"It's not Tom. He wouldn't drive over here this late and besides he'd park right near the door. I wager whoever's in there parked his or her car behind the building."

Hogan didn't have to tell me what he was thinking. It was obvious. Billy's killer was rummaging through the brewery for something he or she missed the first time.

"Do you want me to call the sheriff? Oh hell. I don't have my phone. I don't know what I'm thinking."

"It wouldn't make a difference, Marcie. Remember? Biscay is a virtual dead zone as far as cell phone calls are concerned and that's during the day. Nighttime is even worse."

"Oh my gosh. *The Biscay Triangle*. I totally forgot about that. Now what?"

"Rose and Lila have a landline. I'd knock on their door but I'm afraid the two of them would make such a commotion it would give whoever's at the brewery the perfect opportunity to get the heck out of there. Listen, I'm going to back my truck into the diner's driveway. Lock the doors and wait for me. Here, take my watch. Give me ten minutes. If I'm not back, pound on the Barton's front door and grab the nearest phone. Whatever you do, don't walk over to the brewery."

"You're not going in there, are you?"

There was no way to hide the panic in my voice.

"No," Hogan said as he grabbed my wrist. "I'm going to sneak quietly around the back and try to get a look through the windows."

"Then what?"

"Then we drive to Hutchinson and get the sheriff."

FORTY

WITHOUT THE HEADLIGHTS ON, it was virtually impossible to see anything. There were no streetlights, only a hazy moon that was barely a sliver. I watched as Hogan crossed the street before disappearing into the darkness. Instinctively, I pushed the lock button for the doors and waited.

Minutes later, a nondescript car rolled slowly down the block and kept going. I used those few seconds to see if I could catch a glimpse of anything in the car's beams. Nothing. The street was quiet and dark. Four minutes had passed. It felt like forty. I took a breath and waited. He said ten minutes. Ten minutes. If he wasn't back by then it would mean… I tried not to think about it but my mind wouldn't let me. All I could picture was someone aiming a gun straight at Hogan's head, the same way they did to Billy.

Damn! We should have just driven to Hutchinson. Six minutes. Still nothing. I forced myself to picture the walk-in tank room with the notebook on the wall. I was missing something but I couldn't quite figure it out. To make matters worse, I felt totally responsible for putting Hogan in danger. Why was I so stupid to leave my smartphone there? What was I thinking? No one makes a move anymore without one of those things. Heck, even my mother owns one. Of course she only uses it to make or take calls, but still, she's got one. This isn't the 1980s. And unlike Iris Krum, most people are familiar with the phone's other functions. I tried to picture where I left mine and then I remembered something. Something that had crossed my mind and kept on going. Until this second.

The smartphone was also a camera. No one needed to steal the notebook. Whoever broke into the brewery didn't plan on murdering Billy Hazlitt. They planned on obtaining information. And in fact, they did. Only they didn't carry it out with them. They took a photo of it. Only Billy got in the way. Maybe they asked him for the information. Asked nicely. Then not so nicely. Then demanded it. Then…

I could see the scenario in the walk-in as if I were watching a movie. The only thing hidden from view was the assailant. When Billy refused to part with the information, they shot him and took the data with them. That's why Billy's body was slid across the floor. It was blocking the notebook. Blocking the notebook and preventing someone from using their phone to snap a photo of Billy's special formula—the one for that Wild Turkey Bourbon Beer.

That's why nothing was missing. The killer took the information on his or her phone but it wasn't enough. The formula wasn't right so they came back looking to see what they had missed. OH MY GOSH— Addison's call. The snafu! Longfellow Brewery couldn't get the formula right. That's why they were delayed. They couldn't decipher the lowercase letters on the log sheet. It was all making sense. *Ls c lat* wasn't part of a formula. It was Billy's shorthand for Luanne Saunder's Chocolate. That's what I wanted to tell Hogan back at the pizzeria. *Ls c lat*. Luanne had developed a special blend for Billy. A blend no one would ever have. That's why Longfellow Brewery had to postpone their ad campaign. Not a "hurry-up and wait" like Addison grumbled about, but more like a "get back to the Crooked Eye to find what you missed." I had the *what* but the *who* was in the brewery and probably holding the same .357 that tore through Billy's skull.

Damn. Seven minutes on the clock and Hogan wasn't back yet.

I kept my eyes fixed across the street, refusing to let the brewery out of my sight. I figured that the scant light from the moon would be enough to let me see Hogan's silhouette when he started back to the car.

Eight minutes and nothing. I was more than nervous. I had crossed over to that awful place where fear and anxiety meld. It felt as if every part of my body was shaking. Off in the distance I thought I heard something. A rumbling. A constant rumbling that got louder and louder. It took me a second before I could place the sound. A muffler! A car muffler!

It had to be Trisha. Coming back from the boyfriend's house. How many rumbling mufflers could be rolling through Biscay at this hour? Right on schedule to annoy the daylights out of the Barton sisters. It was Trisha all right. I glanced at Hogan's watch. Nine minutes. By now the beams from Trisha's headlights were in full view. I shoved the car keys in my pocket, jumped out of the door and raced to the road, waving my arms. There was no way she could miss me.

The noise from the muffler got softer as the car came to a stop in front of the diner. Behind the wheel, a puzzled Trisha stared at me as I reached for the passenger door.

"Trisha! Quick! Turn your car around and go back to Hutchinson. Get the sheriff!"

"I wouldn't do that if I were you," came a voice from behind me. A female voice. Calm and deliberate. I started to turn my head when I felt a small, cold piece of metal against my neck. The gun. The woman behind me was holding a gun to my head.

Terrific! I found the murderer at last. *Too bad I won't live to tell about it. Maybe I should have stayed at St. Paul's running crime statistics instead of being one.*

With the car door ajar, I could see the surprise on Trisha's face. It hadn't turned to panic yet.

"Trudy? What the hell? OH MY GOD! You killed him! You killed Billy Hazlitt! You lousy lying little witch! And you can spell that any way you want!"

"Always the drama queen, Trisha. Now listen carefully. Open your trunk. Now! Do it!"

Trisha's eyes widened as she leaned over to the button that unlatches the trunk. "Screw you, Trudy! I'm not getting in there. And neither is Marcie. What are you going to do? Shoot us both in the middle of the street? Someone's going to hear you."

"Who? Those batty old Barton sisters? And don't count on the couple with all those kids. They were in the diner the other day and mentioned going to visit her mother in Rochester."

Ugh. That explained why Marisa's house was dark but there was no explanation for Trudy's role in Billy's death. I could still feel the tip of the gun on my neck and wished that for once in my life I was capable of making the kind of move you always see in the last seven minutes of *Hawaii Five-O*.

In an instant I heard a deafening boom. And then it

was as if I couldn't hear anything else except an awful ringing in my ears. Had I gone deaf? Probably not, but for what it was worth, my hearing was definitely strained. Trudy had shot the gun off in the air as if to prove her point. Trisha was saying something but all I could see was the mouthing of words.

Next thing I knew, I was being shoved toward the trunk of the car. This time with the gun tip prodding my back. Trudy only paused for brief seconds when she pointed the gun at Trisha. For the life of me I wished I knew how to use those seconds to unarm my assailant. So much for *Hawaii Five-O*.

The gun blast must have affected Trudy's hearing, too, because she had to shout at the top of her lungs to be heard. "You can climb in or I can do it for you," she said as I stared at the trunk.

It was well past ten minutes and I had a sickening thought. I had no idea which direction Trudy came from when she approached Trisha's car. Could she have shot Hogan in the brewery the same way she did with Billy? Closing the door to the walk-in so it would be sound proof…

Damn it! Hogan wasn't supposed to go inside. He was just going to sneak around and look. Then again, I was supposed to stay inside the truck. So much for that. So much for thinking I could solve this case and bring a murderer to justice. Now all I could think about was Hogan lying face down on the brewery floor.

FORTY-ONE

THE NEXT SOUND I heard was the muffler. Even with my momentary hearing loss. The Barton sisters were right. It was as loud as an F-16 on take-off. While Trudy was ushering me toward the truck, Trisha got back in the car, started it up and sped down the street leaving me staring straight ahead with a gun pointed to my back. Talk about fending for myself. I really couldn't blame her, though. What did I expect her to do? Stay there and wait to be killed by her co-worker? Then again, maybe Trudy wasn't going to blow my head off. Not now. Not with a reliable witness who would tell the authorities everything that led up to my murder. Everything except the murder itself because Trisha decided to ditch me on the street and save herself...

Then, yards away, another gun shot. Louder. Different from the one that echoed in my ears. The brewery! A gun went off in the brewery and this time it wasn't muffled by the walk-in. I don't know if it was the sound of the gun or a shear fear reaction but I used that split second to swing my body around, jab an elbow into Trudy, and kick at her ankle. Adrenaline surged through my body like a gas pump filling an SUV guzzler.

Trudy stumbled back as I strained to see where the gun was. In a flash, her entire body was illuminated by a bright light. The beams from Trisha's headlights. She wasn't making an escape after all. Trisha had turned the car around and was driving straight toward us, muffler blaring even louder. The beams must have temporarily blinded Trudy because she didn't make a move. The gun was now visible, parallel to her shoulders. The perfect position to send a bullet into my chest.

The muffler was now a 747. The last bit of metal that held it together disintegrated into a single ferocious roar resulting in a sound that relentlessly tore through the street. Trudy instinctively raised her hands to her ears. I stepped out of her line of fire just as the car came to a thunderous halt inches from her torso.

Trisha blared her horn and edged the car forward. I used that second to run across the street to the brewery. This time I could see the building.

Whatever you do, Trisha, don't turn off your headlights!

That second gunshot meant one thing—Trudy wasn't acting alone. Duh. The soles of my sandals felt each and every piece of gravel in the parking lot as I raced to the back of the building. I was less than a yard from the door when I heard a soft rustling sound from the bushes behind me. How many killers were out there?

My hands and my knees were shaking so badly that I had to force myself to take deep breaths. *Inhale. Exhale. In—!* I could feel an arm slamming against my waist as someone lunged forward and threw me to the ground.

Inhale! Exhale! The last breath never got started. Someone held the palm of a hand against my mouth so I couldn't speak. Using whatever strength I could muster, I thrashed around on the ground trying to get away. Trisha was still blaring her horn so even if I could get free, she'd never hear me.

A pause. Then the horn. Another pause. Long enough for me to hear something. A man's voice. Hogan's voice. It was Hogan who had thrown me to the ground. Hogan! Was he the killer after all? Working with Trudy?

Trisha kept on that horn and I strained to make out what Hogan was saying in between the blasts.

"Shh! Don't move! Don't scream. Don't do anything!"

He let go of my mouth and I stayed fixed to the ground. I couldn't outrun Hogan and I certainly couldn't escape from him and Trudy. My only hope was that the noise disturbed the Barton sisters sufficiently enough for them to call the sheriff.

My throat was tight and dry. Still, I managed to choke out a few words. "Why? Why are you doing this?"

Hogan leaned his head down and whispered, "Because whoever killed Billy is in the brewery right now. I tried to sneak up quietly but I couldn't see in the dark and they must have heard me. That's why they fired off a shot. To scare me away. I didn't want you to go running in there. Why didn't you stay in the truck?"

Another horn blare. And another. I threw an arm over Hogan's shoulder and pressed myself closer to him.

Will I ever get this right?

"It was more than ten minutes and…"

"Okay, Okay. Give me the short version, Marcie. That's got to be Trisha's car with the horn blowing. I heard her muffler making it to the grave along with everyone else in the county. Maybe someone will call the sheriff."

"Uh huh. It's a standoff. Trudy's got a gun but Trisha could run her over."

"Trudy? That first gunshot came from Trudy? She's in on this?"

"Yes. Trudy."

"Geez. I never would have expected Trudy. GEEZ! If Trudy's part of this, who the hell is in the brewery?"

FORTY-TWO

By NOW MY eyes had grown accustomed to the semi-darkness and I could see the faint work lights in the brewery. I turned my head toward the road and noticed something else.

"Look, Hogan," I whispered. "All of the lights are on at the Barton house. Do you think they called the sheriff?"

Hogan was about to say something when both of us witnessed Lila and Rose stepping out of their front door onto the porch. Trisha was still blaring the horn and Trudy was holding her own in front of the car, the gun still pointed at the windshield.

"Marcie, take a good look at the Barton sisters. Is one of them holding a broom?"

"I'm not sure what she has in her—"

I never got to finish my sentence. The blast from a shotgun answered Hogan's question. It wasn't a broom. Those sisters had come out of the house with a shotgun and it went off.

"My God, Hogan! I saw that gun! At least I think it's the same gun. It was on the wall in their dining room. They said it belonged to their grandfather. It's one of those double barrel things. How many rounds can they get off?"

I half expected to see bodies in the road.

"Double barreled? If we're lucky, they're using

an early model and both rounds go off at once. They wouldn't have time to re-load."

"And if we're not so fortunate?"

"I think the later models didn't allow both barrels to fire at once so they've got another shot. At least that's what I've heard."

Trisha was still in her car, leaning on the horn. Trudy hadn't budged from her spot but had turned to face the Barton sisters. Lila and Rose had gotten off of their porch and were walking toward the car. One of them was holding the shotgun and pointing it directly at Trudy.

"This isn't going to end well," Hogan said. "Stay here and don't move. I mean it. I'm going to run to the road and get that gun away from the Bartons. It's our only chance."

"What about watching the brewery? Trudy's accomplice is going to escape. Or worse, kill us first."

"I don't think so. When I snuck over here I looked behind the building. There are no cars. He or she must have parked behind the diner and walked over. Probably the same way they did when Billy was killed. They're not going to risk coming out into the open. They'd have to shoot all of us. No, I'm pretty certain they'll use the back door to make a run for it through the woods behind this place, then double back to the diner. So just stay here. Don't make a move. Please!"

I couldn't tell if Hogan's lips had brushed against my cheek on purpose or if he had merely leaned close to me when he stood up. "Shh. Listen. That's Lila's voice. It's higher pitched than Rose's."

I held still and didn't say a word. High pitched or not, those sisters were loud.

"If you want noise, we'll give you noise! We'll give you— Oh, heavens, Rose! That girl is holding a gun. A gun!"

"Well, you're holding one, too, Lila. And yours is bigger!"

Trisha took her hand off the horn. Only for an instant. I was certain she had seen the same thing I did— Hogan was racing across the road and Lila was waving her arms.

"They're coming at us from all sides, Rose! What should I do?"

"STAND STILL LADIES!" Hogan shouted. "THAT'S WHAT YOU SHOULD DO! STAND STILL AND GIVE ME YOUR SHOTGUN!"

If Hogan's voice had reached a fever pitch, then Rose's was a full blown explosion.

"SO YOU CAN TAKE IT AND KILL US DEAD IN THE ROAD? YOU AND YOUR GUN MOLL?"

"WHAT? She's not my gun moll! I'm not a killer. I'm the one trying to stop you and your sister from getting shot!"

"Lila and I need to talk this over."

"NOW? YOU NEED TO TALK THIS OVER NOW? YOU'RE NOT PICKING OUT A FABRIC FOR YOUR SOFA! CAN'T YOU SEE WE'RE ALL ONE STEP AWAY FROM TRUDY FIRING OFF HER GUN?"

I tried to remain still but my body was stiffening up from lying on the ground. I had started to shift my weight when I had the awful feeling I was being watched.

FORTY-THREE

WITH MY HEARING gradually returning to normalcy, I was intent on listening to the situation in front of the diner. I never heard the back door to the brewery open. Unlike the road where Trisha's headlights allowed us to see what was going on, it was too dark and shadowy to get a good look at the person who approached me by the side of the brewery. Only the sound of footsteps gave him away.

Scrambling to stand up, I was face-to-face with the killer from the brewery. Any light from the sliver of the moon was obscured by trees and brush making it impossible to see who he was. But the darkness couldn't hide the voice. I knew it was a man's. It was surprisingly soft as he yanked me by the wrist, pulling me toward him.

"If you can't see in the dark, you can still recognize what this is. Or do I have to shoot it off again?"

He jabbed the gun against my arm, making sure I wouldn't mistake it for anything else. *Terrific. Two guns in one night.* I stumbled forward, edging away from the trees. Now, in the scant, visible moonlight, I was able to get a decent look at the man's face. Something about it was familiar. I had seen that face before. On more than one occasion. But my mind wasn't cooperating. It was as if an off switch had been turned on. I tried to think, but nothing. I read somewhere that when the brain is stressed, it doesn't process information. Even recall. I let out a slow breath and practiced the rhythmic breathing I had learned in every stupid exercise class I ever attended. Then I looked again. Tyler. It was Tyler's face.

"Move it, walk straight to the brewery. Don't make a sound or you'll regret it."

Tyler? Something was off. It was his face but it didn't sound like him. The voice was older, yet the person prodding the gun at my back sure looked like Tyler. It wasn't until we were both inside the brewery that I could see who it was. The resemblance to Tyler was remarkable. Why hadn't I noticed that before?

"You won't get away with this," I said, using a hackneyed line that every victim, police officer or detective must have used since the discovery of dirt.

"Oh, I'll get away with it, all right, but first you're going to help me find what I came here for. Damn lousy timing. Billy wasn't supposed to be here that night. No one was. If he had only given me what I wanted, he'd still be around."

"So you came back tonight to give it another try?" By now we were at the brewery's back door.

"Yeah, you could say that. Crappy timing the second time around, too. But that's not going to stop me. That little stand-off in the street will keep your buddy Hogan busy long enough for me to get what I need and get going. And you know what the funniest part is?"

I shook my head as I stepped inside.

"That's not even a real gun Trudy's holding. It's the starter pistol for her college swim team."

"Oh my God. Rose and Lila don't know that."

"Ain't my problem. I'm getting out of here," he said.

"And how are you going to manage that?" I said, my eyes refusing to lose contact with the gun that was pointed right at me. "It would seem you and Trudy parked the car behind the diner. Can't very well cross into the street without being seen, can you?"

"Trudy. The blabbermouth of the Triangle Diner. They should have put a sign on the door: *Customers Beware—Anything you say will be overheard and spread around like manure.* She had to stick her nose into this. Couldn't leave things alone. That hyena threatened to go to the sheriff if I didn't let her in on the deal. I knew she'd find a way to screw it up so I had a back-up plan. That's *her* car at the diner. Mine's parked behind the woods. A path I could take in my sleep. Once I get what I need, I'll be on my way. A quick cruise down the highway and I'll be out of this state by morning."

The only thing I could do was stall. "So, um…this isn't, I mean, *wasn't* your original plan, was it?"

"Give the detective an A. No, it wasn't. Thanks to you, I'm moving on to a better plan. One where I won't have to work every day catering to a bunch of jerks. I'll have enough money to sit back and watch the other suckers sweating it out. Enough yacking. I don't suppose your blue-eyed dream boy told you where he keeps the real information about the formulas?"

I didn't know whether or not to give myself an "attaboy" for guessing right, or the "stupidity of the year award" for ignoring the one suspect who actually turned out to be the killer—Frankie, the short order cook.

"What did they promise you at Longfellow Brewery? Wait. You don't have to tell me. You'd be in charge of an entertainment hotspot that would net you a pretty sum of cash but only if you delivered the right recipe for their next brew."

"I'm impressed. The lady did her homework."

"Seems you did yours as well. It must help with those family connections of yours."

"Guess blood is thicker than water so they say, even if I haven't been on the best terms with my brothers. Or should I say *half-brothers* to be more accurate?"

"Which one of them promised you this deal? Harold or Stanley?"

The gun was still squarely aimed at my chest but I had the strange feeling it wasn't going to be used. Not at that moment, anyway.

"Does it matter? Let's just say it was a family affair and leave it at that. They were both getting restless about the building in Willmar. And from what they told me, those little hearts and flowers hippie throwbacks weren't about to let go of their stinkin' lease. Even after that little woman got threatened right to her face. Too bad for them. We moved up the timeline, that's all."

"And managed to frame Billy in the process, huh?"

"Hey, can't get too creative, can you? It wasn't that hard sneaking one of those beer growlers out of the diner. Kaye's too busy gossiping like the rest of those old hens and George's got his head so up his you-know-what half the time that he wouldn't know if any of his customers walked out of his place with more than they came in with!"

Just then, I heard the sound of someone slamming on their brakes. The squeal echoed through the brewery and for an instant I thought Billy's killer might lower the gun. He didn't.

"Enough gabbing. You know what I'm after. Where is it? Where's the recipe? The *real* one. The formula for that Wild Turkey Bourbon Beer. And don't play dumb with me. You know where it is."

"What makes you think I would know?"

"I'm not stupid. You're an investigator. You probably got that info on day one."

By now we were a few feet away from the walk-in and I could see the notebook hanging from its usual spot on the wall. The work lights gave off an eerie glow and I wondered if it looked the same way the night the gun was fired into Billy Hazlitt's temple.

"Yeah, well so did you. It's staring you right in the face," I said, glancing at the wall. "It's in that formula notebook. I'm sure each and every page is safely stored in the photo album of your smartphone."

"Whoa. Another A for the lady or maybe I should say B-plus. Not all of the information was in that formula. Longfellow made that Turkey Bourbon beer and it wasn't the same. *Ordinary.* That's what they said. It was ordinary. Missing an ingredient. Billy must have changed the ingredients or maybe the ratios. They were sure of it. That's why I had to come back. To get what I missed the first time around. Hey, I asked Billy politely for it. All he had to do was give me the lousy recipe. What difference would it have made? The Crooked Eye wasn't in any trouble of closing. Longfellow is a big time player. But no. Billy wouldn't part with his precious secret. So I got pissed and…what the hell. You know the rest."

I was so intent on keeping the guy focused that I didn't realize one thing—Trisha's horn had stopped beeping and this time, it didn't resume.

FORTY-FOUR

I TRIED TO keep my voice low and calm. "I'm trying to tell you. You have the right information. Billy used lots of side notes. Hogan explained that to me during the investigation. Look, if you lower that gun, I'll show you."

"Don't try anything funny. I mean it."

"I'm not that stupid."

I took the notebook down from the wall and turned to the page with the Wild Turkey Bourbon Beer formula. "Take a good look," I said, "at the side notes."

"Yeah, so what do all those letters mean?"

I stared at the letters and rattled off the first thing that came to mind. Childhood years of tortuous game show watching with my mother finally paid off.

"*Ls c-lat.* It stands for *lightly salted chocolate*. That's what was added to the wort. The numbers are right here. See for yourself."

I pointed to a spot on the sheet that listed pounds of grains to gravity points (whatever that was) and hoped that the killer wouldn't question me further. Technically, I was telling the truth. Except that the *Ls* stood for Luanne Saunders. If I was certain of one thing, her specialty chocolate would not have been salted. I held my breath and waited for him to say something.

"Crap. I had this all along. Damn Billy and his idiotic side notes. Doesn't matter. Longfellow's going to pay me plenty for this tidbit. So what if I don't stick around to make a fortune off of their entertainment empire. I'll have enough money to start my own."

The room got quiet. I didn't say anything and neither did he. Worse yet, there was no noise coming from the street. Maybe that was a good thing. Maybe the Barton sisters didn't blow off anyone's heads. But the squeal of brakes? Did Trisha back up her car and then decide to charge it at Trudy? At all of them? A million horrific scenarios were playing out in my mind as Billy's killer nudged me forward using his gun like some sort of cattle prod.

"I'm going to make this real easy for you. You're going to step farther into the walk-in and stand still. Then, I'm going to close the door. Got it? Try anything at all and I'll do to you what I did to him."

I shook my head. Actually, I think I was shaking so hard that I think it shook itself. I took a step backwards until I found myself leaning against a small table by one of the tanks. My hand automatically grabbed the table edge as the door to the walk-in closed in front of me. Thankfully, the work lights were still on.

They'll find me in the morning. When they come by to scrape the bodies off the road.

Never before did I feel so helpless, foolish and angry. There wasn't even a word to describe the misery I felt. It seemed like only a few minutes ago when I came into this room to scurry Lila and Rose out of it. Of course they didn't need my scurrying. Hogan had done a decent job of scaring the daylights out of them before I could do anything. Hell, I couldn't even hold on to my own cell phone.

Oh my gosh! My cell phone. I had to have left it in this room. I stopped feeling sorry for myself and started to look around. It took me less than three seconds to spot it where I had left it, on top of the tank nearest to the door.

I pushed the small button on the device and watched as it lit up. The appicons were reassuring as my index finger reached for the green button for the phone. I frantically dialed 911 and waited. Nothing. No sound. No connection. Nothing. A service message with a red icon appeared but I didn't need to read it. I already knew— *Biscay is a dead zone when it comes to cell calls.*

If Biscay was a dead zone where phone calls were concerned, the walk-in room at the brewery was a morgue. Not only was it cold, but it was soundless. Soundless with the exception of a slow hum emanating from the tanks.

My God! In a flash, everything went black and I gasped. A really loud "I'm-scared-out-of-my-wits" gasp but I was the only one who heard it. The room was totally dark and it took me a few seconds to realize the killer must have turned off the work lights when he left. I looked at the battery on my phone. It registered a quarter of the bar. Not very hopeful for a long night.

Not willing to waste what little life was left on my phone, I shut it down and tucked it into my pocket. I remembered seeing a small stool near one of the tanks and fumbled around like one of those blind witches from Greek mythology who shared one eye. At least I had tactile memory going for me and it led me to the stool. Thankfully I didn't have to sit on the cold floor. Not that this was much better.

For some ridiculous reason, the expression "under the cover of darkness" came into my head and I laughed. I had to keep reassuring myself that any hour, any minute, someone would burst through the door and let me out. Maybe I'd seen one movie too many and was overly optimistic.

My eyes were able to discern the readings on the tanks. Small knobs with backlit numbers that meant something to its brewers. Swiveling my head around, I tried to see if anything else was visible. A thin, faint line of light appeared in the doorway. Probably from one of the nightlights that I had seen strategically placed on some of the floor outlets.

I was about to dismiss it when I realized what I was seeing. That faint light meant that the door to the walk-in wasn't latched. It didn't catch. It couldn't have or there would be no light. I jumped up from the stool so quickly that I knocked it over. In seconds I was at the door.

Please dear God, let it be unlatched.

As frantic as I was to try the door, I forced myself to wait, figuring the killer might still be in earshot. I flashed on the phone to see what time it was. Eleven forty-five. Okay. Fine. I decided to wait a full five minutes and at precisely eleven fifty make a move to get out of the walk-in. At least I had a plan. A five-minute plan.

It was agony and it made the ten-minute wait in the truck seem like a pleasant pastime. Sitting in the dark, I had nothing to distract me except for my thoughts and they were bordering on the insane. When I pushed the button to the phone again, only two minutes had passed. I tried to focus on a sequence of action if I could get out but all I could think of was whose gun was going to go off first in the road.

Eleven forty-nine. Only one minute to go and it was worse than waiting for the results of a pregnancy test.

For the life of me, I prayed Frankie had left. He had what he needed and was probably halfway through the woods and on his way out of state. After all, this wasn't a horror movie where the deranged lunatic waits around to bludgeon another victim. And this guy wasn't psychotic. Cold and ruthless maybe, but in full control of his actions. I reached my hand to the spot where the handle should be and gave it a pull. The walk-in door opened without any resistance and for a minute I was dumbstruck. *It opened! The door actually opened!* I could see the nightlights and wanted to rush straight ahead.

Again, I restrained myself from charging through the back door and into the open. Instead, I cracked the door open slightly and listened for any sounds in the road. No horn blaring but lots of shouting. I yelled loud enough to be heard back in New Ulm.

"IT'S NOT A REAL GUN. TRUDY'S HOLDING A STARTER PISTOL!"

Screaming that sentence over and over again, I raced toward the melee in the street. Trudy might not have been holding a real gun, but that didn't mean the new player in the game wasn't holding a weapon. A second car had come to a screeching halt an instant before the killer ushered me into the walk-in. I had no idea who was behind the wheel but I was certain of one thing. It wasn't a deputy sheriff. Those guys love to blast their sirens, and that was the one sound I didn't hear. I took a breath and charged into the street.

FORTY-FIVE

IT COULD HAVE been anyone behind the wheel. A motorist who had to get off the highway, a resident who was returning home from a late shift, or with any luck, a good Samaritan. Wrong. Wrong. Wrong on all counts.

As it turned out, it was Trisha's boyfriend. It took him all of three seconds to charge into Trudy the minute he heard me shouting. I watched as he grabbed for her pistol while Hogan tried his best to get the shotgun away from the Barton sisters. No surprise for any of us. Rose and Lila refused to part with it and why Trisha got out of her car was anyone's guess.

If it wasn't for the fact that a stone cold killer was making his way through the woods and out of Biscay at that very instant, the whole scene might have been comical. Everyone was yelling at once. Voices were carried through the night air with such clarity that I swear if someone had their windows open in Glencoe or Hutchinson, they could hear what was being said.

"DON'T HAND OVER GREAT PAPA'S GUN, ROSE! STAND YOUR GROUND!"

"YOU'RE GOING TO WIND UP SHOOTING SOMEONE! PUT THE DAMN THING DOWN!"

"EVERYONE'S UNARMED EXCEPT YOU, ROSE! PUT THE THING DOWN!"

"HOW DO WE KNOW THIS GUY ISN'T THE KILLER?"

"HE'S MY BOYFRIEND!"

"OH? SO I'M YOUR BOYFRIEND, NOW? A HALF HOUR AGO YOU SAID YOU DIDN'T WANT TO SEE ME AGAIN!"

"YOU KNOW I NEVER MEANT THAT!"

"QUIT WAVING THE GUN, ROSE! YOU'RE GOING TO BLAST IT OFF IF YOU KEEP THAT UP!"

"YOU CAN'T KEEP RUNNING OFF EVERY TIME WE HAVE A FIGHT!"

"TRUDY'S THE ONE RUNNING OFF! GRAB HER!"

I watched as Trudy made a mad dash to the back of the diner where she had parked her car. Huffing and out of breath from running, I still managed to yell out to her.

"DON'T BOTHER. YOUR BUDDY-BOY'S PROBABLY ON THE HIGHWAY BY NOW."

Trudy turned her head for an instant. I yelled again. "WHAT ARE YOU GOING TO DO? CHASE HIM ALL THE WAY INTO IOWA?"

At that moment Trudy stopped in her tracks and started to walk back toward us. The starter pistol, now lying on the ground near Trisha's car, was no longer a threat. I wished the same could be said for the Barton family shotgun.

Rose kept waving it around, pointing it first at Hogan, then at Trisha's boyfriend, and finally at Trudy. Like Russian roulette, we had no idea who the next lucky target would be.

Trisha ducked below her car door to make sure it wasn't her. "You can go ahead and shoot Trudy for all I care," she said. "It would serve her right!"

"I'm not the one who killed Billy, Trisha. I swear. The only reason I got into this was for the money."

"She's right," I said, praying that Rose Barton didn't decide to make a sudden move. "Billy's killer was in the brewery all this time. That's why I flagged you down on the street."

"NOW WILL YOU PUT DOWN THAT GUN, ROSE?" Hogan shouted. "THE KILLER IS PROBABLY ACROSS THE STATE LINE BY NOW!"

"Not necessarily," Trudy said as she reached into her pocket and held up a piece of wire. "I never trusted him so I disconnected the distributor cap to his car while he was in the brewery. He thought he was putting one over on me by parking his car way behind the brewery. I knew what he was up to all along. Once I disabled his ride I snuck back to my own car behind the diner. Everything would have been hunky dory if all of you didn't show up."

"Come on, Brodie," Trisha said as she motioned to her boyfriend. "He should be easy to catch. He'll be the one swearing under the hood of his car. We can circle around the woods to the other side in minutes."

I held up my arm to block the guy from getting into Trisha's car. "What? Are you crazy? He's got a loaded gun and believe me, it's no starter pistol."

Then, like some bizarre scene in a Hollywood action movie, Rose Barton held out her shotgun and spoke. "Take this and shoot his toes off! Then move farther up his body until you reach his—"

At that second, Lila let out such a loud gasp that I thought she was going to have a stroke.

Hogan moved in quickly, seized the gun from Rose and said, "No one's going to shoot anyone's parts! Rose and Lila, if you want to be useful, go back inside your house, lock your door and then pick up your phone and call the sheriff. You *do* have a landline, right?"

"Of course we do," Lila said, sounding more indignant than ever. "And just what should I tell him?"

Trisha spoke up before any of us could say anything. "Tell him to be on the lookout for Skip Gunderson!"

FORTY-SIX

"SKIP GUNDERSON? That was Skip Gunderson in the brewery with you?" Hogan asked as he made his way toward me. He was still holding the Barton shotgun, only it was pointed toward the ground for the first time in what seemed like hours. "I couldn't get a good look at the guy when I snuck around the place."

"NO! It wasn't Skip Gunderson," I said, "It was—"

All of a sudden Trudy took a step forward and finished my sentence. "It was a flaming jerk who thought he could pull one over on me. That stupid grill monkey, Frankie." Then she waved the ignition wire in the air again, as if to prove her point. I glanced at Trudy, then in the direction of the Barton sisters.

"Rose! Lila! Wait!" I yelled, hoping to prevent them from giving the sheriff the wrong information, but it was too late. The sisters had already gone inside their house and closed the door behind them.

"I still say we should drive behind the woods," Trisha said. "Because we can... OH MY GOD! He's back in the brewery. See for yourself!"

Trisha had been facing the Crooked Eye while the rest of us were staring at each other and the Bartons. Now it was our turn to gasp. The lights in the brewery were flashing on and off and I wondered if Hogan had the same thought I did—Frankie's going to set fire to the place like he did to Hearts & Flowers in Willmar.

Surprisingly, Hogan managed to stay calm as he turned to Brodie. "How long will it take you to drive to the sheriff's station in Hutchinson?"

"Twenty minutes, maybe fifteen if I gun it."

"Gun it! I'm not counting on the Barton sisters to get this right. God knows what they'll tell the sheriff, or worse yet, if anyone will believe them."

"You got it! Come on, Trisha. Grab your keys and let's go! Get inside my car. Now!"

Wordless, Trisha jumped into the seat of Brodie's car and slammed the door behind her. I watched as he turned the car around to face north before speeding toward Hutchinson. That left Hogan, Trudy, and me on the street staring at the brewery.

I started to clear my voice when Trudy directed her comments to Hogan. "He won't think anything of setting your brewery on fire. That's what he did in Willmar, you know. Got ahold of those specialty growlers of yours and turned them into Molotov cocktails. Bragged about it when he thought no one else could hear us."

"My God, Trudy," I said. "Didn't you feel the least bit bad about that?"

She shrugged as if I were complaining about leaving dishes in the sink. I couldn't believe what I heard. "It's not as if anyone got killed. Besides, the insurance companies will pay for all the damages. Businesses do that all the time. But don't get me wrong, I felt badly about Billy's death. Really, I did. He was a nice guy. Still, once it was a done deal, I didn't see anything wrong in me getting a piece of the profit. Hey, all I did was threaten to go to the sheriff if I wasn't cut in on the deal. I'll probably get off with probation and write a book about this."

"Did you leave me that cryptic message, too? You know, the one about *sniffing the wrong bush*?"

"Sniffing bushes? What? No. I don't know what you're talking about."

Hogan made some sort of guttural sound as he moved the shotgun level to his waist and took a step closer to me. "Marcie, I know you have a hard time listening to me, but please, stay here with Trudy. Stand next to Trisha's car and wait. Or get inside the car for that matter. It shouldn't be too long before someone from the sheriff's department shows up. And Trudy, if you think of hightailing it back to your car, think again. You wouldn't want to add 'leaving the scene of a crime' to your list of misdemeanors."

Trudy didn't say anything this time. She let out a short breath, opened the passenger door and plopped herself on the seat. Hogan had started to walk across the road before turning to face me.

"Don't look so worried, I'll be fine. Chances are this shotgun is a later model. The other bullet's probably still in here."

FORTY-SEVEN

ONE SHOT LEFT in the gun? That was supposed to make me feel better? What was he planning on? Shootout at the OK Corral? I watched as he disappeared across the road only to catch a glimpse of him by the side of the brewery. The lights inside the place were no longer flashing on and off. They were on. All of them. Including the front porch light.

With the passenger side door wide open, Trudy stared at the brewery, too, before speaking. "You might as well sit inside the car. There's nothing else you can do."

Yeah, thanks to you, Trudy.

I didn't say anything and I refused to move from my position leaning against the hood. As much as I hated to admit it, Trudy was right. There was nothing I could do. My cell phone was useless and I certainly didn't carry a weapon with me. Unless lipstick and car keys are now on the TSA list for forbidden items.

The scene across the road looked almost serene. A quaint little brewery, all lit up in front of the woods. How long before the illumination would change from lights to flames?

How long before…? A strange thought crossed my mind and I moved away from the car. Without a Molotov cocktail or gasoline or any other incendiary device, it would take quite a while to catch something on fire. Heck, we couldn't even manage a campfire when I was in the Girl Scouts. And that was *with* a lighter. The wood wouldn't catch. Maybe there was still time.

"Listen Trudy. I don't give a hoot if you stay here or get in your car and leave the country. You'll be found one way or the other. But I'm not going to sit here and watch while the livelihoods of some decent guys are destroyed."

"You're as reckless as Hogan. The two of you make some team."

For once in your sorry life, I hope you're right.

I grabbed my car keys and darted across the road. I wasn't as optimistic as Hogan about the Barton shotgun having one round left. And there was no need to give the killer a well-lit target. I knew exactly where the electrical panel box was located and one quick move on my part would save Hogan from the same fate as his partner. Theoretically, it was a decent plan. Practically, it was another story.

The good news was that I didn't smell anything burning. The bad news was that I hadn't thought any further than the moment I crept to the rear of the building. Armed with "great papa's shotgun," Hogan had apparently gone inside through the back door, leaving it cracked open. I could hear his voice as well as Frankie's.

"Toss me the keys to your truck, Hogan, and I'm out of here. No one needs to get hurt."

"Like *that's* going to happen."

"You wouldn't take a shot at me and I know it. I know guys like you. So maybe, just maybe, I ought to start shooting up your precious little brewery. Hey, what's a few holes in those tanks going to do?"

"You've got me wrong, buddy. I'm not a killer like

you but the law will be on my side if I have to use this gun to stop you."

Tip-toeing to a side window, I looked in. I was pretty sure no one would see me and I was right. Frankie was standing in the middle of the walk-in and I could see the gun in his hand. Hogan was a few feet from the counter, the Barton shotgun pointing straight into the walk-in. If he moved quickly, he could duck under the counter.

I slipped away from the window and headed to the breaker box. Opening the panel door, I slid the breakers, one by one, to the opposite side. I wasn't sure where the master breaker was, so I painstakingly turned each one of them off, using the laser light that was attached to my car keys.

That revelation came to me as I fumbled through my bag looking for something a bit more menacing, only to realize that week-old used tissues and some credit cards were as good as it was going to get. Somewhere between touching the tissues and wondering if I had sent in my Bofa payment, I remembered my mother's words when it came to my key chain—*"You never know."* In that split second, I knew exactly what I was going to do. I only hoped that Hogan would use this to his advantage and duck for cover.

He didn't. At least I don't think he did. Seconds after the brewery went dark, I heard a shot, followed by a crash and the sound of glass shattering.

FORTY-EIGHT

THERE ARE LOTS of explanations for insanity but I prefer mine—not thinking past my nose. I flicked on the laser light and headed into the brewery. I knew exactly where I was going to aim that beam and I did! *Warning—direct exposure may cause flash-blindness.* Yeah, I read the label. The label and the note from my mother.

"Be careful where you point this, Marcie. Don't point it at the audience if you ever have to give another presentation. Naomi Weintraub's nephew in the seventh grade pointed it at someone and they got retina burns. So be careful. It's still better than using one of those wooden pointers."

Thank you, Iris Krum. The laser light caught the killer off guard long enough for me to speak. He had stepped out of the walk-in and had no idea Hogan had maneuvered himself right behind the guy.

"If you don't want to be permanently blind, you'll drop your gun, Frankie! I mean it. And where are you going to shoot anyway? I know you can't see a thing."

"I can still—"

Without warning, Hogan dropped the shotgun and rushed forward, knocking the Triangle Diner's cook to the ground and sending his gun clear across the floor.

I expected a thank-you but what I got instead was a reprimand.

"Damn it, Marcie. You could have been killed. You could have gotten both of us killed!"

"I... I..."

"It's okay. It's okay. Frankie's not going anywhere. I've got him."

I don't know how Hogan managed it, but in the dark he was able to retrieve the shotgun and hold it directly over Frankie, who was still sprawled on the floor.

I swear it was one of those scenes you see in a movie where the hero says something romantic and then kisses the heroine. The most romantic it got, however, was Hogan telling me to go back outside to flip on the breakers.

The rush of adrenalin had left my body and I was getting twitchy. It had to be at least an hour since Trisha and Brodie took off for Hutchinson. Where the heck was the sheriff? And what about the phone call that Lila and Rose were supposed to make?

Hogan wasn't budging from his position standing directly over Frankie. Frankie. Of all the suspects I had considered, Frankie wasn't one of them. Now, looking at him closely for the first time, I could see the strong resemblance to Tyler and the rest of the Evans family. So this was the half-brother. The one Alice Davenport told me about. Only she thought the name started with an H. That's why I jumped to the conclusion that it was Hogan.

"So you're Tyler's uncle, isn't that so, Frankie?" I said. Not waiting for him to answer, I continued. "Why didn't you mention that?"

"In case you haven't figured it out, I wasn't always welcomed into the fold. It was only when Harold and Stanley figured out I would be useful to them that they decided to extend the olive branch. Some branch, huh? I should have told them where to go and minded my own business but the thought of flipping burgers for the rest of my life was a nightmare."

I did remember someone, Kaye maybe or perhaps Trisha, but someone who told me that Frankie was studying to be a chef but had to change his plans in order to take care of his mother. Seemed no one else in that family was available or willing to do so.

"You must have really resented your well-to-do brothers when they left you to take care of your mother."

"Yeah, you could say that and make it *half-brothers*. I'm not an Evans. The name's Frankie Malory. *Harrison Francis Malory* to be exact; but who the hell wanted a name like Harrison?"

Harrison! Started with an "H." Darn it if Alice Davenport wasn't right after all. Now she'll wind up telling me she solved the murder and next thing I know, she'll be invoicing us.

"What the heck's taking that sheriff so long?" Hogan said as he shifted his weight from one foot to the other. "I thought we'd be hearing a siren by now."

I was about to answer when I heard the unmistakable sound of car tires crunching across the gravel parking lot.

FORTY-NINE

THE SIDE DOOR, which was partially ajar, now swung with such force that it banged against the wall. I turned to see a trooper from the Minnesota State Patrol followed by Lila Barton.

"That's him, officer. That's the man who took great grand papa's shotgun!"

"For heaven sakes, Lila," Hogan shouted, "I did *not* take your gun. Well, in a manner of speaking. I took it away from you so no one would get shot and I told you to call the sheriff!"

Lila was absolutely piqued. "We have the state patrol number listed by our phone. I wasn't about to bother looking up the sheriff's phone number."

The trooper wasted no time approaching Hogan, who quickly explained why he was holding the gun to Frankie, who was still flat out on the floor of the brewery.

"I'll be happy to hand over this relic," Hogan said, "but you'll want to keep you own weapon on this guy. His .357 is on the floor over there, within arm's reach. It's got his prints all over it and I'm sure the bullets will match the one that killed my partner, Billy Hazlitt."

The trooper leaned into the radio device on his shoulder and started to speak when we finally heard the sheriff's siren.

Minutes later the small room in the brewery was

filled to capacity with two sheriff deputies, another trooper, Trisha, Brodie, and the Barton sisters. The only one missing was Trudy. I figured she was on the run but surprisingly enough, she was waiting it out in Trisha's car.

It wasn't until three in the morning when the entire mess was sorted out. Since the murder was in the county jurisdiction, Frankie was taken to the sheriff's station in Hutchinson. Hogan and I had to answer a multitude of questions as well as assist Lila and Rose as they tried to give their statements. Trisha and Brodie wasted no time implicating Trudy, who was also escorted to the sheriff's office.

The trooper made sure that there were no bullets in great grand papa's shotgun before returning it to the sisters. As it turned out, it was an early model gun and that first shot had used all the ammunition. Talk about a close call for Hogan.

By the time everyone had left the brewery, I felt as if I was about to collapse. I fell into one of the stools at the counter and used the palm of my hand to prop up my head. Hogan swept up the broken glass from the small window in the back and hammered a piece of plywood over it.

"Guess that'll keep till tomorrow. Huh? Good thing we had some plywood sheets out back."

I nodded. "I've never had a night like this in my entire life and I never want to ever again."

I watched as he locked the side door to the brewery and walked toward me. "You *do* know that you could have gotten us killed with that crazy stunt of yours, don't you?"

"Yeah, well, you were the one running off with an unloaded gun."

"The killer didn't know that."

"Heck, *you* didn't know that, and the killer would've found out soon enough."

"What do you say we call it a truce, Marcie? We might as well celebrate. You actually solved the case!"

"I think it kind of solved itself, but as far as our client is concerned, Blake Investigations will be happy to take the credit."

"We could toast to your victory with any of our brews or would you rather I drive you back to Glencoe for your car? Of course I've got a better idea."

"Better than drinking and driving?"

"Yeah. Sleeping. I'm opting for sleep and lots of it. Sure, we're both wired but once we start to crash, we'll be exhausted. Last thing I feel like doing is nodding off behind the wheel. And you've got a longer drive back to New Ulm. Listen, this isn't some kind of come-on. Although I could make it convincing. Seriously, my place is a few minutes from here and you can catch some sleep."

"At your house? Sleep at your house?"

"Uh-huh. You heard right. Look, now that you know I'm not a murderer, you don't have to fear for your life around me. I can tell I make you nervous but you can relax now."

Oh believe me, it wasn't the killer thing that made me all jumpy around you.

"Hogan, I—"

"I swear I won't try any funny stuff. Hey, and even if I wanted to, I'm beat. Another half hour and I'd need toothpicks to pry open my eyelids. So what do you say?

Your car will be fine parked in Glencoe tonight. I'll drive you back first thing in the morning. I've got a guest bedroom whose only occupants are my two cats when they get bored sleeping in my room. And the bed's got a new mattress, too. Not that the cats would know the difference. Heck, they sleep on crumpled newspapers if I let them."

"Cats?"

"Foxy and Lady. Domestic shorthairs. Very friendly. Um, I hope you're okay with felines."

I thought of Byron and let out a sigh. "I'm more than okay and I've got one, too. A big guy named Byron. Right now he must wonder where I am. He's got plenty of food and water and two litter boxes but he's used to sleeping with me."

Hogan smiled. "I can understand why. Look, I'm sure he'll be fine for the night. Cats are amazingly resilient. So, what do you say? The sun will be up in less than three hours."

I was absolutely exhausted and everything he said made sense. Unfortunately, I could also hear another voice. My mother's. "Are you insane? You spent the night in a strange man's house? What's the matter with you? Is that how I brought you up? You could've been killed."

"If I was going to be killed, it would have happened already."

"Huh? Are you all right? No one's going to kill you. We got the bad guys."

"Sorry. I was just thinking out loud. After all we've been through tonight, this really shouldn't have much bearing on whether or not I stay at your place but it kind of does."

"What does?"

"I don't have a toothbrush."

Hogan shook his head and laughed. "Is that what you're worried about? A toothbrush? I've got a whole drawer of them. Souvenirs from the dentist. Got lots of toothpaste, too. And soap. And shampoo. Plus hot and cold running water and something we call 'electricity.'"

"Very funny."

"I'm serious." He looked dead on his feet but nothing could dim those blue eyes of his. Was this how it was going to be? Me falling for the proverbial man-trap?

"Promise you'll let me sleep," I said.

"Scout's honor. Oh, and lest I forget, I was an Eagle Scout. I'll prove it to you when we get back to my place."

"Oh, don't you worry. I can always verify with Alice Davenport."

As soon as Hogan turned the key to his front door, I raced for the phone to leave a message for Max. It was four words. "We caught the killer." Then I sank down on Hogan's couch. I never did get to sleep on that new mattress of his, or any mattress for that matter. I must have closed my eyes the minute I sat down because when I opened them again it was daylight and my head was resting in the crook of his arm.

"You're awake," he said stretching out his arm. "Any longer and I was afraid I'd lose all feeling from my shoulder to my wrist."

"You slept here next to me?"

"Um, yeah. I didn't want to leave you alone in a strange place on a strange couch, especially if you had a nightmare. I don't know about you, but I'll have recurring visions of Rose and Lila sneaking into the brewery with their spatulas and slotted spoons to 'help out.'"

"Ew, yeah. That really is disturbing. I should have stopped them from going inside. Sorry."

"Don't be. If it wasn't for you, Frankie would have gotten away with murder." Hogan sighed and bit his lower lip. "Frankie. Of all people. It's always the ones no one suspects. And Trudy, talk about cold blooded and opportunistic. I knew businesses like Longfellow were prone to that kind of behavior but when it's up close and personal, well, let's just say I'm still unnerved. Anyway, it's over now."

"Uh-huh."

Hogan stood up and walked to the kitchen. "I'll go make us some coffee. I left you four different toothbrushes to choose from and two different kinds of toothpaste. Clean towels in the bathroom, too."

A small gray and white cat brushed against my leg.

"That's Lady. She's the overt one of the two. Foxy will most likely check you out from a distance before she becomes a pest."

I stroked the cat and got up. My body felt weird and stiff from sleeping in one position. "Thanks. Coffee sounds good. I'll join you in a minute."

Hogan's house reminded me of one of those décor magazines. Everything neat and in its place. My eyes darted from bookshelves to the media wall. What the house lacked in cutesy, it made up for in style. The guy had decent taste and was anything but a slob. I don't know why I was scrutinizing the place. It wasn't as if I was going to see it again, or Hogan, for that matter.

I washed up quickly in the bathroom and brushed my teeth. With my toothbrush in hand, I walked into the kitchen. "Um, I guess I should just throw this away, huh?"

Hogan shrugged. "You could always label it and stick

it in the drawer with the other forty or so toothbrushes from my stable of women."

My mouth opened and I didn't say a word.

"I'm kidding. I'm kidding. If you want to know the truth, you're the only woman who's been in this house in years. It probably looks it, too."

"I think it looks fine."

"Only because I went on a cleaning binge the other day. Usually it looks very lived-in."

"Lived-in is nice," I said.

Hogan handed me a mug of coffee. "So, I guess I won't be seeing you anymore since the case is solved. Unless of course there's paperwork I'll need to go over and I suppose the sheriff will send a deputy for that."

"Yeah, I suppose so."

"Of course you could always stop by for a beer tasting. We'll be introducing new brews in the next few months. Oh what the hell. I don't want you to stop by for a beer tasting like some nameless customer. Geez, this is coming out wrong."

He walked over to me and put his hands on my shoulders. I all but dropped the coffee mug. "What do you mean?"

"I mean, I want to keep seeing you. Do I *really* have to explain it?"

I shook my head, looked him directly in the eye and answered him. "The way I see it, you owe me a hamburger. But I don't want to wait twenty or thirty years for Frankie to grill it, and that's if he gets a light sentence."

"He won't. So what do you say we forget the hamburger and make it a steak? Lots of good places in New Ulm and I don't mind the drive."

"It's a deal."

It wasn't exactly a kiss-me-on-the-lips moment but it was a start. He gave my shoulders a squeeze and muttered, "Good, then."

FIFTY

"YOU COULD'VE GOTTEN yourself killed!" Max shouted the minute I walked into the office. He was standing next to the coffeemaker but hadn't turned it on. "I got the whole story from the sheriff's department in Hutchinson. Bad enough there was a killer with a gun, but the Barton sisters with their grandfather's rifle? Lucky they didn't shoot the entire street up. What on earth were you thinking? Because you weren't. Next time give me a shout-out before you go off on your own. I don't care what time of day it is. Deal?"

"Deal."

"And while I'm at it, you really should carry a gun. You're licensed. You can't afford to be vulnerable."

"Uh-huh."

"Fine. Guess my lecture for the morning is over. You must be whipped. I can't believe you came into the office today. Go home. Get some sleep. Angie will be here any second and she can handle all the calls and walk-ins."

"I already slept. And I've been home. To shower. I'm fine. Honestly. And all I need to handle is a final report for our client."

"Your instinct was right, kid," Max said. "About Billy's innocence in all of this. But it isn't always going to be that way."

"I know. Still, I just had a feeling."

"I did, too, when I took you on. It was the right choice. Now go get started on that report before Alice Davenport swoops down on us."

"We'll both have to learn to duck."

BY WEEK'S END I had sent Alice her complete report. Chronologically and grammatically correct. Left justified and double spaced. Frankie had confessed to the murder, along with breaking and entering two businesses, ours and the brewery. He was being arraigned in court along with Trudy. I later learned that she was right about her prediction. She was going to get probation.

The only one who got off the hook was Skip Gunderson and Trisha was furious. It seemed the "payola" Skip was referring to in the diner was the money Frankie owed him for putting a scare into Luanne Saunders. The polished thug turned out to be Skip after all. Not that it mattered. It was up to Luanne to press charges and she wasn't willing "to waste another moment" on the matter. Something about bad karma and negative forces in the universe. Too bad she didn't have Trisha as her lawyer.

According to Addison, Longfellow Brewery was still "on-hold" regarding the release of their specialty beer but that didn't stop them from advertising their new hipster hot-spots, *soon to be popping up all over the state*. I had half a mind to anonymously mail them the fake formula with the salty chocolate but decided otherwise.

As for Rose and Lila's alleged phone message from Hogan, the sisters listened to it carefully again and it was from their washing machine repairman who said, "I'll be there at eight."

Everything seemed to have fallen into place with the

exception of one detail. One nagging, annoying little detail. If it wasn't Trudy, then who put that note in my bag about sniffing the wrong bush?

That annoying detail plagued me up until the holidays when I went into a local bookstore to find a children's book for my niece. As I glanced at book covers with frogs, princesses, and teddy bears, a bright green book with a picture of a dog stood out. It was titled, *Stop! You're Sniffing the Wrong Bush.* Was it that simple? Had I mistaken a mere book title for someone's cryptic message?

I called the office and got the phone number for Marisa, the lady with the kids who lived across from the Crooked Eye. After ten minutes on the phone she told me she was still freaked out about the thought that the killer snuck into her house to hide while waiting to get into the brewery. As a result, she and husband had a state of the art alarm system installed. I finally asked her if she remembered writing a note about *sniffing the wrong bush.*

"My gosh, I do, Marcie. One of my friends told me about that book and I wrote it down in a hurry. I couldn't find a pen so I had to use a marker. Then for the life of me, I couldn't find that note. Why do you ask?"

When I told her, she burst out laughing. "What a riot! And all this time you were worried about it. One of my kids probably dumped the note into your bag when you stopped by that first day. Isn't that odd!"

Yeah, it was odd all right. I swore I shook my head all the way back to the office.

"There's a call for you on line one, Marcie," Angie said as soon as I got to my desk. "I think it's your mother. Should I put her through?"

I knew what the call was about. I'd been avoiding it for days but it was time for me to deal with it. I picked up the receiver and said hi.

"So, what have you decided? Should I start telling everyone my daughter's a detective? I left you a message at the house and one on your cell phone. I know what you're up to, Marcie. You think by avoiding your mother you won't have to make any choices."

"Um, actually Mom, I did make up my mind."

"So? Are you going to go back to campus security or are you going to do whatever it is you people do in order to be an investigator?"

"I'm applying for my private detective license. I've already met the six thousand hour requirement and Max's going to pay the thousand dollar fee."

"A thousand dollar fee? What's wrong with the state of Minnesota? Who's got that kind of money?"

"Licenses are expensive. That's the way it is."

For one long minute the line was silent. "What's the matter, Mom? I thought you'd be happy about this. I'll have a long and interesting career."

"Does it mean you have to walk around with a gun?"

"No. Why?"

"Because Erma Gottlieb's grandson was carrying a gun in one of those holster things and the next thing he knew, it shot off his right toe!"

I took a deep breath and counted to ten. It was going to be a long day, but there was one bright spot. She didn't ask me if I was seeing anyone. I figured I'd spring Hogan on her after New Year's. No sense ruining his holidays.

* * * * *

ENDNOTES

The Biscay Triangle really does exist. It's a little over an acre in the Biscay area and for unknown reasons, cannot receive cell phone service. Other strange phenomena including a slower growth rate for plants and crops and changes in funnel cloud patterns have also been reported. Check out http://en.wikipedia.org/wiki/Biscay,_Minnesota for further information.

J.C. EATON IS THE pen name of husband and wife writing team Ann I. Goldfarb and James E. Clapp. A former teacher and middle school principal from upstate New York, Ann always had a passion for writing. As a sideline to her career in education, Ann wrote for a number of trade journals before turning her attention to mysteries. She got her feet wet writing YA time travel novels and then joined forces with her husband, James Clapp.

With a background in construction, a degree in business and a successful tour of duty with the US Navy, James never envisioned himself writing cozy mysteries along with his wife, Ann I. Goldfarb. In fact, the only writing he did was for informational brochures and workshop material for the winery industry where he worked as a tasting room manager in his home state of New York. When he and his wife left the Snow Belt for the Arizona desert, he was hit with the writing bug.

The couple resides with their four-legged friends in Sun City West, Arizona, where sunshine doesn't need to be shoveled.

Visit jceatonauthor.com and timetravelmysteries. com for more information.

Get 4 FREE REWARDS!

We'll send you 2 FREE Books <u>plus</u> 2 FREE Mystery Gifts.

Harlequin Intrigue books are action-packed stories that will keep you on the edge of your seat. Solve the crime and deliver justice at all costs.

FREE Value Over **$20**

Get 4 FREE REWARDS!

We'll send you 2 FREE Books plus 2 FREE Mystery Gifts.

Harlequin Romantic Suspense books are heart-racing page-turners with unexpected plot twists and irresistible chemistry that will keep you guessing to the very end.

FREE Value Over $20

Get 4 FREE REWARDS!

We'll send you 2 FREE Books plus 2 FREE Mystery Gifts.

Love Inspired Suspense books showcase how courage and optimism unite in stories of faith and love in the face of danger.

FREE Value Over $20

YES! Please send me 2 FREE Love Inspired Suspense novels and my 2 FREE mystery gifts (gifts are worth about $10 retail). After receiving them, if I don't wish to receive any more books, I can return the shipping statement marked "cancel." If I don't cancel, I will receive 6 brand-new novels every month and be billed just $5.24 each for the regular-print edition or $5.99 each for the larger-print edition in the U.S., or $5.74 each for the regular-print edition or $6.24 each for the larger-print edition in Canada. That's a savings of at least 13% off the cover price. It's quite a bargain! Shipping and handling is just 50¢ per book in the U.S. and $1.25 per book in Canada.* I understand that accepting the 2 free books and gifts places me under no obligation to buy anything. I can always return a shipment and cancel at any time. The free books and gifts are mine to keep no matter what I decide.

Choose one: ☐ **Love Inspired Suspense Regular-Print** (153/353 IDN GNWN)   ☐ **Love Inspired Suspense Larger-Print** (107/307 IDN GNWN)

Name (please print)

Address   Apt. #

City   State/Province   Zip/Postal Code

Email: Please check this box ☐ if you would like to receive newsletters and promotional emails from Harlequin Enterprises ULC and its affiliates. You can unsubscribe anytime.

Mail to the **Harlequin Reader Service:**
IN U.S.A.: P.O. Box 1341, Buffalo, NY 14240-8531
IN CANADA: P.O. Box 603, Fort Erie, Ontario L2A 5X3

Want to try 2 free books from another series! Call 1-800-873-8635 or visit www.ReaderService.com.

Visit
ReaderService.com
Today!

As a valued member of the Harlequin Reader Service, you'll find these benefits and more at ReaderService.com:

- Try 2 free books from any series
- Access risk-free special offers
- View your account history & manage payments
- Browse the latest Bonus Bucks catalog

RS20